SEP 19

P9-CDA-450

A Deadman's Cross

Rhys Davies

Books by Sherrilyn Kenyon

THE DARK-HUNTERS

Dragonswan
Night Pleasures
Night Embrace
Dance with the Devil
Kiss of the Night
Night Play
Seize the Night
Sins of the Night
Unleash the Night
Dark Side of the Moon
The Dream-Hunter
Devil May Cry
Upon the Midnight Clear
Dream Chaser
Acheron

One Silent Night
Dream Warrior
Bad Moon Rising
No Mercy
Retribution
The Guardian
Time Untime
Styxx
Dark Bites
Son of No One
Dragonbane
Dragonmark
Dragonsworn
Stygian
The Dark-Hunter Companion

DEADMAN'S CROSS

Deadmen Walking
Death Doesn't Bargain

At Death's Door

THE LEAGUE

Born of the Night
Born of Fire
Born of Ice
Fire & Ice
Born of Shadows
Born of Silence

Born of Fury
Cloak & Silence
Born of Defiance
Born of Betrayal
Born of Legend
Born of Vengeance

CHRONICLES OF NICK

Infinity
Invincible
Infamous
Inferno

Illusion
Instinct
Invision
Intensity

At Death's Door

At Death's Door

SHERRILYN KENYON

TOR

A TOM DOHERTY ASSOCIATES BOOK

NEW YORK

AT DEATH'S DOOR

Copyright © 2019 by Sherrilyn McQueen

Interior illustrations by Dabel Bros.

A Tor Book
Published by Tom Doherty Associates
120 Broadway
New York, NY 10271

www.tor-forge.com

Tor® is a registered trademark of Macmillan Publishing Group, LLC.

The Library of Congress Cataloging-in-Publication Data is available upon request.

ISBN 978-0-7653-8574-1 (hardcover)
ISBN 978-0-7653-8575-8 (ebook)

Our books may be purchased in bulk for promotional, educational, or business use. Please contact your local bookseller or the Macmillan Corporate and Premium Sales Department at 1-800-221-7945, extension 5442, or by email at MacmillanSpecialMarkets@macmillan.com.

First Edition: September 2019

Printed in the United States of America

0 9 8 7 6 5 4 3 2 1

To my boys. For there is nothing covered, that shall not be revealed; and hid, that shall not be known.

And never forget what I've always quoted to you:

When I returned, and I saw vanity under the sun . . .

There is one alone, and there is not a second; yea, he hath neither child nor brother: yet is there no end of all his labour; neither is his eye satisfied with riches; neither saith he, For whom do I labour, and bereave my soul of good? This is also vanity, yea, it is a sore travail.

Two are better than one; because they have a good reward for their labour.

For if they fall, the one will lift up his fellow: but woe to him that is alone when he falleth; for he hath not another to help him up.

Again, if two lie together, then they have heat: but how can one be warm alone?

And if one prevail against him, two shall withstand him; and a threefold cord is not quickly broken.

Better is a poor and a wise child than an old and foolish king, who will no more be admonished.

Together, we will rise, and we will overcome. You are my lights in the darkness and never has any mother been prouder of her sons. I love you now and forever.

And for my grandfathers, who each taught me different life lessons.

As always, to my most awesome Tor team for everything they do! You guys are the best! And for Robert, Linda, and Claire for being there! Thank you so very much!

At Death's Door

PROLOGUE

"Oh great Ghede, rise up! Come to us and do what we say!"

Valynda Moore rolled her eyes at Helena Day as she and her sister, Prudence, danced around the small beach fire in sheer chemises. Their loose, pale blond hair trailed about their plump shoulders as they drank rum and frolicked in the moonlight. "Your father will kill you if he sees you like this."

Taking another deep drink from the bottle before

she passed it over to her sister, Helena scoffed at her. "Don't be such a ninny prig! Come and join us."

Seated on the ground beside Valynda, Margaret Latimer turned to another page in the book she was reading. She glanced up toward Helena. "It says here to scatter the white rum with herbs to entice him from his sea kingdom."

Pru quit dancing to blink at Margie. "Scatter it where?"

"The fire, no doubt." Helena grabbed the rum back from her sister's hand, and before Valynda could warn her that it was highly flammable, slung it at the flames.

The girls shrieked as it exploded toward the heavens and caused hot, sparkling embers from the sea breeze to rain down on them.

Except for Valynda, who never screamed, and especially not over such foolery. Rather she thought them ridiculous in their drunken revelry.

"Now toss in the herbs!" Margie reminded them.

Herbs which also turned out to be highly flammable, as there was no telling what those silly lunatics had gathered for their summoning ritual so that they could entice the ancient being they wanted to ask about their future husbands.

As if!

After shrieking and hollering some more over the small explosion they caused, they returned to singing their lude chant to invoke their Voodoo spirit.

Her ears ringing from the raucous cacophony, Valynda sighed in irritation. It was more than she could take. It was one thing for her friends to tell her they planned to be this ridiculous, it was another to witness it firsthand and lose all respect for them. She'd tried on multiple occasions to tell them that the ghede Nibo was the spirit for the dead and wouldn't know anything about their would-be husbands. Still, they kept insisting . . . provided he existed at all, which Valynda highly doubted. Such was her very nature.

And they call me *ridiculous for my sanity.*

Worse, they'd ignored her completely, while they went around the island compiling a list of what they'd need to perform a hokey Voodoo ritual from the hodgepodge of people Val was rather certain had been mocking them.

Unable to stand any more acoustic abuse, Valynda pushed herself to her feet, intending to head home.

Helena tossed more rum on the fire. "Oh great Ghede, come to us and do what we say!"

Valynda ducked the flames as the fire exploded around her. Enough already! They were about to summon the watch and be caught.

Just as she was ready to caution them again over the folly of their actions—and their would-be arson—a huge shadow appeared on the dark beach before them. Like some great fulsome demonic beast, it rose to tower above them, twisting and writhing in a way that made even Valynda gasp. Its cape billowed out as a cane appeared by its side. A cane topped with a skull that matched his evil face. Opening its bony mouth, the cane appeared to scream, then it vomited fire.

Margie screamed.

A second later, she fainted onto the pale sand.

Helena ran, leaving her sister behind to fend for herself. Shrieking and waving her hands over her head, Prudence wet herself before she ran in the opposite direction, with her book forgotten on the beach. Bemused by it all, Valynda stood frozen.

Deep, masculine laughter rang out as that hideous skeletal face turned into one of a handsome, fetching man. One with a riot of dark curls that hugged a perfectly sculpted jaw dusted with whiskers and eyes so vivid and playful, they were beguiling. This was exactly what her friends had been trying to summon and yet he mocked them for it.

Indeed, the infernal beast dared to laugh over the very chaos and panic he'd caused. The humiliation her friends had suffered at his callous hands.

And that set off Valynda's anger that he'd dare such at their expense, especially given the blatant disregard he showed her friend who lay passed out at his feet. "Really? Is this how you entertain yourself? A grown man, frightening schoolgirls? What's wrong with you?"

His laughter died instantly. With an unearthly slowness, he turned to face her, which only confirmed what she'd already noted. He truly was the most handsome man she'd ever seen in the flesh. There was a most unnatural aura of power that clung to him. One that set off the hairs on the backs of her arms and made them stand upright. It let her and everyone else know that he was not one to be reckoned with. Rather, he was used to doing the reckoning. "You dare chastise me?"

Her common sense told her to back down and be the meek maid her father had tried his best to make her, but it wasn't in Valynda to cow to anyone. Male or female. So she spoke her mind and prepared herself for whatever dire consequences might be about to rain down on her. "For being a churlish knave? Aye. Of course I do."

Nibo was aghast as he saw the tiny woman who stood in brave defiance. Never in all the centuries he'd lived after his death had he met a human who wasn't a little intimidated by him. Terrified, point of fact. Most scurried away at his approach, and those were the ones who wanted a favor from him and had dutifully invoked him with gifts.

Until now.

Confused and baffled, he stared at the puzzle who was only passably attractive. While her body was comely enough, she was a bit lanky for his tastes. Her nose rather narrow and long. The only really striking thing about her was her eyes. A rich dark brown, they were searing with their intelligence, and raw with curiosity.

Marked by her condemnation.

For him.

Seriously? How dare she, a mere human, give him such a look! "Do you know who I am, girl?" More to the point, *what* he was.

She narrowed that censoring gaze with an audacity that was quite cheeky and bold, if not downright foolhardy given that he'd feasted on the flesh and bones of creatures that made monsters cry. "Aye. The giant cod-dangle who scared my friends within a quarter inch of their lives."

He scowled at the unfamiliar term. "Cod, what?"

"Dangle," she repeated, then lowered her gaze to the center of his body to illustrate what she was calling him.

While Nibo was amused by her reckless spirit, the most astonishing part was that he actually felt his body stirring.

15

What the hell was that?

She aroused him? How?

This mere slip of a human piece? A pasty pale skirtling who insulted him and looked at him as if he were the cloying slag caught on the hem of her best gown? Surely Anansi and Papa Legba were playing mehen over this, and betting against him right now.

Yet there was no denying the sudden hunger for her that he felt. Especially when he stepped closer and caught the lily scent of her dark brown hair that was tinted with just a hint of red in it—like fire captured in an evening sky. While she wore it tightly coiled and pinned about her head, he wondered what it would look like were he to free it of that cantankerous knot that seemed to be an offense to the curls surrounding a face that was suddenly growing on him.

Aye, she was much more fetching than he'd first thought. There was something about her that drew him in and warmed a deep, cold part of his soul.

Did she have any idea how very dangerous that was to one of his ilk? "Tell me, girl, why did you summon a ghede?"

For the first time, he saw a hint of fear flash through her dark gaze. "W-What?"

"You heard me. What is it that a European daughter would want with one of us?"

Valynda hesitated as she realized he was staring with a peculiar interest down at the cross she wore about her neck. Her jaw went slack as she stepped back and took another look at the beautiful man in front of her.

A real ghede . . .

They weren't just stories made up by the islanders to scare them. They were real! And he was one of them. Holy saints!

Could her lunatic friends have really summoned him to this world? Was it possible?

Trying to calm herself, Valynda wasn't quite sure what one would look like, but certainly not this fine specimen of male attractiveness. It just didn't seem plausible or right given the effigies and drawings that were strung up all over the island.

At well over six feet in height, he was the last thing she'd ever expect of such a terrifying entity. Dressed in a loose-fitting light blue shirt, he had sun-kissed caramel skin that covered a body taut with rippling muscles. Amber eyes that were searing with their intelligence and torment, as if he had a secret that only he knew. A riot of dark, shoulder-length curls framed a face that had been sculpted to masculine perfection. Indeed, she'd never seen anyone more handsome. There was an air about him of power and charisma unlike anything she'd ever beheld before. Something that made her want to walk into his arms and at the same time turn and run as far away as she could. He was terrifying.

And beguiling.

Because there was no doubt that he was equally as lethal as he was beautiful. And his fashion showed that he didn't give a fig what others thought of him. Indeed, he had a number of long pheasant feathers attached to his hair that fell over his chest to trail to his waist. Along with a light beard and an earring that gave him the appearance of one of the pirates her father's stepbrother was so fond of convicting and hanging in cages to rot along the shoreline as a warning to others who dared to venture here to their island home.

Swallowing hard, Valynda shook her head and made a solemn observation she prayed she didn't live to regret. "You're japing. You're not really a ghede."

He arched a brow as a devilish grin lifted one corner of those delectable lips. A low, musical laugh rumbled from his chest. "I'm not just any ghede, gel. I'm the leader of the dead."

Now she knew he was messing with her. Surely a psychopomp would have much better things to do than torment her and her friends, given the number of people slain in and around the islands in this day and age. Rolling her eyes, she crossed her arms over her chest. "On with you now. I've no time for this."

"You don't believe me?" he asked incredulously.

"That a ghede has nothing better to do than scare schoolgirls? Nay, sir, I don't believe you. Now, if you'll excuse me, I needs see about my friends."

As she started to help Margie, he appeared in front of her.

Out of the blue.

Startled and alarmed, Valynda pulled up short. "How did you do that?"

His grin turned teasing. "Told you. I'm Ghede Nibo." He held a small silver ring toward her. "You've intrigued me, Valynda Moore. Check on your friends, and when you're ready to learn more about me, call my name . . . without the theatrics."

An instant later, he was gone and the ring was on her finger.

Suddenly shaking, Valynda stood beneath the light of the full moon in complete shock. Her jaw went slack as she held the ring up to see the skull and crossbones that had been impressed deep into the band. It was beautiful, in a morbid way.

A silver ring of mourning.

"How did he know my name?"

1

1717 Port Royal

Nibo stared down at the scars on his finger where his old silver mourning ring used to rest. A ring he'd placed on his hand as a memorial for his beautiful Aclima and had once vowed to never remove. He still had no idea what had possessed him to hand it off so recklessly to Valynda the night they'd met. Not after he'd spent centuries guarding it so.

He hadn't even thought twice about letting her have the one thing he treasured most. . . .

Strange how he could still feel it there even though he'd given it over so long ago to a mere slip of a woman to hold for safekeeping.

Along with a part of his anatomy he'd deny having if anyone was stupid enough to ask. 'Course it wouldn't be a lie to deny its existence now, given that Val had possession of that damnable organ he'd never had any use for as it had never done anything other than lead him into the fiery pits of damnation.

Still . . .

He missed that ring.

Sadly, he missed Valynda more.

Valynda Moore . . .

The mere thought of her name made him smile.

And *that* instantly made him sneer in disgust, as he realized what the hell his body had done without consulting him.

Again.

"Ye gods," he muttered to himself, "I've gone mad."

Perhaps he'd handed over his brains as well as his heart. What would he lose next? His bullocks?

His dignity?

Shite! To this day, he still didn't know how it was that he'd managed to let himself be dragged into the mess that was his wretched existence. Or come to care for a human the way he did his Val.

And was it any wonder given what his love had done to her?

He'd ruined her life.

Nay, he'd ended it.

Just as he'd done Aclima. He winced at a memory he could

never bear to think about for long. If he did, it would drive him mad.

Furious at himself and the very gods who conspired against them, he downed his rum and fought against the raging anger that had become his constant companion, instead of the one person he'd wanted most by his side.

"What's this? You're looking a bit gloomy, aren't you?"

Nibo glanced up from the spiced rum he was drinking to see the tall, dark menace who'd decided to join him in the crowded tavern where he sat alone at this midnight hour. Alone by choice, not because he was a mutant like the beast before him that everyone avoided because he was an ass. Which was why Nibo had deliberately chosen his solitary table that was tucked back into a shadowy alcove, thinking it would provide him with some degree of privacy and anonymity.

Bugger that. He should have known better. The damned, along with everyone else, were forever seeking him out. For all manner of reasons. Most of which normally pissed him off, and none as much as whatever stupidity would soon be spilling from this creature's lips.

With an annoyed sigh over this unwanted interruption, Nibo raked a bored glare from the top of the dark hair, past his mismatched eyes, to the tips of his scuffed black boots. "Stating the obvious now, are you, mate?" After all, Nibo was the loa of the dead. Gloomy rather came with the territory.

As did a raunchy temper. And derelict disposition.

Though, given enough rum, he could be persuaded into bouts

of cheeriness and debauchery. In fact, he could be downright giddy if the occasion called for it.

This, however, wasn't such an occasion.

Though a good and thorough gutting and denutting of the beast before him might serve to cheer his spirits. At least for a moment or two.

"Come now, is that any way to greet an old enemy?"

Nibo smirked as he modified his welcome to a feigned mixture of jolly alacrity. "Jaden . . . as I live and breathe. To what do I owe this particular hell?"

A slow, beguiling smile curved his lips as Jaden stepped forward into the dim, buttery light cast by stinking tallow candles that made his one green eye glow with mischievous intent. That eye was a stark contrast to its deep, dark disconcerting brown mate.

They were the only imperfections in an otherwise well-proportioned face, framed by a mass of black wavy hair that fell loose about his wide shoulders in defiance of the modern fashion of powdered wigs or queues. But then Jaden had never cared what others did. Or what they thought of him, or of anything else for that matter.

Indeed, like Nibo, he'd left his black shirt untucked and open at the neck. There was no lace or trim of any kind. Or hat, either, as practical fashion could sod off for the night. Jaden's heavy wool coat was plain except for the brass buttons that bore skulls on them. His black breeches were tucked into a pair of scuffed and worn boots. Plain and simple.

But there was nothing else plain nor simple about this warrior god. The worn ancient sword at his hip said as much, as did the threadbare leather hilt which testified to the number of lives lost to this god's nefarious short temper.

More than that, 'twas oft speculated that a million virgins had lost their maidenheads to this scoundrel. As well as another million demons, who had vied for a place in his bed to curry a favor from him.

Nibo didn't doubt that last bit at all. There was something about the demon broker that made him appealing to everyone. Even creatures like him who found the bastard repellent and intolerable. Yet, like a massive catastrophe, it was impossible to look away no matter how horrified one was of the blood and gore of the situation.

Jaden compelled. It was his sick gift.

Oblivious to the growing danger, Jaden stepped forward with his unique predator's lope and sat down at the table across from him. Then, with a reckless disregard for his life, he reached for Nibo's rum and took a leisurely swig.

"We have a problem."

Nibo arched his brow. "Aye, we do. An asshole just stole me rum, and I want it back."

With a laugh, Jaden downed the last of it and poured himself more. "The Malachai has escaped Azmodea."

Nibo scoffed about that.

As the old saying went, *kirast kiroza kirent*. Conceived in violence to do violence and to die violently. That was the Malachai curse, and the code they all lived and perished by. Born of the purest, darkest evil—a trio of gods, Kadar, Azura, and Apollymi, who had brought them forth into existence to fight against all that was good—the Malachai fed the three primal dark gods and lived for nothing except to cause as much suffering in the universe as they could. Because of that, the last one in existence had long ago been trapped and imprisoned.

"I should think that a good thing." After all, if Adarian was missing from Kadar's hell realm, then he'd be unable to feed the powers of all evil. Thus it would weaken the old bastard who plotted the death and dismemberment of all living creatures, and his return to supreme power. Rather a win-win for the world, if you asked him.

Not that anyone ever did.

"Perhaps, but in the process of escaping it seems he took a bit of fluff with him."

"Azura?" The queen of all evil and shadows. Given that she was Kadar's sister and lover—sick as that was—it made sense that the Malachai would kidnap her on his way through the gates of hell and into the human world.

A special little trophy, as it were, to get back at the two of them for keeping him prisoner all these centuries so that Adarian could maintain their powers while they tortured him.

But Jaden shook his head. "Think closer to home . . . *mate*."

He could have done without the bastard's mocking. "I'd say your mother, but you didn't have one." Least none what would claim him.

Father neither, for that matter.

Jaden passed him an unamused glare. Then slid his gaze down

Nibo's chest to where a small treasured trinket lay exposed on a chain, resting near his heart. Just as the woman herself did. Always.

Instinctively, Nibo covered Valynda's cross with his hand.

Strange how no one had ever noticed his odd feminine fashion choice that matched nothing else he wore.

A horrendous sense of dread turned his stomach as he caught Jaden's meaning. Nay, surely not even Adarian would be so stupid as to dare that affront. "What are you saying, demon?"

"I'm saying what I'm saying. You just don't want to hear it. Adarian has your Valynda . . . and Marcelina."

An indescribable rage took hold of him. One that burned so deep and dark that it actually caused Jaden to flinch. No easy feat that, given his own dark and lethal nature. Indeed, Nibo hadn't even known Jaden had it in him to back down.

Until now.

That would be scary if he were able to feel fear. But he and fear had parted company a long time ago. The only emotions he had these days were more potent.

And destructive.

"I see."

With the bitter taste of unspent rage scalding his tongue and a deep need to rip something down to its basest atoms stirring in his belly, Nibo rose. He reached for his rum and downed it, daring Jaden with his eyes to speak another word. His breath came in a ragged cadence. That sound alone betrayed his fury that urged him to go on a rampage. Unable to speak, he headed toward the door while the sound of rushing blood filled his ears.

"Where are you going?"

To make sure that he didn't lose another woman he cared about.

Nibo froze before glancing back at the demon broker who watched him with those peculiar mismatched eyes. "To kick the shit out of the idiot who dared to try and take what is mine. No one makes me out a liar. I won't rest until I'm baptized in their blood and bile and am tying me shoes with their guts."

No one threatened him. Ever.

If anyone knew anything about him at all, it was that they should never come after what he loved. Not if they had any kind of self-preservation or even a shred of common sense.

There would be a reckoning for this that would make Lucifer himself flinch and cower. One to make the demons from the lowest pits of hell hide in fear.

Good-bye. Good luck.

For the one truth to Nibo was that he had no ability to forgive any slight, and he wouldn't rest in a world where the one who'd wronged him lived.

His own twin would testify to that. Which had always made Nibo wonder how it was that everyone feared Qeenan so, simply because he'd been designated as the hitman to the loa. How could they forget the fact that he and his brother were identical twins? Cut from the same set of cells.

He harbored every bit of the ferocity, venom, and bloodlust of Qeenan. The only difference? Unlike his brother, he didn't whine about life's inequities. Nor did he flaunt his skills, which was what made him the deadlier of the two of them.

No one saw him coming.

Qeenan was brute force, and he was Le Beau Mort. Elegant in every way.

Unless it involved Valynda.

Aye . . . things were about to get bloody and people were about to get dead.

Jaden didn't move as he watched Nibo leave. In fact, he didn't breathe until he heard someone clapping sarcastically over the din of mundane conversations. Irritated, he turned to see the last person he'd expected to find in this dismal, dank place that catered to human sailors and their wanton slags.

Tiny and petite, she watched him from shadows that were as dark and mysterious as the lady herself.

And as treacherous.

It was something the two of them shared. Ever shifting in loyalty. One never knew where they stood with them.

Not even their own children.

Some days, not even he knew where he'd put his chips.

Which was good, as it kept everyone on their toes.

"What are you doing here, Cam?"

With skin that was a pure cocoa and eyes that were a startling and unexpected shade of green in contrast, she approached him slowly and with the grace of a mythic queen. She wore bright orange, rust, and yellow skirts that were hemmed in bells that jingled lightly with her fluid movements. Her long Senegalese twists fell to her waist and were held back from her face in a sophisticated chignon. Beauty incarnate, she was tiny to such a degree that most would discount her. But Jaden was well aware of his sister's power.

And her lethality.

In that, they were like-minded creatures.

While she considered herself a force for good, she was as quick to kill and harm as any of those who pledged their hearts and swords to his evil overlords.

"I go by the name Menyara these days, brother, and your powers of subtle manipulation never cease to amaze me. No wonder Kadar and Azura were so hell-bent to get you enslaved to them."

He scoffed at her words and tried to ignore the barb that stung deep, as he would never grow used to being enslaved to their siblings, no matter how many centuries passed. Like Cam, he was technically a god of protective powers who hated what he was forced to do in order to survive. "That wasn't subtle. Trust me. That was the most heavy-handed abuse of my powers ever."

"Perhaps. But impressive nonetheless."

He would argue, except that he didn't like to waste time. And no one ever won an argument against Cam. "You're avoiding my question."

"I'm here for the same reason you are."

To stop the Malachai from rising to the height of his full power that would enable him to destroy the world, and to keep their brother and sister imprisoned.

Good goal that, given that it was the least they could do for everyone's sanity and sakes.

Jaden glanced around the crowded Caribbean tavern that was filled with humans who were oblivious to the fact that they were on the verge of total annihilation. One step shy of oblivion. While Port Royal was about as filthy a hole as any he'd ever seen, he still had a peculiar affinity for humanity. Why? He had no idea. They'd never been particularly kind to him. Had been even less so to his children.

And the human vermin were rank bastards to each other. Surely such a repugnant species should be beyond any form of redemption, and yet . . .

He, like his sister, was counted among the Kalosum—the powers of light or so-called good. At least until he'd made the fatal mistake of enslaving himself to his brother and sister in a sad effort to spare the life of his own grandchild.

And for what?

In the end, evil always seemed to get the upper hand and slap them in the face.

Then give them a staunch middle finger.

Trying not to think about it, he sighed. "Have you found Adarian?"

Cam shook her head. "He's a crafty bastard."

Nay. He was a paranoid one. Much worse, in his opinion. Crafty could be outsmarted. Paranoid was much harder to overtake, as those bastards trusted none and saw danger in every passing shadow and fart. He should know. He'd been paranoid for centuries. It was why he was still alive. Not that that was a particularly good thing. After all, he'd be better off dead at this point.

Damn him for his paranoia.

And damn Adarian for his.

"We've got to trap him and clip their powers, Cam. They're getting way too strong for us to corral. The balance is shifting fast to their favor."

Her eyes darkened as she realized what he already knew. They were in trouble and their side was losing. The balance was ever a delicate thing. A certain amount of evil was necessary in the world to motivate humanity to be good and do what they should. They needed to fear the things waiting in the dark to feast on their souls.

It was good for them.

But too much of that evil, and they would be destroyed. It would overwhelm them.

Worse? It would overrun him and his sister and reshape the entire universe into a vast besmirched vacuous hole where demons would rule and they would all be enslaved to endless torment. He gave an involuntary shudder at the thought.

Having lived for centuries in a realm where his brother and sister had no restraint or anyone capable of reining them in, he was terrified of seeing that unleashed here. It was the last thing he wanted.

Although, with Adarian Malachai around to fight them, it could get entertaining. Provided one avoided the cross fire.

And raining body parts and entrails.

"So what are you thinking, little sister?"

Cam smiled. "I think we use the tools we have to snip the devil in the balls."

He arched a brow at the last words he'd expected to hear her say. "Pardon?"

"We need to kill the Malachai before he raises the dead."

Jaden's blood ran cold as he finally understood what she was saying. "Lillith?"

She nodded. "Since he can't locate Apollymi, that's his answer. To bring back the mother of all monsters."

"Can he do that?"

She shrugged. "Let's just say I've no wish to find out."

Neither did he. Because if Adarian brought back the original evil who'd first crawled into existence and she learned what they'd done to her, they'd all be dead in the next heartbeat.

Lillith was an unforgiving bitch that way, and he had the scars to prove it.

However, they did have one tiny problem. . . .

"You know we can't kill the Malachai. Not until he has a son to replace him." That was the sacred covenant they'd made thousands upon thousands of centuries ago to end their bitter blood feud with their siblings. "They" being the light powers and their siblings being the corrupted darkness that conceived the unholy Malachai army that had almost destroyed everyone on the planet.

The only way to bring about peace and ensure the safety of all was to put down all the demons with Malachai blood. Unfortunately, there'd been a tiny problem in that the Malachai leader, Monakribos, had been the son of their one sister. And Apollymi had refused to see her son dead.

Mothers tended to be unreasonable that way.

Like their sister, Lillith, she was petty and selfish, seeing only her own wants and desires, and not the greater good. Apollymi would have burned down the whole world to save her son.

So, they'd agreed to spare his life and to guarantee him one child to placate their sister-goddess. The sole catch being that only one Malachai could live at a time. Once the son grew in power, he was required to kill his father and replace him.

That was an unbreakable law that stuck in Apollymi's craw to this day.

If their bloodline died out, Apollymi could rise up and strike down the primal gods to exact her revenge on them for what they'd done to her and her husband. It was something they'd all been trying to avoid since the dawn of time.

Damn his sister for her bitchy ways. But that pact had enabled him to save the life of his own grandson, so he couldn't really complain.

Yet one corner of Cam's crimson lips lifted into an evil, quirky grin. "Adarian has a son . . . or it might even be his brother. The point is, there is another Malachai."

Jaden shook his head. It wasn't possible. If anyone else had that kind of malevolent power, they'd all know it. "How? Who?"

"He lives as a cursed god. Deprived of his emotions by Zeus."

He froze for a moment to digest her words. "You're serious?"

"Indeed." She smiled widely with that. "So you see, we can kill Adarian and not break our pact. He has a replacement."

Aye, but there was still one not-so-small problem.

"The last god who went up against Adarian was swallowed whole."

"Then I suggest you pick one you don't like." Patting him on the cheek, she wrinkled her nose and vanished.

Jaden growled low in his throat. "You're a menace, Cam."

Menyara, she whispered in the air around him.

Whatever she wanted to call herself, it changed naught. This was a fool's quest they were about.

Although . . .

His gaze shifted down to Nibo's cup. If anyone stood a chance to stop Adarian, Nibo might work.

After all, raising the dead was what the psychopomp did best.

We're doomed.

Ignoring the echoing sound of reason in his head, Jaden went for the door. Either to fetch Nibo or run for the hills.

He still wasn't completely sure which course was the wisest.

2

Valynda paced the small cell where she and Marcelina had been tossed. And with every step, her fury mounted. Not just because their enemies had violently seized them from the *Sea Witch II* that was part of Marcelina's Deruvian body, and brought them into this dark, dismal hell against their wills, but because . . . well, Mara was just so damned tranquil about it.

As crazy as it sounded, that made her feel betrayed.

She paused in her pacing to glare at the taller woman. "Why aren't you angry?"

Mara lifted her amber gaze to arch a perfect brow. Her white-blond hair shimmered in the darkness. As did her unblemished, porcelain skin. That combination made her appear like some elfin queen holding court. The woman was absolutely flawless in composure. Not that Valynda should be surprised, given that Marcelina was born to the fey Deruvian race. They were known for their poise, grace, and beauty. It rather went with the fact that the Deruvians were a unique tree species that were able to bond with wood and become any wooden object. Therefore, Mara sat all stiff and so elegant.

Rigid. And it was starting to seriously piss her off.

"Anger would be counterproductive." Mara gently smoothed her lace cuff.

Valynda glared at her. "As one motivated by its fiery force, I completely disagree. It gives me clarity."

"Your clarity gives me agita."

In spite of their dire situation, Valynda laughed at her dry tone that caught her off guard. As did the rat that started chewing on the straw that made up her right leg. Growling, she shooed her skirts at the furry little beast. "Off with you! Find something else for your nest!"

She turned to catch the sadness in Mara's eyes as she watched her. Dropping her skirts, Valynda felt the twinge of pain that would have once been in her chest. Only she didn't have a chest anymore. Just a hollowed-out husk of braided straw, thanks to the curse that had been laid upon her by a hate-filled rogering bastabule with nothing better to do than ruin her life for no apparent reason, other than he was a rank arseling.

I'm repugnant.

But she hadn't always been thus. If Valynda closed her eyes, she could still see herself as she'd once been. Tall and thin, with lush, dark hair and perfect skin to rival Mara's. While not as pale, it'd still been clear enough to cause the local poets and dandies to write odes to her. Her only flaw had been the nose she'd inherited from her father. Yet not even that had been enough to detract completely from her looks. At least not as much as the fact that she'd been impoverished.

While her uncle had been Midasarianly wealthy, her father had not. Fool that he was, he'd spurned the trappings of his wealthy youth and turned his back on his family's fortune, forcing her and her mother to live in poverty. She'd tried her best not to resent him for it.

But that had been easier said than done. Especially as she'd grown older. For she'd been a girl of many wants. Like her friends, she'd dreamed of fancy gowns and shoes. Jewels to adorn her neck, wrists, and ears. Pretty hats and elegant balls. Of dining amongst the elite.

Petty things, true. Yet they had seemed immensely important to her at the time.

Until Nibo . . . or Xuri as she and a precious few knew him. He cared nothing for fancy trappings, unless it was to lure others or trick them.

Closing her eyes, Valynda still remembered the night he'd whispered his name in her ear. His coarse whiskers had tickled the flesh of her lobe, spreading chills all over her. He'd held her close to his heart while he was buried deep inside her body. His breathing ragged, he'd tensed ever so slightly as he caressed her cheek. She'd moaned out his name in a desperate cry. "Nibo."

"Call me Xuri."

Startled, she'd stared up at him with a frown. "Xuri?"

"My real name . . . known by only a few."

It was only later that she'd learned how precious a gift he'd given her. By calling out "Xuri" she could summon him. Anywhere. Any time.

He had made himself hers. The elusive loa who had sworn to never be held down by any, who swore fealty to none, had bestowed upon a mere mortal the key to command him any way she wanted. It was a rarity that was unheard of in his world, and something never given lightly.

Most mortals would have bragged about it.

Valynda had never told a soul that she had the ability to call for him. Not because she was embarrassed, but because she respected him that much. He was a private loa, and for it to be known that he'd given a human such authority would make him a laughing-stock among the others of his kind. And she would never hurt her Nibo.

No matter the cause or reason. Because he had always been there when she needed him.

Most of all, because he was there when she didn't.

"Valynda?"

She flinched as Mara's voice lured her back to their dank, dark cell. "Aye?"

"What are you thinking?"

That she wanted to be back in Nibo's arms so that she could show him how much she loved him. Most of all, she wanted the ability to taste his lips and feel the warmth of his skin sliding against her own. Small things really, but Lord how she missed them now that she couldn't have them anymore. "How much I loathe being made of straw."

Besides the fact that it itched constantly. Why couldn't *that* sensation have been taken away, too?

Mara stood and took her hand. Because Valynda wasn't made of flesh, she could barely feel it. Her straw body lacked nerve endings. It was hard to describe to others how she felt, though they'd often asked her. Curiosity being what it was, everyone wanted to know how it felt to be something living that wasn't human.

Though if you asked her, there were many in the world who wore the guise of humans wrapped in flesh who didn't qualify for that title. The man who'd trapped her into this damnable state was most definitely one of them.

Wretched bastard.

And for what? To make her love him? He certainly hadn't thought that one through, had he? In what realm had the beast thought that taking away her free will would make her fall madly for his lack of masculine wiles?

Drugging a woman to force her to do a man's bidding was no way to win her to his side, or gain anything more than her eternal hatred. If she lived to be a million years old, she'd never understand Benjamin Sparke's twisted logic. Or why he'd done what he'd done when it'd benefitted neither of them in the long run.

"We'll get out of this. You know we will."

She wanted to believe that. But she was running a bit low on optimism. Unlike Mara, luck had never been her friend. Rather, it was a fickle bitch who teased and abandoned her at the worst moment possible.

Hence her current stint where she was trapped as a living Voodoo doll. Well, not quite, but it certainly felt that way most days.

Valynda covered Mara's hand with her own and tried not to notice the difference between Mara's smooth flesh and her pale straw extremity. While she wasn't technically a Voodoo doll, she was definitely an abomination.

Why? Because she'd dared to fall in love and trust the wrong man. She'd let her guard down and this was her punishment for trying to be happy. For attempting to have the one thing that others had all the time without punishment.

Love. Happiness. A future of her own.

You're not other people.

True. She was cursed.

All of a sudden a blinding light flashed in their bitter darkness.

One second Mara was there by her side, and in the next she was gone. Ripped from her very grip with nothing more than an almost inaudible gasp!

Valynda panicked more than usual, given that this was what happened to her over and over again in her life.

Everyone she loved vanished on her, without warning. Seldom was she ever given a reason for it. One moment they were there. The next they were gone and she was left behind to pick up the pieces. Alone. With nothing and no one to help her through the madness and pain.

"Mara!" Forcing her hysteria down, Valynda turned around, searching the room with her gaze. Not that there was much to search. The tiny cell was definitely empty. Yet she felt the need to try and find her friend. To reclaim her from the darkness that threatened to swallow them whole. "Mara!" she shouted again, praying she could find her.

It was useless.

Mara was gone.

How could this be? She was alone again. In the dark. Without warning. For no reason. Panic crashed through her like a tidal wave that threatened to tear her apart.

How could she have ever forgotten this desperate feeling? Yet somehow the crew of the *Sea Witch* had driven the horror from her heart. They had given her a false sense of hope and security.

Because the truth was, due to them and their kindness, Valynda hadn't been alone since the day she'd been resurrected from her death.

Nay, since the day Benjamin had killed her.

You will love me. She could still hear his maniacal insanity as he insisted she give him what he hadn't earned. So afraid of the world and of her running away from his repugnant form, he used to stand on her feet to keep her planted by his side. Psychotic to the extreme. How could no one else see it? Everything about him was wrong, and yet her father had insisted she marry him. From the moment she'd met him and had first stared into those dark, soulless eyes, she'd known something about him hadn't been right. He'd lacked empathy for others. Lacked any kind of caring for her.

Sanity for himself.

And on that fateful night when his need to control her had gone too far and he'd slipped over the edge of all human decency, he'd stabbed needles into the body of the poppet he'd used to represent her. Every one had shredded her and torn through her flesh. The pain had been relentless. Unbearable.

She'd screamed for him to stop, but he'd taken no mercy upon her. Then as now. No one ever took mercy on her suffering.

Because no one cares, a disembodied voice whispered in the air around her. It was a haunting sound. Chilling and emotionless.

Worse, it was true.

That was what she hated most. Not because she was being self-pitying. Because it was the truth. Not even her own parents had cared about her. Sad though it was, she'd known that from the moment she'd entered this world and taken her first breath. Her parents had provided for her out of duty and nothing more.

Now . . .

She froze as she heard a sudden sound. Someone was here.

Or something.

"Who's there?"

Echoing laughter answered her whisper.

That only made her panic more, which then angered her, because she hated her own weakness. Fear was ever a useless emotion. It robbed her of what little intimidation she could muster.

Valynda stepped back against the wall to prevent anyone from attacking her there.

"Do you want your freedom?" This time, the voice was loud and commanding. Yet still the creature didn't show himself.

Which made her wonder if it was a trick question. Some bizarre phantom conjured by her mind that didn't want her to be left alone. "Who are you?"

The darkness continued to obscure any trace of Mara or the creature who was speaking.

Instead, her eyes burned from trying to create something for her to focus on in the abysmal blackness. All they provided were peculiar stinging dots of light that chased each other around.

Until an eerie red light appeared. It spread out to form a giant demonic beast before her. One that made her antsy with anticipation. This wasn't just any monster.

It was a Malachai.

The red and black on his skin swirled together and would have been pretty had he not oozed such an unnatural aura of evil and misery. There was never any mistaking such a creature. For they were torture and suffering.

Everything about him screamed ultimate torment and pain. The kind that crawled through the night seeking victims. That turned best friend against best friend. Father against son. Brother against brother. He fed on such turmoil and treachery. It was mother's milk and he lapped it up like a starving kitten.

Had flesh still covered her body, it would be crawling from being this close to his ilk. As it was, she shivered in revulsion. As any normal person would. She had no choice, as his evil permeated the air around her.

Ironic, really. Most assumed Xuri to be this type of destructive creature. Her own father had denounced him as such and forbidden her to be near him.

Yet Xuri, for all his temper and moods, didn't even begin to compare to this. He was actually quite mellow so long as no one crossed him.

The Malachai skidded across the floor to tower over her with eyes that glowed.

"Bet you've scared many a felon into church."

His golden eyes flashed red in the dark, letting her know that he didn't appreciate her humor. "Are you not afraid, chit?"

Not really. Hard to frighten someone who couldn't feel pain and whose significant other was a psychopomp immune to preternatural bullies. So . . . "Been to hell already. Not much more you can do."

He made a noise that might have been a snort. Or indigestion. Hard to tell, really. "Do you not know who I am?"

"Adarian Malachai."

"Then you know to fear me."

Now it was her turn to scoff. "Pish to the posh on that. I don't believe in catering to male egos. Figure yours is large enough already. Why make it grow larger?"

A blast of hot air blew against her, plastering her gown to her straw body. It was so fierce, it caused her to stagger back against the damp stone.

"I could rip you to shreds!"

And she wouldn't feel it. He was missing the point. She wasn't human. She lacked the physical sensation of others. Hence the whole straw-body nightmare that made up her existence and why she really didn't care if he did end her. At least that would put her out of her misery and end this epic horror once and for all. Because, honestly, she was so tired of living like this that eternal death was beginning to look good to her.

Most of all, she was sick of creatures like Adarian, Benjamin, and her father using her for a pawn in their sick games and for their sick goals.

In spite of her current form, she was human, not a trophy or a prize.

Or a means to an end.

When would someone see her as a person with feelings? As someone to be loved and not used?

Was it really too much to ask that one person, somewhere, just once, cherish her?

All her life, everyone around her had done nothing save shove her and threaten her if she didn't please them or do what they told her. Be a lady. Be silent, etc. Her father had spent her entire childhood beating her every time she questioned him or didn't do exactly what he wanted.

Her mother had never allowed her an ounce of breathing room. *Sit properly. Say nothing. Be a good little piece of eye candy to catch a good husband.* And all that training had culminated in Benjamin's insane ultimatum—*marry me or die.*

She was done with it and with being pushed around and disregarded.

"Do you have a real point for your visit or is your ego so fragile that you have an innate need to build it up by preying on a pathetic human creature you're keeping in a cage like some pet bird you've dragged home?"

Hoping to God that someone finally put her out of her never-ending misery, she lifted her chin defiantly and glared at him.

Please, God, have mercy and kill me!

"Go ahead, Adarian. Do your worst."

She wanted him to blast her into oblivion. Nay, she needed him to so that the constant pain in her heart would finally cease and leave her be. She braced herself for it and waited.

And waited.

Instead of giving her what she wanted most, the wretched, heartless bastard pursed his lips and narrowed those demonic eyes as if he were assessing her mettle.

Or something worse.

Without warning, rats burst up from the floor, rushing around her feet.

Shrieking, Valynda danced around, trying to avoid them as they did their best to shred her legs and climb up them.

"So, you are at least squeamish."

She did her best to keep them at bay as she glared at him and beat them away. "No one likes a rat." Especially not a six-foot-something demonic red asshole of one who thought this funny!

Her breathing ragged, she cursed them and him as she continued stomping.

"Unless it's another rat."

He had a point, she supposed.

Suddenly, the two of them were outside the room.

Valynda jerked her skirt out of the paws of one last rat, which sent the little beast tumbling away from her. It scurried off.

Bright light blinded her as she found herself on an island beneath a bent palm tree. Grateful she was no longer under assault from the furry little rodents, she held her hand up to shield her eyes from the glare.

The Malachai seemed even taller here. Somehow more massive even though they weren't in a confined space. And that said a lot for his presence and powers.

His skin faded to that of a normal man. Well, "normal" was a stretch given that he was exceedingly handsome with eyes so clear and blue they'd rival the very sky for its cerulean clarity.

Her jaw went slack.

An evil smile curved his lips. "Transmutation is only one of my many powers."

She snapped her mouth closed, unwilling to feed his massive ego any more, lest it grow larger. "Am I supposed to be impressed?"

"Depends. Are you ready to be human again?"

3

Valynda held her breath at an offer that was too good to be true. Aye, she knew that adage and then some. Looking a gift horse in the mouth never turned out well. It made enemies all around.

And when things were too good, people turned into Voodoo dolls and life slid straight into the very bowels of hell.

"I wasn't born yesterday, sirrah. No one makes such an offer without exacting a dear price for it." And having already paid a price so dear that it left her soul raw and bleeding, she had no desire to repeat such a mistake.

She had no more blood to give. Literally and figuratively.

"True. There is something I want."

Of course there was. No one gave because they were altruistic. There was no such thing as a "good" Samaritan. Better than anyone, she knew that. So, she braced herself for the repercussions of refusing him because there was no way she intended to play this game with something like the Malachai when she knew she was going to lose. "And that is?"

"You to join my ušumgallu."

Stunned to her very straw core, she stared at him. Was he serious?

Well that's something new. And not what she'd been expecting.

The ušumgallu were the main generals who led his demonic army. Powerful beyond belief, they were the very things she and Mara, and the rest of the Deadmen, had been fighting against lo these many, many bloody months. Horrible beasts, one and all. It was what Thorn had resurrected them for—to keep the Malachai and his evil forces from taking over the world and swallowing it whole.

They were the blackest guard who wanted to enslave mankind and watch the world burn. Literally and figuratively.

"I don't understand."

"I lost my Šarru-Namuš." *Death King.* The moment Adarian said the name, she saw a glimmer in his eye that said he hadn't lost him so much as he'd probably either sacrificed said being . . .

Or brutally killed him or her. Probably for nothing more than breathing the same air. Adarian was, after all, the Malachai. Killing off his generals and replacing them with another poor unfortunate soul wasn't unheard of. It was rather a blood sport of sorts for his kind, as they held no value for anyone, not even those who served them.

"And I can think of no better replacement than one such as yourself, given your need for vengeance upon this world for what it's done to you." Adarian lifted her chin so that she was staring up into his glowing, feral eyes. "Provided you bring me Nibo's crook."

There it was.

The rub that would get her killed if she was discovered, for that was the one thing Xuri would never part with. He'd gut her himself should she dare try to take his staff from him, as it held mystic powers she couldn't even begin to fathom. She felt her stomach twist at the very thought of what Adarian asked.

And she wasn't dumb enough to fall for it. "You're the Malachai. Why not get it yourself, Lord of Infinite Powers?"

His eyes turned a vibrant red and his brow darkened as if he were about to hit her for her insolence. And he wouldn't be the first to lay fist to her cheek. Her father had raised her on that tactic.

So, she braced herself for the impact.

But it didn't come. Rather, he seemed to catch his temper at the last second, and took a deep breath.

To her even greater shock, he laughed and stepped away from her. His huge black wings expanded out from his back while he paced. They twitched to show his irritation. "It's enchanted. *I* cannot remove the crook from his possession. But *you* . . . you can go in there and pull it out for me."

She laughed out loud at the thought. Nibo's crook that he wore as a small charm about his neck was deemed sacred. The one time she'd accidentally brushed it with her fingertips out of curiosity, he'd actually hissed at her and pulled back as if he were a cobra. His reaction had been so swift and instinctive that it'd scared them both.

To this day, she knew better than to go near it. Either when it was around his neck as a charm, or when he held it in his hand as a walking stick.

He would definitely kill me.

"Would he?" Adarian asked.

She gasped at the fact he'd heard her thoughts.

Stepping forward, he turned her around on the beach so that she faced a tall, intricately carved looking glass that rose up from the sand. Her eyes widened at the sight of her in her old body, dressed in the finest ball gown she'd ever seen. Tears shimmered in their dark depths because they were no longer that hateful demonic red caused by her unholy resurrection.

Her eyes were once again the dark brown of her human lifespan.

She reached up to touch the flesh of her cheek to make sure it was real skin.

It was. As was the dark auburn hair that she'd missed so much. Thick and soft tresses that twined about her fingers like silk, not horrid straw that crinkled and broke. For the first time in her life, she didn't even mind the size of her nose, because it was hers and it was real. This was no illusion or dream.

She was human again.

Falling to her knees in the sand, she wept in relief, grateful beyond measure to feel the wetness on her cheeks and to endure the stuffy nose and swollen eyes that came with it.

Adarian watched her with a cold, calculated stare. "I want his crook and Thorn's sword. Get them for me and I will ensure that you maintain this appearance you so covet."

Damn him for knowing the one thing she'd betray the world for. She wiped at her eyes with the back of her hand. "And if I can't get them?"

"You're a beautiful woman, Valynda. There's nothing you can't get from a man if you set your mind to it."

She hated him for that, as she'd never been the kind to use her looks or wiles that way. It wasn't in her to be manipulative or to use another person for personal gain. She found it petty and cruel. Heartless. In truth, she'd always hated the attention her looks had caused. The distraction. The animosity and trouble. From the moment the other girls had realized that she turned male attention away from them toward her, her life had become hell. Especially because she'd been poor.

Whore. Gold digger. Tart. Slag. She'd been called every name imaginable.

All except the one she'd wanted . . .

Friend.

The men had been even worse. They hadn't seen her as anything more than a pretty object to be claimed. A token they wanted to ruin and sully, and then cast away once they had their pleasure and were done with her. Because she had no money, she was of no value to them as anything more than a passing curiosity. She'd spent her entire mortal life being treated as if she had no feelings.

Put down and belittled as some trifle to be ignored at best and berated for sport at worst.

She'd learned to hate the world. To lash out anytime someone got too close.

Until Nibo.

How ironic that it'd been a spirit of death who'd taught her about life. Who'd given her a reason to live and to love. A reason to want to be a part of the world that had done its best to make her feel unwanted.

He alone had seen past her flesh and not been taken in by her beauty. Rather, it was her heart and soul that beguiled him.

Just as she'd fallen in love with his.

Nibo had given her a cold once-over on the night they'd met . . . *"You're passing enough, I suppose. For a human."*

Most women would have been insulted. She'd been intrigued. Nibo hadn't seen her external beauty until they became close. That was his curse. He couldn't see the physical appearance of anyone. He only saw the truth of their soul. It'd been her inner fire that had attracted him. The fact that she'd called him out for his inappropriate behavior and made him act better whenever he was with her.

She'd demanded he rise above his baser mischievous arrogance and treat people with regard and not the disdain he was famed for.

He was an insufferable ass, but he was her ass.

"Why should I be human, Vala? I'm a death loa. We've never been polite. To anyone."

"Because there are enough assholes in this world, Xuri. Why should you strive to be another?"

A tear ran down her cheek as she remembered the first time Xuri had kissed her. The possessive passion he'd shown. The love and desire. Fired not just by lust, but by real care and something so much deeper. She could still taste his lips. Feel his hesitant arms around her body as he drew her close to his side.

He who knew no fear or doubt had been bashful the first time he'd tasted her lips. And that was a part of him that she would always cherish. The part of him that she alone possessed and held sacred.

For she had seen him vulnerable.

She had seen him human.

"I could never betray him."

Adarian leaned down to whisper in her ear. "He betrayed you the minute he let another man lay claim to your life and take it while he did nothing to protect you from Benjamin's madness. Why didn't he fight for you?"

Pain shattered her heart over something she did her best not to think about. Ever, as the pain of it all was so much more than she could bear. It was true. Xuri should have protested her father's actions and taken her away from a fate so much worse than death. Why hadn't he fought when the pastor came and demanded her hand from her father?

Instead, he'd said nothing when she told him her father had arranged her marriage to a stranger.

His dark eyes had held no emotion whatsoever. Neither had his flat and even tone. "It's for the best."

How could he ever say such to her? Wish it on her when he was supposed to love her above all others?

Valynda had been outraged. "I don't love him, Xuri. How can I marry him when I'm married to you?"

"We have a spiritual marriage. It's not the same, Vala. You know that. What you share with a loa transcends human marriage. It can never be the same."

Those words had torn her heart out and left it bleeding at his feet, where he'd stepped on it and ground it into the dirt beneath his heel. After everything they'd shared, she'd stupidly deluded herself into thinking that they had something more than a simple tawdry affair. That Xuri had been different than the other men who'd made advances toward her. Surely she hadn't bought into his lies. Deluded herself into thinking he was better than the others, only to find out that he wasn't. Yet as they continued to argue, she had come to the horrible realization that he'd been using her as a mindless tool.

In the end, he'd been no better than anyone else.

Another lousy user out for himself, who saw people like her as nothing. Not even human.

He'd wanted her virginity and he'd taken it. What happened to her after that hadn't mattered to him. The laws of man that would denounce her as a whore were irrelevant. What did it matter to a loa who lived beneath the sea in his happy little kingdom, where the laws of man didn't apply? He would always be untouched by what they'd done.

Meanwhile, she was ruined. Her future destroyed. He'd singlehandedly set fire to and annihilated every plan and dream she ever had.

And the worst part?

He didn't care. Nibo had looked her dead in the eye and not blinked or shown any remorse for his actions. That utter lack of regard had shattered her heart.

It had destroyed a part of her that would never heal again.

That was the day she'd learned what true hatred was.

The pain had been more than she could take. To know that no one had ever loved her. That after all this time, she'd allowed herself to be taken in by a pretty face and honeyed, lying tongue. That she'd wasted her love on a heartless bastard . . .

How could she have been so incredibly stupid? Was she really so desperate for love that she'd allowed herself to become his prey so easily? The pitifulness of it all had been more than she could bear.

Furious, she'd gathered her skirts and moved to leave him. "Then I will marry no one! I denounce even you!"

That was what had gotten her into this fix. Her stubborn tongue and independent fire that had refused to heel for any man.

Even her father.

The moment the "good" Christian pastor had learned of her connection to a loa, and of her determination to avoid her marriage, not only to him, but anyone, he'd become a crazed monster. One bent on her complete and utter destruction. Whatever the cost to both their lives and souls. He'd lied and gone after her with a fanatic zeal that had made no sense.

She'd never understand how people could be so callous toward each other. How one person could set out to destroy another without any regard for them or their family. All that mattered was their own selfish gain. Their own wealth and wants. To hell with the person they were destroying.

Surely there was a special corner of hell reserved for such wretched bastards. A place where all the world would see them for what they were and know them by their lies and deeds, where they would be stripped bare to be eternally mocked for it all.

They were the true whores of Babylon. For they took the hearts of the faithful and crushed them with their cruelty, causing those of faith to doubt the existence of all goodness and kindness in this world and beyond. Removing them from the path of right and the hand of God to pull them toward the darkness.

Forever lost to the cruelty of their actions.

So here she was.

Twice cursed.

Betrayed. And with no hope of anything better.

"Don't you deserve to be loved?" Adarian's question hung in the air between them.

Valynda felt more tears stinging her eyes as she stared in the looking glass that reflected her perfect, serene image on the beach. A clear sunny day that was at odds with the storm brewing inside her.

Of course she did. All creatures deserved love. It was a basic right that came with the first breath of life, and yet it seemed to forever elude her. What a tragedy that so many were forced to fight for it. Even more were denied its crucial sustenance. And why?

Because of the brutality of others.

What was wrong with this world that so many were caught

up in their own pain that they sought to lash out and inflict their misery upon all they met? How could people be so mean?

Aye, she wanted blood for what had been done to her. Just like they did. It wasn't fair what had happened. It wasn't right. She'd never asked to be turned into a monstrosity because of one man's selfishness.

Surely, she deserved some happiness. Just once.

Something for herself. Was that really so selfish?

Thorn had promised her a body and yet she'd seen the doubt in his eyes whenever he spoke of it. As if he feared his ability to keep his word.

No one had ever once kept their troth to her. Unless their word had been to inflict pain and harm. That promise they'd abided by and then some.

So how could she trust anyone? She'd been lied to the whole of her life.

By everyone. Her mother. Her father.

Xuri.

Charlatans, all. Her beleaguered heart was scarred beyond all recognition at this point. She didn't even know how it was capable of beating anymore, given the abuse it'd taken.

So weary was she that she knew better than to even hold out a snail's snot of hope that this beast before her would keep faith in what he was telling her. 'Twas Sam's folly to even dabble with the notion that he be honest.

If his lips are moving, he's lying. . . .

Aye, that was the one truth she could believe.

"How do I know you'll keep this bargain?"

Adarian laughed bitterly. "That's the rub, isn't it? You never know what set of lips are false or true. The world is filled with liars and thieves, beggars and whores, all out to take what they can while assuring you that you can trust them to do no harm. Each one stealing a bit of your soul with everything they take until you have so little left that you become one of them. Or something far worse."

He was right. That was the hardest struggle in life. To maintain a grip on your soul when you were done wrong, especially by someone you trusted. To not let the beasts rob the last of your goodwill. Your decency.

It wasn't the scarecrow she feared being anymore.

'Twas the shadow overtaking her heart that caused her to wake up screaming at night.

Because, deep inside, she knew she had so little goodness left that it wouldn't take much to tip that scale over and render her useless and dark for the rest of eternity.

To make her one of the beasts she hated most. The beasts they were commissioned to stop from preying on others.

But to take from the two men who had helped her . . .

She couldn't do it.

Adarian tsked. "Here, love. Let me help with your decision."

The image in the mirror turned sinister. Swirling. No longer was it her reflection. Rather, it became a dark, raucous tavern that looked similar to those she knew Xuri had a peculiar penchant for. The kind he'd never allowed her to venture into because he claimed that he didn't want her tainted by their tawdry ways.

"You are far too pure for such, *lanmou mwen*. You don't need to be sullied with my bad habits. I'd rather you lift me up than I drag you down." His words had always touched her.

It wasn't until she'd joined the Deadmen crew of the *Sea Witch*, who were charged with hunting down demons and returning them to their respective hell dimensions, that she'd ventured into such human hellholes and learned what Xuri had meant. Only then had she fully understood his reluctance for her to enter such places.

He'd been right. They were disgusting. And it did nothing to salvage her low opinion of the people who had spent her entire lifetime tormenting her and trying to prey on her innocence and poverty because they saw her as less than nothing. Thought her an easy mark because her father had picked his pride over her future. Honestly, she couldn't fathom what Xuri found so evocative about them.

The stench alone was enough to keep anyone with a nose far away.

Yet Xuri was an easy one to pick out of the thick crowd in the smelly room. Not just because he was there with his two companions she knew so well, Oussou and Masaka, who were impossible to miss on their best days, but because he sat with Papa Legba and Baron Samedi.

A chill went down her spine that the gathered loas were all away from their precious island, Vilokan. The loa homeland that existed below the seas where they took the dead and lived in peaceful accord with each other until they were summoned into the human world. Rare was it for them to be gathered in such a manner.

And this was no happy outing.

They wore the grim faces of the reaping they were known for. Sitting in a semicircle, the four men reminded her of a murder of crows. A cloud of cigar smoke encircled their heads while Papa Legba and Samedi swapped rum glasses.

As the sole female of the group, Masaka was tall, with dark skin and eyes that flashed with intelligence. Her red brocade coat was embroidered in the same gold that matched the trim of her tricorne hat. But like her brother, she remained silent while the older spirits talked.

Legba narrowed his gaze on Xuri. "You weren't to be dabbling with her kind, you know that, son."

Sullen in his silence, Xuri twisted his glass as a tic started in his jaw.

"What were you thinking?" Legba lit a new cigar while he glared with dark, soulless eyes.

Dressed in a bright purple brocade coat, the baron shook his head. "She's not one of us. She can never be one of our kind."

Xuri met the baron's gaze without shirking. "Neither was Maman Brigitte."

An earthquake went through the room, causing the humans to shriek and seek cover. It was so deep and fierce that even Valynda felt the fury of its shivering.

Xuri didn't flinch.

Papa Legba lowered his cigar and reached for the rum nearest him. "What are you saying? Are you to marry her, then?"

Xuri shook his head. "You know better. She's human. There's no place for her in our world. Least not so long as she's alive."

Samedi cut his gaze to Oussou. "Go to Erzulie. Find his human a lover and take her off our brother's hands. Sooner rather than later."

Valynda held her breath as she waited for Xuri to stop his little minion from obeying. To do something other than sip his herb rum and ignore the other spirits.

He didn't.

Rather, he just sat there, doing nothing.

Nothing!

Her heart sank as she felt the horror of the one piece about her fate that she'd never known. Xuri had taken a personal hand in her damnation. No wonder he'd been so quick to help Thorn bring her back.

Not out of love.

Out of guilt!

Fury rose up and choked her. How could he have done this to her? How! She'd loved him more than anyone. Had trusted him. Given him every piece of her heart and soul. And how had he repaid her?

With treachery! He'd worked against her and had sicced her worst nightmare upon her. Sold her out to an embittered old bastard for sport because she'd meant nothing to him.

Never in her life had she felt so stupid.

So . . . so . . .

Words failed her.

Pain filled her.

Truly, she wanted to die as emotions battled each other for supremacy and she couldn't tell which one she should give in to. The hurt, the rage, or the confusion.

All she knew was that her life had been torn apart and she'd done nothing to deserve this. Nothing save love a creature she thought loved her back. That shouldn't have cost her everything and more. Love shouldn't be paid for with blood and bone. Never should it cost someone their soul.

He'd taken everything in the world that was precious to her and more. Therefore, it only seemed right that she should return the favor. If he didn't love her or care about her, she knew one thing he did give a damn about.

One thing he couldn't stand to live without.

It would be as precious to him as her body had been to her.

Her breathing ragged, she turned to meet Adarian's gaze. "You want his staff? I'll get it for you."

Xuri would only be lucky if she didn't ram it someplace extremely uncomfortable first!

4

Valynda wasn't prepared to return to her straw body after her blessed respite. The sheer cruelty of it . . .

It made her want an even larger piece of Xuri's hide over his betrayal. But that also built up her resolve to see this mission through no matter what it took. To not let her feelings for Xuri intrude on what had to be done. To be as cold toward him as he'd been toward her when he made the decision to sell her out and leave her to die.

After all, why shouldn't she? He'd put himself first. Why shouldn't she do the same? Even her own father had cast her off for his own gain. Used her as a bargaining chip as if she were a mindless thing.

Be good. Do as you're told. 'Twas all she'd ever heard. *Cause no problems. Just be a pretty little thing.*

She'd been cast as a doll long before Thorn had brought her back in a poppet's straw body.

No one had ever given a fig about her, and she was done with this wretched world and the callous way it had always treated her.

Thorn had brought her back to protect mankind. Yet at the moment, she wasn't feeling particularly charitable toward anyone else. Not while her heart was so broken. She might not be able to feel physical pain, but she could feel this splintering inside her that hurt so deep to her soul that she feared she'd never be whole again. And she was tired of aching like this. Of being used and used up.

Of crying while no one cared about the damage they did to her.

At least until she saw Mara surrounded by a group of jumbies—demonic creatures who lived to inflict pain and prey on the life forces of others. Parasitic beasts with no regard for anything save themselves.

With her powers, Mara had fashioned two sets of circular blades for weapons so that she could fight them off. Still the jumbie demons came at her, trying to overrun the pregnant Deruvian who'd protected the Deadmen for all these many months as their mothership.

In a weird way, their vicious attack on Mara made sense. She was part of an ancient tree race and the jumbie were part of the silk cotton trees. They were of similar species and probably had a common ancestor somewhere. Perhaps defeating her would give them additional powers and strengths.

Let them have her. What do you care?

For once, she was feeling *that* selfish and brutal. Like the rest of the world and like most everyone had been toward her.

But Mara was her friend. She'd never been unkind to her, and that meant a lot to Valynda. Particularly because Mara had nothing to gain by being nice. It was merely her nature to be that way. Such people were so rare that she refused to see her harmed. Nay, not this day, and not while the good captain relied on Valynda to protect the one thing in this world he loved above all others.

Kindness should never be rewarded with betrayal. Such a rarity should be protected at all costs.

By life and limb, and especially those exceptionally rare few who gave it for no reason whatsoever.

Growling with the weight of her betrayal, Valynda rushed forward to join the fight. Not to mention it gave her an outlet for her own pent-up rage at this callous life that seemed to begrudge her every breath. Aye, she needed this!

More, she wanted to taste their blood and let it quench her fury. While she might not have the powers that Mara had, Valynda could cut the heads off any demon who came after her, and she had the added bonus of being an immortal who could feel no physical pain. Let them try their best, for the jumbies weren't so fortunate. They could be banished back to their hell realms by separating their heads from their bodies or piercing their eyes. And if her mood were foul enough, she could even take their life force and extinguish it entirely.

Which was why she used a long, thin rod to hold her straw hair up from her neck. Made it easy to keep a weapon handy. Sliding it free, she ignored the straw braid that fell forward as she used the long blade to pierce the eye of the first jumbie she reached.

"Take that, you heartless bastard! Pick on a pregnant woman, will you! To the devil, let you burn!"

It made a piercing, horrendous scream, then burst into a shimmery veil of dust. That gave the obnoxious fiend next to it pause as it realized what had happened. And by whose hand death had come.

When the other demon tried to run, Mara threw out one of her "limbs" and wrapped it around him to trip him and haul him back toward them. Now that made Valynda wish *she* could turn into a tree and grow her arms at will.

Oh, to have those talents with her straw! But then everyone had their own unique skills.

Hers appeared to be chafing the gods. Why else would they punish her so?

"Val!"

She turned at Mara's call to see three jumbies headed for her. Valynda barely caught the first she-bitch that reached her before it sank its fangs into her arm. Not that it would have mattered really, given that she couldn't truly feel such bites the way normal people did. Still, it was nice to be warned. She elbowed the demon in the throat, then caught it with her rod.

"How many of these are there?"

Mara sighed. "Enough to be annoying."

She'd give Mara that. And they seemed to be multiplying like a hydra. Kill one, find ten more. 'Twould be terrifying to most. But at the moment, 'twas most edifying to her, as she had a lot of pent-up fury she needed to purge.

So she welcomed the extra targets.

"Give me more!" She tore through the demons with a glee that, judging by Mara's face, must be a bit shocking. And why not? Valynda had always been one of the quieter, meeker members of their crew.

Until now. But then betrayal had a way of bringing out the witch in even the gentlest of creatures. There was nothing more motivating than a need for blood vengeance.

She understood that now.

Especially when all the demons were dead and gone, and she found herself standing in front of Mara, and Valynda took note of the alarmed expression on her friend's beautiful face as she stared at her as if she were a stranger.

"Are you all right?"

Valynda hesitated as she wondered what Mara saw that gave her such concern. "Aye. Why?"

"Just . . ." Her voice trailed off while she glanced around the darkness, where blood was smeared all about. "You seemed a little bloodthirsty there. Much more so than usual. Been hanging with Kalder a bit?"

She snorted at the mention of their ship's striker. He could be a bit intense in a fight as he'd been one of their rougher members.

Especially now that he'd claimed Cameron as his bride. While he'd been protective of the crew before, he'd jumped to a whole new level of insane protection after his marriage. One that had only intensified with his wife's pregnancy.

Before Valynda could comment on their similarities, a portal appeared beside them. The light was almost blinding in the darkness. Mara summoned her sharp wooden daggers again as Valynda made ready to attack whatever new creature was coming for them. Though to be honest, she was growing a bit weary of the battle. Why couldn't something nice come out of the portal for once? Like maybe soft butterflies.

A piece of pie or music?

Just as Valynda made ready to rush and attack whatever new monster hell had decided to spit out at them now, she paused to see an incredibly tall, handsome demon stepping through. One with red, evil eyes and coal-black hair that begged for a woman's fingers to be twisting through its curls. More than that, his lethal predator's lope said he was here to kick the ass of anyone foolish enough to cross his path.

And Valynda had seen him do that enough to know he was more than able to make good on that threat.

Mara ran into his arms with a delighted cry.

With a deep grunt of relief, Captain Bane scooped up his wife in one arm, while holding out his sword with the other, ready to stab and kill whatever creature had made her so hysterical. He scowled in confusion as there was nothing left to confront him, then paused as he caught sight of Valynda, who watched them with an amused smirk.

Behind him, Blackheart Bart and William Death slowed down their rush to fight as they realized they'd missed the threat, too.

Stepping forward, Valynda clapped Bart on his broad shoulder. "Day late. Pound short, gentlemen. We ladies already took care of the nasty beasties. Thanks for not being here."

With a mane of long brown hair that he wore tied back in a tight queue, Bart had the bluest eyes of any man Valynda had ever known. And like Xuri, he fancied jewelry to such an extent that he wore a ring upon each finger. What was more, he'd not only pierced both ears, but also his left eyebrow, where he wore a small gold hoop.

Even so, he was still unbelievably handsome. Same as William, what with his black hair and hazel blue eyes that had seduced many a maid past her common sense and out of her knickers. Much to the maid's later chagrin. And to hear Will tell it, his too, many times.

Those men were just three of the reasons being a member of the *Sea Witch* wasn't so bad. She had to give it to Thorn, he'd picked a mighty handsome crew for this venture. Or perhaps that was the thing about evil.

It liked to corrupt pretty things.

Come to the dark side, we have luscious booty.

Bart tsked. "Are you telling me that we're too late to play hero? What good are we then?"

"Not a bit, mate." Will winked. "It's what I keep telling you." He sheathed his sword before he grinned at Valynda. "Are you all right, milady?"

"Aye. Thank you."

The three of them ignored the captain and his wife, who were locked in a bit of an awkward display of affection. So much so that Bart began to whistle and clap his hands together. A bit loudly, as if trying to separate them, and remind them that they weren't alone in the dreary darkness.

"Thinking we should head back to the ship, eh?" Will volunteered loudly when Bart's tactic didn't work.

Bart nodded. "Definitely." He passed a meaningful look toward the captain and Mara. "Anyone got a crowbar?" He smirked. "Bucket of cold water?"

Will let out a scoffing snort. "I dare you, mate."

She couldn't agree more, as such a move would be all kinds of suicide. Not to mention, she didn't want to dawdle, as more jumbie friends could come back at any moment.

"We'll just leave them to it, shall we?" After all, Captain Bane was more than capable of dealing with anything their enemies could toss at them.

With one last look, Will led the way back toward the portal.

Valynda didn't hesitate to follow. Last thing she needed right now was to see a happy, loving couple. That only reminded her of how badly Xuri had done her and how much she wanted to cut off a piece of his anatomy and hand it to him.

With her regards.

Bloody bastard.

He'd deserve it, too, for what he'd done.

They all would. Every last one of them.

Their ship's pilot, Sancha, was right. Men were the worst sort of philandering beasts, one and all. Their cod-dangles were nothing more than dowsing rods bent on seeking trouble and women of low virtue. Their lips might claim to want one thing, but their actions spoke of something else entirely. Why Valynda had ever sought to protect one of their questionable species, she had no idea. Some of her stuffing must have come loose in her noggin and left her seriously lacking.

That was her thought, until they returned to the ship and she was greeted by more hugs and well wishes than she'd ever imagined. Her head spun as she was grabbed up, squeezed, and then passed to the next set of arms.

It wasn't until she got to Cameron and Kalder Dupree that she came to a staggering halt. Laughing, Cameron drew her into a warm hug. "You poor wee thing. You look a bit dazed."

Valynda smiled at her friend. Since Cameron had married Kalder, she'd stopped dressing as a man, and had begun to wear the trappings of a woman. Gowns looked good on her, as did the dainty bonnet that framed her lovely face and brought out the curve of her flushed cheeks, which had grown rounder with her pregnancy. "How did all of you find us?"

Kalder inclined his head to someone over Valynda's shoulder.

She glanced over, expecting to see a crewmember or Thorn.

It wasn't.

To her eternal shock and dismay, Xuri was there, towering over her. He'd covered his curly dark hair and those feathers he wore braided into them with a black linen headscarf that strangely made him seem tame. Subdued. For the first time, she saw the guilt in his amber eyes and knew it for what it was.

Guilt for his part in condemning her to this fate. Damn him for it.

More than that, he'd tamed down his dandy fashion to a faded light purple linen shirt and a plain black overcoat. Black breeches and scuffed, unremarkable boots. He was more akin to the captain than the arrogant peacock he normally appeared whenever he made his presence known among humans. The only accouterments to betray his loa identity were the elaborate necklaces layered around his neck and the studded leather belt with a large silver skull buckle. And of course his bejeweled rings. They alone were the usual fare that she'd never seen him part with.

Meanwhile, Oussou wore his pale hair pulled back from his handsome face. He stood to Xuri's right, dressed in his typical elaborately embroidered black brocade jacket and satin breeches. His purple vest stood out in vivid contrast to the somber colors. As did Masaka. But then, she always stole the show and drew everyone's attention. Her dark skin glistened in the light even though she'd painted the outline of her skull over the top of her flesh so as to scare those who saw her. It was, after all, what she loved to do most—

Frighten anyone foolish enough to cross her path. The more screams, the better. She counted that as her personal badge of honor.

Yet like their master, they were subdued today.

Sincerity burned in Xuri's eyes as he approached her slowly. Almost as if he were afraid of how she'd react to him. "I'm glad they found you."

She gave Xuri a cold smile. "As am I. Would have been most rotten had they not." She was torn between anger and hurt . . . but really, it was mostly hurt. A deep, agonizing pain that burned straight through her heart and made her want to put as much distance between them as she could. Right now, she needed time to think about what she'd found out. Time to consider what he'd done and if she could really forgive him for tearing her out of her body and leaving her as this horrific shell of a creature.

Could she forgive him? And if she did, was that worth giving up a chance for a real human body again?

So, she brushed past him to head toward the stairs that led belowdecks.

Nibo stood completely stunned as Valynda left him with a sudden brush-off the likes of which she'd never done before. What the hell was that? Especially after everything he'd done for her!

He could tell Masaka wanted to say something but knew better than to speak in front of the others. After all, he wasn't one to take insubordination lightly. While he could be laid-back, he did have a temper.

Right now, that temper was climbing.

Nibo passed a look to his companion that dared her to break her common sense and speak one single word. The mood he was in, he might hand Masaka's tongue to her if she dared. This wasn't the reception he'd expected. Valynda was supposed to be grateful to him for her rescue. Throw herself into his arms and kiss him blind. Declare her undying love. Maybe not to the extent of Marcelina and her public mauling of Devyl Bane on his left, but still. A happy medium between an all-out orgy on the deck of the ship and the cold brush-off he'd just been given would be nice.

Unable to stand it, he headed after her.

But he didn't get far. As soon as his feet hit the lower deck, he found the tiny little sorceress Belle Morte planted squarely in front of him. The look in her amber eyes said that she wanted to give him a resounding lecture, though why, he couldn't even begin to imagine.

Her dark skin was a stark contrast to the white shirt and exposed corset she wore over a bright red skirt. She tsked as she shook her head at him. "What have you done?"

That tone irritated him and called for a sarcastic response. "Came below."

She rolled her eyes. "There's a secret you be harboring. Be wary what you keep. For nothing is secret that shall not be made manifest. Neither anything hid that shall not be known and come abroad."

Nibo stiffened at her audacity. Those words sent a chill down his spine. Secrets were what he kept best and appreciated most. At least when they were his and not someone else's. He had more than he could begin to catalogue, and personally he liked it that way, as it kept others on their toes. "She wouldn't understand."

"People don't understand lies. The truth is usually easier to swallow and causes a lot less choking."

That was what she thought. In his experience, it wasn't always so. The truth had once gotten him killed.

So, he sought to divert the sorceress from this discussion to a new one that was much more palatable. And a lot less dangerous. "I owe you for helping to bring Valynda back into this world. But never mistake that gratitude for leniency."

Belle frowned at him. "Meaning?"

"I don't like to be questioned, Mistress Morte. Not by anyone, and especially not by Deadmen walking." He stepped around her and headed after Valynda.

Then wished he hadn't. The minute he entered the bunk room and she saw him, she cursed him and his parentage.

"Love you, too," he said simply.

She cast him an annoyed grimace as she straightened the blanket on her rough wooden bunk. "Is there a purpose to your harassment?"

He hadn't meant to harass her. "I was hoping for a bit of a warmer reception."

"And I was hoping not to die. Really hoping not to live as a scarecrow. So, I guess we're all disappointed, eh?"

Nibo bit his tongue as he realized the mood she was in and the fact that he'd walked right into the midst of a hurricane. Naked and unprepared for it. There was no way to reason with her when she was like this. He knew that from his years of dealing with her and still, like a fool, he found himself trying anyway, because he was an idiot and he didn't like to see her upset. "I came for you as soon as I could."

"*You* didn't come for me at all, now, did you?"

Technically, she was right. But . . . "I came as close as I could."

She paused in her frenetic cleaning to right herself and glare at him. "Really?"

He'd never realized before how much that one word could be weaponized. "Vala—"

"Don't you even try to charm me right now, Xuri. I've no mood for it."

He ground his teeth in frustration. This was not how he'd seen their reunion going in his mind.

At all. Rather, he'd envisioned a lot more kissing and sweet-talking.

In the past, there would have been a lot more nudity.

"What do you want from me?"

Pain flickered behind her reddish eyes, and that singed his soul. Never had he wanted her harmed in any way. She'd been so innocent when they met. So full of fire and joy. In all his life, she had been the one pure thing he'd wanted. The only real thing to make him happy.

And happy was all he'd ever wanted to make her.

So, whenever she looked at him like he was her nightmare, it cut him to the marrow.

"Nothing, Xuri. I want nothing from you."

Her lips might be saying that, but the rest of her . . .

She was angry and he'd done something that had seriously pissed her off. He knew that tone, and she definitely wanted him to do something to appease her mood. Some sacrifice to the angry goddess before him. Too bad she wasn't telling him what it was that she wanted him to do to make it up to her.

Damn it.

I am in so much trouble. Too bad he didn't know why. Or how to undo it.

Wanting to please her, he held his hand out and manifested a single red rose. "I'm here for you, Vala. If you need me."

For once, she didn't take it. "But you're not . . . and you weren't." She shifted her gaze from the rose to him. "Were you?"

With that last hurtful question she brushed past him to leave.

Xuri had never felt worse, which, given his past, said a lot.

"She thinks you've lied to her."

He turned sharply at the unexpected voice in the doorway. It took him a second to remember the name of the Dark-Huntress Janice Smith. Her lyrical accent was smooth, like her dark skin and beauty. She had the kind of lush curves and sweet scent that had once driven him to madness and lured him into all kinds of trouble.

Before Vala.

Now . . .

He only craved one lady and she was currently furious with him. "What do you know of it?"

Dressed in dark breeches like a man, along with a long over-coat, she came into the room, careful to avoid the sunlight that was deadly to her kind, and sat down on a bunk to his left. She glanced to the porthole someone had left open. "Would you oblige?"

He used his telekinesis to close it and seal the room in total darkness so that the rays would threaten her no more. Though to be honest, he'd always thought that particular restriction from Artemis for her warriors was a bit shortsighted. While Nibo understood why Apollo had banned the Apollite race the god had created from sunlight after they'd attacked Apollo's mistress and slaughtered her and his son, and then cursed them to prey on each other for blood sustenance, he'd never quite understood why the goddess Artemis had done the same for the hunters she'd created to police them. After all, he'd have gone insane too, over such a betrayal by his people. But Artemis's insanity made no sense given that the Dark-Hunters were supposed to keep the Apollites from eating humans.

But then Artemis seldom made sense.

"Thank you." Janice watched him with a strange curiosity.

He inclined his head to Janice. "Why does Vala think I've lied to her?"

"You have, haven't you?"

That was beside the point. "Everyone lies."

Janice shook her head. "Nay, Nibo. They don't. Whoever walks in integrity walks securely, but he who makes his ways crooked will be found out. In all things, show yourself to be an example of good deeds, with a purity in doctrine, dignified, sound in speech which is beyond reproach so that your opponent will be put to shame, having nothing bad to say about you."

He rolled his eyes at her quote that had almost made bile rise up inside him.

Still, she gave him no quarter. "You have a problem with that?"

"Aye. You seriously misjudge the wickedness of a corrupted tongue out to court mischief. Those who seek to sow strife for the sake of misery and entertainment need no more reason than that to do so."

"And by that tongue they are always undone and found out. For nothing is hidden, except to be revealed. Nor has anything been secret, but that it would come to light."

She was as naïve as Vala had once been. "You've no idea of the depths some will go to to keep their secrets buried."

Janice snorted at him. "I'm a Dark-Hunter, Nibo. Born of vengeance and violence. Made such because I was so betrayed by the one I trusted most in this world that upon the hour of my death, my soul screamed out so loudly for retribution that it summoned forth a goddess I didn't know existed to offer me a bargain to strike back at the one who had wronged me. Do you really think I know nothing of the lengths people will go to, to keep their bad acts buried? But what they underestimate is the determination of those who have been so greatly betrayed to repay that debt in full and in kind. For Nemesis wields a mighty sword, and she is fueled by a fury so great that it can and will defy the grave itself to ensure justice is done, and that those who have done wrong against them will pay for their sins in this world and in the next. May the gods have mercy upon them, for those of us who are wronged will not."

Her heartfelt words sent a chill down his spine. Not just because they resonated within her and he knew she meant them. But because he knew of his part in what had happened with Valynda.

That had been an accident.

Did it matter?

He'd known better than to care for anyone. That was his punishment. He knew of the curse. Had he simply dallied with her and moved on, she'd have never been harmed.

They had killed her because he made the mistake of caring. Because he'd been unable to walk away.

Forever damned.

He might as well be one of Apollo's Apollites who was cursed from birth over something he'd had no part in. For he was caught in a vicious cycle he didn't know how to break, and like a spoiled toddler he lashed out at everyone around him. Even Masaka and Oussou because they were part of it.

No one was immune. If he felt anything for them, they would pay for it. There was no hope for him and he knew that, too.

"Janice?"

Nibo moved aside as Belle leaned in through the door to have a word with the Dark-Huntress.

"Captain wants to speak to everyone. We're meeting in the galley."

Janice got up to follow after her. That was probably his cue to leave as well. If he had any common sense, he'd have gone the moment Vala brushed him off.

Damn his lack of self-preservation. It'd been getting him into trouble since the dawn of time.

And today that lack of sense found him following after the women to the crew meeting where, for once, he didn't really stand out with the motley bunch of miscreants who called the *Sea Witch II* home. How strangely comforting.

And disconcerting. He was used to being one of the strangest people in the room, but given Rosie with his dark blond dreads and mismatched island wear mixed with a brocade coat, and Cookie, their oversized cook who barely fit into the room, Nibo definitely didn't stand out here.

Silently, Masaka came up behind him like a shadow to rest at his back.

She dropped her chin on his shoulder and placed a possessive hand on his hip while Oussou stood on his left. There were many who mistook her actions for those of a lover. But they were closer than that. More akin to siblings—they even fought as such. And while Masaka was viciously beautiful, she had never attracted him sexually. Mostly because he knew the darkness of her past equaled his own and feared falling into that bottomless abyss that would suck him in and leave him even more soulless than he already was. The last thing either of them needed was to feed each other's hatred of this world and those who dwelled in it.

Rather, he chose those like Vala who made him want to see beauty. She was his glimmer of light when the darkness began to close in and he couldn't see a way out again. She kept him grounded so that he could find his way through the hate and bitterness to something better.

If Vala closed him out and left him adrift . . .

Pain savaged his heart. He couldn't bear the thought of losing her love. Of being cast back into the place where he'd lived before he'd found her.

He was an animal and she was the only one who tamed him.

If he had any doubt about that, all he had to do was look about at the others and see the fear in their eyes as they glanced at him. This fearless crew who had faced down the worst of evils.

A crew made up of insidious Deadmen.

They were terrified of *him*.

Except for Devyl Bane. The World-King who had once led an army for the Lord of All Evil himself. Bane feared absolutely nothing and no one. He met Nibo's gaze as an equal. Because he was as evil as Kadar had been on the moment the bastard had been spawned.

"So what pissed down your leg, Bane?"

Devyl let out an irritated sigh at Nibo's question. "Why are you still here?"

Nibo shrugged. "Morbid curiosity."

"Well now, you know what they say about curiosity."

"It's the ruin of good men, but I see no such here."

Masaka bit his shoulder to warn him to silence.

Bane's nostrils flared as if he were the one she'd just taken a chunk out of.

That was Nibo's one flaw—well, maybe not one. He did have many. Still, it'd been ever his nature to rankle. He couldn't seem to help himself.

Today was no exception.

"As I was saying . . ." Bane cleared his throat. "Vine has taken refuge with the Malachai's army . . . at Death's Door."

A whisper of protest went through the group at the mention of the infamous gate that had been holding back some of the worst evils of the world, including Bane's first wife.

Vine.

Rotten to the center of her being, she had murdered him, and in retaliation, Bane had reached out from the grave to capture her and imprison her so that she couldn't harm any more innocents.

But when the Malachai had escaped, the gate had fractured, and Vine, along with countless others, had escaped, and they were now preying on mankind.

"You've got to be japing," Bart groaned. "For the love of all that's unholy, tell me you're joking, Captain."

The grim look in his eyes said he wasn't.

Will sighed. "Is it too late to tell Thorn I quit? I say we summon his buddy Michael, jump overboard, and let our damnations take us. Be quicker, less painful, I'm thinking."

Nibo snorted at the mention of the archangel who was a friendly enemy to Thorn and the Deadman crew.

Sancha Dolorosa scoffed at the men. "Ah, you big bunch of crybabies! What is it with you? We've faced down greater things than this. Besides, we got a mermaid!" She pointed to Kalder.

"Myrcian," he corrected.

"Ah, don't get your gills in a wad." Sancha jerked her chin toward one of the older members of the crew. "And we got Sallie and his soul in a bottle. I say we head for it. Let's show 'em what we're made of."

Devyl nodded. "But first we need to take on supplies and leave behind—"

"Nay!" Mara cut him off, knowing exactly what he was planning. "There will be no leaving behind of your crew, Captain. Especially if that means me or Cameron."

"Aye to that." Cameron turned a vicious glare toward Kalder and then to her brother, Paden, who turned sullen at her defiance. The former blond captain had never been able to corral his sister, hence how she'd become a member of this wayward crew.

Nibo chuckled until he caught the glare from Valynda, who had joined them. He started toward her, but Masaka tightened her hand on his waist.

84

Leave her alone.

He winced at Masaka's voice in his head. Normally, he'd balk at her orders and disregard them. But something inside told him to pay heed.

So he stood down, even though it was the last thing he wanted.

Much like Bane. The reluctance glowed deep in his eyes before he nodded. "Fine, then. We'll take on supplies before we see this met."

"And perish abysmally. Again." Will sighed heavily. "Poor Will Death. We knew him well. He died in anonymity and none knew of his sacrifice."

"Will you shut it, Will?" Bart elbowed him in the stomach.

"Easy for you to say. No one ever loved you."

Bart scoffed. "None ever loved you, either. Not even your mum."

Will opened his mouth, then snapped it shut. "You're right. I'd deny it, but for the truth."

"As I was saying," Bane said loudly over them. "We have a few days, and we know not what we're headed into. Make peace and rest. Most of all, prepare."

"Prepare, he says," Will mumbled. "For what, we do not know, other than our doom. And demons . . . lots and lots of demons."

Bart shoved him forward as he grumbled under his own breath.

Ignoring them, Nibo headed for Valynda, but she was again having none of him.

Masaka cut off his path. "You're embarrassing yourself," she whispered. "And you're embarrassing us!"

Those words set fire to his temper. "I don't care."

Masaka's dark eyes glowed purple. "Think, Nibo. They've already killed her. Turned her into that monstrosity to get back at you. What do you think they'll do next?"

That gave him pause. She was right and he hated her for it. He could never show his emotions. Never show anything.

He knew it.

Weaknesses were always used against him. *For what you've done, you are damned.* He could still hear his brother's voice in his ear. Right before he'd cut his throat.

The pain of that betrayal was forever etched in his heart. And for what? Because he'd wanted to be loved? Dared seek happiness?

Nibo let his gaze follow after Vala, and he knew that he had to let her go. It was the only way to see her happy and to let her escape this hell intact. She deserved to be happy.

I destroy what I love.

That was his curse. There would never be any way to break it. The gods would never have mercy on him and he knew it.

Worse, he couldn't fight it.

5

Valynda sat quietly, returning in her mind to the days when she'd believed in something.

Believed in *someone*.

Closing her eyes, she was no longer on board the *Sea Witch II*. Rather, she was a girl back on her island home, filled with wonder over the simplest things because that was all she'd been allowed to know. The only demons in her world those days had been the ones the preacher used to frighten them with on Sundays. Nebulous things that had only existed in fables and nightmares.

Nothing tangible or real. Just figments of an overactive imagination that caught glimpses of shadows it twisted out of proportion.

"Valynda? We're going to swim. Would you care to join us?"

"Not today." She'd waved her friends off and headed away from them. Her goal was to pick shells from the shoreline. A hobby that went back to her childhood when her grandmother had told her tales of how she could hear the war of sea creatures inside conch shells if she could find the right ones. Or free a trapped jinn who would grant wishes. All she had to do was rub his magic shell to free him, and then he would be hers to command.

Valynda had tried to tell her grandmother that it was a lamp she needed to find to free the jinn, but her grandmother had insisted lamps were a stupid home for such miraculous creatures. Shells made much more sense, as they traveled the world on the brilliant sun-kissed waves, and no one could set fire to those and burn down their homes.

She supposed that made sense.

So here she was, seeking her jinn to free her of her insipidly boring life of endless chores.

Tucking her skirt up so as to protect its fragile, worn hem from the salt water, she began to wade out into the shallow waves to seek her treasure. While she'd never found a jinn, she had found a number of pretty pieces that she used to create jewelry that she could sometimes sell for profit to travelers who were making their way from Europe to the colonies.

Without thinking, she hummed to herself as she searched the glimmering, turquoise waves until she found a magnificent pinkish-blue shell. Pulling it up from where it was partially buried in the thick, wet sand, she rinsed it in the water, then tried to blow through the end of it to clean it. With a scowl, she dipped it back in the water, rinsed it again, then cradled it to her bosom and rubbed it in her hands.

"I've never envied a shell before."

Valynda shrieked in startled alarm at the deep voice behind her. She was so shocked that her skirts tangled in her legs, and between that and the waves, she was caught off balance and sent crashing to the ground, where she landed in a most undignified heap. If that wasn't embarrassing enough, another wave rushed over her just then, almost drowning her. She sputtered and coughed, then pushed herself up on unsteady feet. Brushing her soggy curls out of her eyes, she looked up to find her irritating loa staring at her with a quirky, charming grin.

"It would be you."

That made him laugh. "Why does everything you say feel as if it insults me?"

Still sputtering, she twisted her sopping hair up into a knot on her head. "Probably because it does."

"And why is that?"

She shrugged. "Maybe because every time we meet you're doing something that annoys me."

His smile widened. "You're a cheeky little thing, aren't you?"

Ignoring his question, Valynda searched the waves for the shell she'd been holding. Sadly, she'd dropped it in the commotion of his unexpected appearance.

"You haven't contacted me."

Annoyed, she straightened to give him a peeved glare. "Was I supposed to?"

Nibo followed after her while she searched. "I told you to."

"And everyone does what you tell them?"

He shrugged nonchalantly. "Most do, aye."

"Lucky you." No one ever cared a single fig what she thought or wanted. Case in point, here he was being a burr in her nether regions for no reason whatsoever when all she wanted was to be left alone.

She turned away from him so that she could continue to seek her shell.

"Whatever are you doing?" Now he sounded as annoyed as she felt.

"Hunting my shell that you caused me to drop."

"Why?"

"Because I liked it and I want to find it again."

Suddenly, laughter rose up from the depths of the water where she stood. Cold and gurgling, it'd been unlike anything Valynda had ever experienced in her life. Too shocked to react, she'd stood there until Nibo had wrapped his arm about her waist and pulled her back against him. She'd been startled by the unexpected intimacy of his embrace. And by how hard his body was in contrast to hers. He was a solid wall of lean muscle. While he comforted her, his metal necklace had let out a strange melody that haunted her. But what startled her most was that his eyes glowed the same shade as warm brandy. They were haunting and searing in their unique beauty.

If that wasn't startling enough, his two companions appeared from the waves behind them. Two psychopomps Valynda knew by their fierce reputations that were recounted on the island in song, verse, tales, and, at times, in fear-filled whispers. She could barely leave her father's modest home that she didn't come across poppets or wangas their followers had fashioned for them and left in strategic places throughout the island in hopes that the loa would intercede with the Bondye on their behalf to grant them wishes and favors—in much the same way as offerings made to saints or pagan gods.

Given that, there was no mistaking who and what they were.

Masaka, a sorceress of extreme power, was said to be capricious and bold. Her followers feared her wrath as much as her sexual appetites, though Valynda wasn't supposed to know anything at all about the latter bit.

Any more than she was supposed to know about the rumors that said Masaka might not be a woman, but rather a man dressed as such.

Without a word to her, or any real acknowledgement, Masaka moved to guard Nibo's right flank as Oussou moved to shield his left. In perfect synchronicity, they turned around to protect Nibo's back.

"What's going on?"

Nibo tightened his hold on her. "An old friend wants a few words with me. 'Tis all. Think nothing of it."

He made it sound so simple, and yet the raging waters that percolated said this was no friendly matter. As did the tenseness of his companions. They were ready for a battle.

"Nibo!" That angry shout rocked the ground beneath them.

He passed Valynda over to Oussou as if she were a doll. "Careful with her, brother. Keep her safe."

Inclining his head, he took her from Nibo, then peeled off from the other two to take her back toward shore. Once they were safely ensconced on the beach, he set her down and stood in front of her as if she were his new mission.

Unsure of what to make of it all, Valynda took a step toward the sea.

Oussou countered her actions with an angry hiss that caused her to retreat to where he'd put her. His stark white braids rattled like bones against his pale flesh. His black grave-digger's coat was a startling contrast to the eerie pallor of his skin and hair. To his eyes, that were every bit as lacking in color. Each sleeve of that chilling frock was marked with a large purple cross, as was the back of it. Smaller animated crosses appeared to dance along the edges of his black tricorne that was trimmed in vibrant purple.

He was a peculiar sight, no doubt. Everything about this encounter was strange.

And Masaka was no less odd. For she was as dark as he was pale. Her skin every bit as iridescent against the bright waves. But where Oussou's linen shirt was white, hers was black, and where his jacket was black, hers was the color of human bones, and decorated with skulls. The same was true of her breeches and hose. Even the buckles of her shoes were bone hands that held the leather in place. She looked more pirate than spirit, especially with the trailing black scarf that came out from beneath her tricorne and the baldric that held three flintlocks across her chest.

No ordinary flintlocks either. They were the rare type with rotating barrels that allowed their user to have more than a single shot at a target. Costly and deadly, those weapons were the bane of her uncle and his watchmen.

When the waves rose up around Masaka and Nibo, she lifted one of the dangling drawstring bags from her belt. Her voice was deep as she began to chant words Valynda couldn't even begin to understand.

As Masaka did so, Nibo pulled a braided leather belt from his lean waist. He unfurled it with a vicious snap that caused it to turn into a long shepherd's crook.

Valynda's eyebrow shot north.

Defiantly, Nibo faced the turgid sea. "You want a word with me, Aggie?"

"I want many words with you, you unfit dog!"

"Told you not to sleep with his wife," Masaka snarled over her shoulder at Nibo.

"Not my fault."

Masaka gaped at him. "Whose then?"

He passed her a charming grin. "You knew better than to leave me unattended."

She was aghast as she seemed to forget they were in danger and turned more toward Nibo in the water. "You're not seriously blaming me?"

Leaning against his crook, he gestured toward Valynda and

her new companion. "Well, I can't very well blame Oussou. He wasn't there, now, was he? Nay, he'd gone off alone. 'Twas you who were there last, and you knew better than to leave me alone with La Sirene! As if anyone, particularly *moi,* could resist her."

Masaka scoffed. "Since when do you need an excuse to jump into a woman's bed, Brave Ghede? Oops, I tripped and fell on top of her? Nay, I think not. Your problem is staying clothed. I swear, I don't know why you bother to dress at all."

"You're a fine one to talk. As if you've—"

A loud thunderous roar cut their argument short. The sea rose up to form a giant wall in front of Nibo, who appeared less than impressed by the display. "You little bastard!"

Nibo grinned. "Better than being a giant bastard or big asshole."

"You've been accused of both," Masaka said flippantly.

Nibo cast her a glare that said she wasn't helping and that she really needed to keep her opinions to herself.

The waves fanned out into giant spikes that rushed toward Nibo as if to pierce him through. Just as they would have reached him, he held his crook up and caught them, then sent them back toward his attacker. "Can't we talk about this?"

"We cannot! I want what you took!"

Nibo and Masaka passed a confused frown between each other. "Pardon? I'd think you'd be getting a piece of that fair regular, being married to her and all."

Aggie screamed out in fury. "You motherless, futtocking dog! Not *that*! Me kiman, you rotten ass!"

"Oh . . . *that*." Nibo nudged Masaka, then sobered. "There's a bit of a problem there, mate."

"How so?"

He screwed his face up. "I rather drank it all. Was quite tasty. Really good recipe that, you know?"

"You did *what*?"

"Couldn't help meself, really." He passed an amused, twinkle-eyed stare to his companion that made her roll her eyes before he sobered a bit more. "Had a nip, and the next thing I knew all these rogue little bitches started coming up and out from everywhere. Places *I* didn't even know. Had a party with them. Went to town, if you know what I mean. And you probably don't. Well, long story long, because that's normally the only kind I tell, we killed a few things, gutted an enemy, and ended up naked in a ditch. No more kiman, but one incredible night out that left me wondering what the hell elephant ran me over and if there were any witnesses to it."

"I hate you, you daft, arrogant bastard!"

Nibo didn't seem the least bit concerned by the fact that the other loa wanted to kill him. "Now, now, Aggie, don't be like that. You know you don't mean it."

"Of course I do! Why wouldn't I?"

"No particular reason really, other than I'm cute and you might need me one day. Never know what fight might be brewing. Gatekeepers come in handy. Healers even more so."

"That was a mistake," Oussou breathed under his breath an instant before the water exploded all over Nibo. Only it wasn't water.

It turned into blood.

And something a little more disgusting.

Unable to stand the sight, Valynda turned away as her stomach heaved violently. More from the smell and sound than the sight.

Oussou caught her against his side. "There now, me pet. It's not so bad really." His hand faltered. "Well, perhaps it is, but still. Best you keep looking away for a bit longer, eh?"

Agreeing with his wisdom, she didn't know what to think. Not until Nibo appeared in front of her, toweling himself off as if he'd just stepped out of his bath. Not one flit of a care about what had just happened or why.

Valynda kept her hand pressed to her lips as her stomach began to settle. "This happen a lot to you?"

He grinned. "The blood and guts, not so much."

"Jealous husbands, all the time," Masaka said under her breath.

Which caused Nibo to glare at her. "Do you mind?"

"All the time," she repeated. "Do you care? That's the real question here, love. And the answer there is nay, because if you did, you wouldn't be getting me into all these messes of yours, or poor Oussou either."

Oussou cleared his throat. "Leave me out of this, please. Last time I was dragged into one of your fights, you two almost had me gutted. So, I'll thank you both to leave me over here where I'm feeling awkward and alone enough, thank you very much."

"Poor Oussou," Nibo said with feigned sympathy. "Don't you know, man, that's the lie we tell ourselves each day. Even when we're in a crowd or surrounded by what we think are our friends and family, we're all still standing alone. Always feeling awkward."

Valynda found his keen insight astounding.

"And you, young miss." Nibo sighed heavily as he leaned against his crook in a way that really was unbelievably sexy and alluring. She didn't know what it was about that man, but he could make breathing evocative. There was something about him so incredibly sexual that it made everyone around him want to reach out and pull him near. She'd never seen anything quite like it. "In the future, please be avoiding the conch shells of the sea, if you don't be minding. As you can see, blowing into them, they're a bit hazardous to your health and my sanity."

It took everything she had to focus on the conversation and not how much she wanted to take a bite out of his succulent flesh.

Valynda glanced over her shoulder toward the sea. "Should I ask who the big blowhard was? Just so I know who to avoid in the future?"

Masaka rolled her eyes. "She don't even know what it is she done. You see what you get when you mix with mortals, man?"

"Relax, Saka. Breathe." He straightened, and his crook disintegrated back into a belt that he quickly wrapped around his lean waist and buckled over a piece of his anatomy Valynda tried really hard not to notice, as it was a rather large piece. One that grew even bigger in size while her gaze lingered there. Aye, he was a fine one, indeed.

And that made heat sting her cheeks as she quickly averted her gaze.

Nibo laughed. "That was Agwé, and he's a nasty bugger."

"When you sleep with his wife."

He glared at Masaka for her added comment.

"Just saying." She was completely unabashed.

Nibo arched a brow. "Why don't you try saying that from somewhere else?"

"Such as?"

"Europe would be a nice change of pace, man. Or back in Vilokan, how's that for you, eh? Yeah, I like that thought for you a lot. Why don't you both take some of me rum and go bother Legba or one of the others for a bit?"

Crossing her arms over her chest, she scoffed. "I say you're a daft, loon bastard thinking with his pizzle. And you might as well go and calm your coconuts, as Kal will be slurping milk out Erzuli's belly button afore this one opens her gate even to the Brave Ghede. You're a-wasting your time, brother. Ain't no way she'll up her goods to the likes of *you*."

His eyes and nostrils flared with annoyance. "Ain't nobody here talking to you or your brother. Now off with you before I decide to make a sacrifice of you both for the sake of me sanity. I'm sure there's some sea serpent be wanting some indigestion." Nibo waved his hand and a huge, glowing slit appeared in the air between them. It looked as if someone had ripped a hole straight in the air. "Go!" he barked.

Oussou obeyed without hesitation.

Masaka rolled her eyes, then leaned in to Valynda. "Take me word, gel, if you do decide to let him in, make sure you get a piece of him to hold on to that'll always be yours. Don't be the fool that others have been. His is a fickle heart. Off to the next before he's even left you. Heed my words or you'll pay a dear, dear price."

Valynda smiled at her kindness. "Trust me, I know. And I appreciate your candor. But it's not necessary. I'm not one to go milking any coconuts from anyone, no matter how handsome the tree."

Masaka laughed, then winked. "I like this one, Bo. She's a spicy girl." And with that, she vanished through the portal.

Nibo clenched his fist and sealed it shut before he tsked at her. "I see you're going to be a handful for me, aren't you?"

"Not planning to be a handful to any." And with that, she flounced away, intending to keep herself clear of the loa and his scheming coconuts and accomplices.

If only it'd been so simple.

Valynda sighed as she came back to the present to find herself on board the *Sea Witch II,* staring out the porthole into the murky waves.

So much had changed since that first day when Xuri had charmed her. She should have listened to Masaka and avoided him like the plague he was.

But he'd been hard to resist. Harder still to ignore. It was why he was the ghede known for sexual encounters. Anytime he'd been around her, his mere presence had set her body on fire and made her want to be his.

Now it just set her temper off, even though she knew she'd have to seduce him if she were to get that damned crook free from his grasp.

How easy her bargain had seemed, but the moment she'd laid

eyes on him, the betrayal had been so deep that she couldn't face him. Let alone charm or seduce him for anything.

She just wanted to rip out his heart and feed it to him. And who could blame her?

How could he do such a thing?

"What does it matter?" she breathed. Like everyone else in her life, he'd abandoned her when she needed him most. He was supposed to be the loa in charge of healing and of untimely death. Yet where had he been when she'd been murdered and her soul ripped from her body? Why hadn't he come to ease her passage and offer her comfort?

Where had his powers been then, huh?

So much for telling her that she could put her faith in him. That he'd be there for her whenever she needed him and all she had to do was call and he'd be there for her. Always. When it'd mattered most, he'd been nowhere to be found. He'd set her up. And here she'd been stupid enough to think he was staying by her side out of loyalty.

Instead, it was guilt.

That was what sickened her most.

I am unlovable.

As much as she'd felt that way in human flesh, with a woman's body, she was even more so nowadays. Now, she couldn't blame anyone for being repulsed by this straw, unnatural form that itched and crinkled. She was an abomination. Abhorrent and foul. She really was the doll they'd once treated her as. A thing to be tossed about as if it had no feelings.

If only. Too bad she wasn't a thoughtless, useless thing. How many times in her life had she prayed to be such a trifle that felt nothing and knew nothing, only to awaken in this nightmare known as life. Alone. Abandoned. Forgotten.

In the darkness, even your own shadow forsakes you.

Nibo's words haunted her now. He was right. It was why her favorite verse had always been found in Romans, when the Lord looked upon those who had sinned and proclaimed to them, *I loved you at your darkest.*

Because that was the one thing she'd always wanted most. The one thing she'd craved since the hour she'd drawn her first breath and hadn't had the God-given sense to make it her last.

Unrequited love. One that didn't judge. Or demand. It simply gave. Not because it was required.

Because it cared. Not because she was beautiful or dutiful. Love that came to her in spite of her flaws, which were numerous. A blind love that was loyal and permenant. *That* was her dream.

And it was one elusive bitch who had taunted her every day of her life. Mocked her so very cruelly. Every time she caught her breath and thought that this day, today, she'd be all right and that no past madness would haunt her, someone or something would come along to remind her that she really was nothing special in this world.

That no one cherished her. If she died on the morrow, there would be no mourners. She'd be forgotten as quickly as a tide.

As Masaka had warned her so long ago, Nibo was a feckless bastard whose head was forever turned to whatever tart came near him. Which was unfair and she knew that. They weren't the tarts, not really.

Nibo was the whore in this equation. Ever selling himself as a cheap piece of ass for a moment's worth of pleasure. Keeping his heart locked away as if terrified to let it be touched for fear of what might happen to it should someone ever lay claim to that icy, petrified organ.

She would feel sorry for him if she wasn't so busy holding a pity party for herself. As it was . . .

Go drown yourself in your misery, you faithless dog.

For that alone, she'd be happy to get his crook and hand it over to the Malachai. It was the least she could do given what he'd taken from her.

But to get the crook, she'd have to play nice with the sodding bugger.

I'd rather have me eyes gouged out.

Nay, she'd rather beat him until he bled.

Yet in her heart she knew the truth. She'd have rather had Xuri be the man she thought he was. Rather have died than learn this harsh lesson . . .

That he'd betrayed her.

Damn you, Xuri. Damn you.

And damn her. She gave a scoffing laugh as she realized it was too late. She was already damned, and there was no salvation for her.

Adarian staggered, then caught himself. What the hell? He glanced about and was grateful no one had been near just then to see his misstep. As the Malachai, he couldn't afford for anyone to see him hold any kind of weakness, and normally he didn't.

However . . .

Something wasn't right. Ever since he'd pierced the veil that separated the worlds and entered the human realm, he'd been weaker than normal. If he didn't know better, he'd swear he had a son here.

Impossible, he knew, since he hadn't been here in centuries.

But that was what it felt like—his powers weakening to accommodate the powers of a rising Malachai.

His replacement. A bastard born to kill him.

Which was why he'd taken care to make sure he had no issue. Male or female. Still . . .

The sensation was unmistakable. A light hum in his ears. Peculiar fog in his eyes that made everything dull, and the weakness of his limbs. Those were definite giveaways that he was growing weaker.

Slower.

"My lord?"

He froze at the sound of Vine's voice. An ancient Deruvian, like her sister, Mara, she was a fiery redhead. One given to extreme tantrums over the slightest provocation. Just not with him, as she knew he reacted poorly to such theatrics.

As in he tended to snap such people in half.

Literally.

Adarian composed himself before he faced her. "What is it?" he hissed.

"Your generals are here. Laguerre and Grim."

That made him feel better. War and Death. Of all his generals, they had always been his favorites, in spite of the fact that the two of them had played a major role in the damnation of the entire Malachai race and in particular his own family. Which was why they were enslaved to him now.

Payback was his pleasure.

Those two personally owed him and his predecessors, and he made sure they paid their debt in full. That they would for all eternity.

True to their style, they entered as if they were the ones in charge. Though Mot was nowhere near as tall as Adarian, the plucky little bastard strutted as if he was. Dressed in black on black, he appeared to be a cross between a funerary attendant and a military commander, hence why most called him Grim. His Colonial-style coat was similar to what the British officers peacocked about in, except for the fact that it appeared to have been dipped in night. Even the buttons were flat black. Along with his feathered tricorne.

Dressed in a bloodred riding habit, Laguerre was even more striking with her jet eyes and long dark hair that fell in spiral curls to her slender waist. The two of them had been seeding exceptional discord in his name, and they appeared quite pleased with themselves.

"I take it I won't be gutting either of you today?"

That caused Mot to back up a step.

As the daughter of all evil itself and a war goddess in her own right, Laguerre wasn't so easily intimidated. She actually smiled.

"The day's still young, but I think you'll be happy with our report."

"Then thrill me." He gestured for her to take a seat.

With an audible gulp, Mot sat down. Laguerre chose to stand in the large room, near the window that looked out onto the sea where Adarian could take advantage of the beauty there. While he'd been held in Azmodea—the nether realm ruled by Laguerre's father, who had tortured Adarian for centuries—he'd been unable to see any kind of beauty whatsoever. There had only been violence and gore. Screams for mercy and pleadings for death.

That had come from his own lips.

The others tortured there had been worse.

Now that he was free, he would burn this world down before he'd ever go back. To hell with Kadar and Azura, and all the old gods. They could all rot, and this world with them.

All worlds, for that matter. None cared for him and he cared even less for them and their outcome.

As if she sensed his darkening mood, Laguerre offered a smile. "It's an interesting time you've chosen to escape in. The world has gone quite mad."

Adarian yawned. "You're boring me. Have you found my mother?"

She shook her head. "Apollymi is still in captivity. And Acheron refuses to release her."

Damn him for it. Adarian wished he could do it, but since he was technically not Apollymi's son, but rather her great-great-great-whatever-grandson plus a few generations, he was too far removed genetically from her womb to have the ability provide her the key to freedom.

Rather, all he could do was remember his link to the goddess, as each subsequent Malachai absorbed the memories of his father whenever he killed his sperm donor and rose to take his place—a special little nasty curse that Mot and Laguerre were directly responsible for since they had cursed Adarian's great-great-whatever for attacking their daughter. As such, no reigning Malachai could ever quite shake the concept that Apollymi was his mother, given that he was directly descended from her first son Monakribos.

If only the goddess returned the loyalty. But as with all things in life, fairness was a fickle bitch, who forever went against his kind.

So, while the Dark-Hunter leader Acheron was viewed as a brother, he was a brother they all wanted to kill for the fact that he was one of the bastards who kept their mother imprisoned and was responsible for making sure the Malachai remained leashed to serve a master they hated while Acheron was free to do as he pleased.

And Adarian was sick of his collar. It'd long ago rubbed through his skin and left a bitter, chafing wound that wouldn't heal. It didn't matter to him that Vine and her Irini friends had opened the gates that allowed him to go free. He felt no sense of obligation toward her or anyone else.

Only an overwhelming need to destroy the world that had done nothing for him or his kind. There were only so many beatings a dog could take before it became rabid and went on the attack. And he'd passed that point long ago.

Now . . .

He wanted the throat of any and all who made the mistake of crossing his path. Particularly one bugger.

"Then bring me the heart of Acheron. We release my mother and she'll burn down this world for us." So what if she killed him in the process. He'd welcome that, too.

Laguerre watched as Adarian launched his wings from his back and then took flight through the grand set of windows. Stunned, she didn't move until Mot rose behind her.

"Um . . . should we have told him that while Acheron's death will definitely release Apollymi's curse, it will leave her exceptionally pissed off at whomever is stupid enough to murder her beloved child?"

She passed a droll stare to her idiot husband. "I don't think he cares."

"Lovely. Then I nominate you for the task, as I've already pissed off and on one primal god too many. Since I'm not the child who calls one father, love, I think you're better suited to the task anyway."

Laguerre scoffed at his cowardice. "Believe me, one doesn't rattle my aunt's cage if one wants to keep their hand attached to their body. 'Tis why I have a wondrous compromise."

"That is?"

Smiling, she went to the door and opened it. "Vine?" she called. "Adarian has an assignment for you."

6

"What's that long face for?"

Nibo paused at the sound of Brigid's voice as she joined him where he sat drinking another round of kleren in the grand hall on their island home below the seas. It was here he was supposed to intercede on behalf of the living and the dead, taking special care of those like Valynda who'd died young and violently because of someone else.

Those like him, who should have left well enough alone and kept their interference out of someone else's life.

There had been a time once when his job had seemed important. But centuries of needless, unending violence had taken its toll.

Now . . .

He was tired. Nibo didn't understand this world. And he was disgusted from trying to figure it all out when really, crazy was crazy. And attempting to decipher fucking crazy just ripped your brains out, threw them on the ground, stomped them into oblivion, and made you join their ranks.

"I thought you'd be off with the others." Nibo used his powers to push the padded chair out in front of him for her so that she could join him.

She accepted his invitation before she reached for the bottle he'd been making liberal use of and poured herself a drink. "Why bother? As you noted, they're all fucking crazy."

He laughed at her notorious "potty" mouth. "Stay out of my head, Maman Brigitte. You know I don't like it when you make my brain your playground."

"Few do." She quickly knocked back the spiced rum before she poured another round for each of them.

As he watched her, his memories went back to the worst day of his afterlife.

He'd been sitting at this very table when he'd heard Vala scream out his name.

Not Nibo.

Xuri.

By that alone, he'd known how urgent it was, as she never used his real name lightly unless they were alone. And usually naked.

Twice so when he'd reached the gates to the human world and Kalfou had refused to let him pass through them. When Legba hadn't answered his call to let him go so that he could help her.

Because of his nature and the rules of this land and his kind, Nibo couldn't cross through the gates on his own. As a psychopomp, he was trapped here or on the other side. One of them had to open the portal for him so that he could pass from one world to the next. Otherwise he would be trapped in one dimension or the other forever.

Normally, no one minded when he wanted to come and go, and there was no problem with opening the portal.

Yet neither had seen fit to oblige him that day.

Instead, he'd been forced to listen to Vala's cries as she died, unable to help her. Unable to stop the ritual that had stripped her soul from her body and left her trapped between worlds, lost and alone, cursing him. That, too, he'd heard every word of.

Damn them all for it.

He'd attacked Kalfou and they'd fought over it, but it'd done him no good. Nibo couldn't leave here unless they allowed him to cross over.

Rules were rules.

And he'd always hated rules.

Sighing, he narrowed his gaze at the petite woman before him.

She was one of the few of them who'd come here from an older pantheon . . . another nanchon.

Her mother had been the raven battle-goddess the Morrigan, which made Brigitte a goddess in her own right. And as such, Maman Brigitte had some of the strongest powers of any of them. "You know, I've never understood why you left your lands to come here and join us."

Maman sighed. "Sadly, times change, Bo. As do people."

He heard the heartbreak that lay beneath that tone. Someone had hurt her badly. And grief and regret were the two things he understood all too well. Better than he'd ever wanted to.

Sometimes he wondered if perhaps those hadn't been the first emotions created by the gods for their perverse pleasure. And then happiness made as an afterthought and given only as a way to increase the pain and depth of emotional suffering. After all, without joy and happiness there to remind people that there could be relief from the agony, someone could become immune to the pain. But nay, just as soon as you felt like you couldn't take it anymore, fate or life threw in just enough happy to alleviate the bitter misery, and just when you thought you'd be all right, it would rip that rug right out from under you and send you back on your arse, to a depth even lower than before. It was an unending seesaw of perpetual anguish.

And how he hated every heartbeat of it.

So aye, despondent heartache must have been the gods' first creation, as it was their go-to place for everything else.

And that bitter, dreadful emotion darkened her gaze as she

fidgeted with the lace cuff on her sleeve. "The world wasn't the same, Bo. People had begun to forget me, and my powers were growing weaker every day. I didn't want to die off like so many others I've known."

Nibo understood and couldn't blame her. That was the most tragic part of all about the old gods. If mortals ceased to believe in them, their powers faded drastically. When that happened, they became vulnerable to the others of their kind, who could then prey on them and take over their territories, absorb their powers, and erase them from existence. Or worse, they would become mortal and their powers would be released back into the universe.

It was a gut-wrenching fate of their kind. To die out as a forgotten whisper. As opposed to the old way, where they'd fought bloody, violent wars and killed each other off at the height of their powers. Now *that* had been a problem. If two gods in their prime went at each other and one killed the other and didn't manage to absorb the powers before they were released back into the universe, it could cause the entire fabric of creation to come undone.

Which meant all life, in all realms, ceased. Everything was reset.

Total annihilation.

The world would fracture, and all life would end.

Nibo shuttered in memory of the Primus Bellum that had led to the death of the Malachai race and all the Sephirii who'd been created to fight them. Those had been wretched times that the world had barely survived.

It was what most of them were trying to avoid now.

Being one of the survivors, he was in no hurry to repeat it. Sadly, not everyone here shared his memories.

Or sanity.

Kalfou was one of them.

As with all those who were young, their blood and Kalfou's ran hot, and they were too eager for war. A war they wanted when they didn't fully understand the cost and consequences. Once that genie came out of the bottle, you couldn't put it back in. For that was the thing about acting in the heat of the moment and letting your emotions lead you astray.

You have to live with the total fallout of your stupidity.

Careful the fires you start in the heat of fervent anger. For once lit, the flames of destruction are just as likely to double back and consume you as they are to engulf the ones you set them upon.

Neither words nor actions could be taken back, and there were a lot of things in life that "sorry" couldn't fix. While words had the power to destroy, they seldom had the power to heal.

Valynda's fate was just one of many of his own mistakes he kept on his conscience.

Not wanting to think about it or any harm he'd done the one person he loved most, he poured himself another drink. "Are the petro still going at it?"

She nodded. "They want to join the Malachai and help him in his madness. They think if they side with him, they'll have a place in his new world."

Choking on their stupidity, Nibo rolled his eyes. Of course they did. What was it with people ever ready to believe such lies whenever they dripped from the tongues of those they had to know were liars, out for themselves? And to be so willing to hang up their lives for them? It made no sense to him that anyone would so recklessly throw away their own life for such obvious idiocy. "There will be no place for any of us if there are no people left."

"You know that and I know that. Sadly, they don't understand the Malachai. In their minds, he's one of us and therefore he'll be merciful and won't kill *them*."

Nibo cursed. While it was true that Adarian was a demigod who drew half his powers from the same place they did, the father of the original Malachai had been a Sephiroth. Independent creatures the gods had used as warriors and protectors to fight their wars for them so as not to weaken themselves when they attacked other gods. Insidious, really. Therefore, the Sephirii didn't draw their powers from humanity or by being worshiped. The source of their powers came from conflict.

Bloodshed.

Just like the Malachai's. And that was what made the Malachai so destructive and invincible. So very different from them. The more you hated him—the more you fought him—the more powerful he became. It was also why his son was the only one who could destroy him. Because the son was the only one who didn't hate him fully. No matter what a father did, there was always that core bit of love in a child's heart for its parent that made the child stupid.

But it was also what made the Malachai lethal, for a father didn't always feel the same for its offspring. Not the way a mother did, at least when she wasn't demonic born. The Malachai would kill its son to protect itself, without hesitation. Hence why Adarian was so old. He'd slaughtered any and every son born to him that he'd learned about. Long before that child could grow to an age to pose a threat to his reign.

Meanwhile, the Malachai existed because Apollymi, being a true mother goddess, had sacrificed everything for her child. She'd even given up a portion of her powers to her firstborn to ensure the other gods didn't renege on their bargain with her. To safeguard him from their capricious wrath. There was nothing she wouldn't do for her child.

The same for her son Acheron. She was imprisoned to this day because the only way she could free herself would be upon his death, and she would rather rot for eternity in Atlantean hell than see her child harmed for her freedom. For all her vicious nature and brutality, her lack of regard for any living thing, she would never harm her own child. It just wasn't in her.

In fact, she would gut anyone who caused Acheron to shed one single tear. And that had been proven, too.

Like Nibo's own mother upon his death, Apollymi had mourned Acheron's premature demise the whole of her life, and it was why he held so much regard for women and for what they went through in their lifetimes. The wretched hand that fate had dealt them all.

There was truly nothing like a mother protecting her young. The sacrifices she would make, or the lengths she would go to. For that was an unbreakable loyalty that nothing else could ever match. The fiercest power ever created. A bonded love that knew no judgment. Asked no sacrifice.

It simply gave because it wanted to.

And because of that, the Malachai had grown more and more

powerful with every generation. More so due to the fact they hadn't just bred with other gods and humans. They'd bred with demons and all manner of preternatural creatures, inheriting the strengths of them all with each subsequent generation until they were an amalgam of the most lethal, unfeeling beings that had ever belly-crawled from the depths of every hell realm. So that now, the Malachai's power was a source unto itself.

The only thing Nibo knew that could still kill Adarian was either the last Sephiroth who was being held in captivity, or Adarian's son.

Slim pickings for their side, especially since a curse prevented the last Sephiroth from killing Adarian, and if his son killed him, then he'd rise to replace him, and usually whenever a new Malachai took his father's place, he was even more psychotic than the last. Worse, he was more powerful, given that he'd not only inherit his father's powers but would have the addition of whatever his mother had been, and she was seldom human, and never born of anything weaker than a demon.

Usually, the Malachai settled down to hide for awhile after the rest of them united their powers to kick his ass, but that took centuries of senseless battle.

Something Nibo didn't want to repeat.

Nibo sighed. "How do we get through to them?"

Maman shook her head. "How does one ever get through to obstinate asses who reinforce their own stupidity with blindfolded sycophants? As soon as you speak reason to insanity they shout you down with their concocted lies and misconceptions that they repeat to each other."

True. They lived in perpetual echo chambers. "Aye. That is the real definition of madness, isn't it? When you turn your ear from the truth to embrace a lie and willfully close your eyes so that you can continue to do wrong for the sake of pride." Too many fought against the sense formally known as common.

Damn them for it.

Maman reached across the table and placed her hand over his. The contact was so unexpected that it caused him to look up and meet her gaze.

"You know I wanted to help you with your Valynda, don't you?"

Odd how they'd all said that and yet no one had done a damn thing. Rather, they'd just stood by and let her die. Stood by and watched him suffer.

Pain rose up inside as he felt the anguish, raw and hungry, gnawing like a sick madness in his gut. There was nothing worse than to love someone and know they needed you and not be able to get to them. To know you could have and would have done something had you been there.

Unlike the ones who'd gleefully remained on the sidelines and taken pleasure in the suffering. Or worse, those who'd gloated over it. Surely, there was a special place reserved for eternal torment for those bastards.

And it took everything he had not to lash out at the goddess he considered a second mother. But then she wasn't his real mother, and this proved it. His real maman would have never allowed him to hurt like this. She would have done something to help them.

That was the difference, after all.

No mother would stand by and see her child suffer. It wasn't in them.

"*Merci, Maman.*" He choked on those words. They were as false as the ones she offered him.

Nibo took a deep breath and rose slowly to his feet. With one last shot of rum, he lifted his hat and headed for the door, unable to stand the false company for another heartbeat.

As he left the stifling hall, he heard the petro in the street as they argued for the war they wanted.

It figured that his brother would be among them, egging them on. If ever there was trouble, his brother gravitated toward it like a bear chasing after honey, bees be damned. It'd ever been his nature to cause conflict.

"*He came from the womb trying to choke himself on my umbilical cord!*" As a boy, Nibo had thought his mother hysterical whenever she'd denounced Qeenan's behavior with those words. But as they'd grown older, he'd begun to wonder if the story hadn't been true.

His brother was just that contrary.

And that suicidal.

Shaking his head, he watched the group that appeared to be entranced by his brother's rampant stupidity. Proud in bearing, Qeenan had the outline of a skull painted over features that were identical to Nibo's. His black coat was ragged with ribbons of bloodred and purple trailing from it as he railed against the others.

But then that was what Qeenan did best. Complain. Everything was always unfair. To a ridiculous level.

So much so that even before Nibo's death, back when he'd been engaged to his Aclima, Qeenan had gone out and claimed Aclima's twin sister, Avan, as his fiancée. Yet even that hadn't satisfied his ever competitive brother. Nibo couldn't even begin to count how many times Qeenan had found Avan lacking, even though the sisters were identical in looks. Within a year, he'd turned a sweet, precious girl into a harping shrew because of his endless and needless comparisons.

But then ruining people and their lives was Qeenan's specialty.

"I'm telling you, brothers and sisters, our time is here. The time is now! Our followers are crying out to us, more and more, every day. And we must act! We grow stronger, while the others grow weaker. We rise with the Malachai and we can own this world!"

"To all things there should be balance." Papa Legba rose to stand at the top of the stairs that led to the main hall where he kept wise counsel. "We are only spirits. The Bondye teaches—"

"The Bondye sleeps!" Qeenan growled. "As do all the gods. They don't care what happens in this world or to our people. This is why we must make sure our wrath is felt and that we teach them to respect us!"

Nibo sucked his breath in sharply as he remembered a time before when such rebellion had been spoken.

It hadn't worked out for those participants either. Such things never did. While there was a time and place to shake up the system, there was also a time and place for negotiation. That was the secret of life. To know when to speak and when to fight.

Never strike at a trained warrior or natural-born fighter when you thought them weak or when they were down, as that only motivated them to defeat you. Like the Malachai. And never fight if you didn't have to. That had always been his brother's biggest mistake, like the day Qeenan had killed him. He had yet to learn the art of finesse.

Strike fast, with a heavy blow, and run—that was Qeenan's motto.

The trouble was, if your enemy got up, and they would, they came at you with everything they had, and you had no choice but to keep running and then die tired once they caught up to you. And catch you they would. Because they would be more determined than ever to ruin you for blindsiding them.

It was why the two of them warred to this day. Nibo had done nothing to warrant Qeenan's hatred. Other than breathe. He'd even tried to make peace, but there was a hatred inside his brother's heart that he'd never understood, and he was grateful for that.

"We are not to start this fight, Qeenan!" Legba swept his gaze around the gathered petro spirits, and the handful of rada who'd come out. Roughly fifty different members of the nanchon had gathered to argue whether they should join Adarian's army or sit the fight out.

Qeenan saw him over the crowd. "Nibo, you'll join me for this fight, won't you, brother?"

Oh . . . *now* they were brothers. He'd choke on that if he wasn't too busy tasting bile.

"Have you nothing to say?" Qeenan couldn't quite pull off that innocent look he was attempting.

Nibo scratched at the back of his skull where his skin was crawling with distaste over the very thought of what they were planning. "I think you rattled me wits when you clubbed me to death. What can I say? My brain hasn't worked right since."

They burst into laughter.

Qeenan glared at him.

Legba smiled in approval. "Brave Nibo. Such wisdom spoken. We should all heed it. Now off with you. Pay no mind to this madness. Let the Malachai have his war. There's no place in this for us."

"Bah!" Qeenan flung his hands out in frustration. "You're a fool, old man. You'll rue this, I tell you!"

Nibo felt his brother's hatred slide over him like a knife, but there was nothing new there. Since the hour of their birth, they'd competed for everything. Such was the way of twins. Ever confused for one another, it was a struggle to find their own identity. Their own place in the world. Everyone assumed because they looked alike, they were the same.

Yet he and Qeenan had never shared much of anything in terms of interests. While Nibo had loved music and poetry, Qeenan had preferred hunting and sports. Nibo had always been slow to anger with ne'er a thing to aggravate him. Qeenan's temper erupted like a volcano, with the slightest provocation and an ever-changing trigger for it.

Hence what had caused his untimely demise. He'd turned his

back on his brother and Qeenan had risen up in fury to strike him down. Because Nibo, like a fool, had thought that his own twin, the one person in life he should be able to trust, would never do him harm.

That was what hurt him so much with Valynda. He'd failed her that same way his brother had failed him, and he knew that betrayal. It was an unending burn that should never be dealt to any human, especially when one had done nothing to deserve it. He'd loved his brother, had shown him nothing but loyalty and kindness, and his brother, out of petty jealousy and unfounded lies whispered by others, had struck out against him and severed a sacred bond that could never be healed again.

Not fully. For trust, once shattered, was eternally gone. Not even time could heal it. No amount of anything could ever bring it back.

And he knew that he'd lost Vala's because of what they'd done.

He couldn't bear the thought of losing another woman he loved. Not after Aclima had killed herself because of Qeenan. His idiot brother who had gone after her the instant Nibo was dead, demanding she marry him instead.

Aclima had refused. Unlike his brother, she'd been loyal to the end.

And her death had caused her sister to hate Qeenan all the more. Not just because she'd lost Aclima, but because Avan had known the truth. Her husband hadn't loved her. He'd only married her because Nibo had been engaged to Aclima.

Four lives ruined because Qeenan was a selfish asshole.

Unshed tears choked him and burned raw in his throat. In that moment, he wanted to join Adarian and help burn the world to the ground for what it had cost him. Aye, he understood the need to strike out. Better than Qeenan or any of the petro spirits in front of him. He knew their anger. The rage that wanted to rise up in indignation over the injustice of it all.

He walked that path every day.

Life was pain and it was brutal. He'd done nothing to deserve any of it.

There for the briefest moment, he'd touched a bit of beauty. Had held paradise in his palm.

Closing his eyes, he reached up and clenched Vala's cross in his hand. Even now her laughter rang in his ears as he'd watched her dance in the surf along the shoreline of her beach in the late-night hours when they'd met long after her parents had gone to bed and she'd snuck out to meet with him. Her bulky dress hiked up to billow in her arms so that she could spare its hem from the tide. Her ample bosom had teased him as she laughed, and it threatened to spill out the top of her corseted bodice. She'd always worn her hair swept up into an elegant chignon with wisps of curls that fell around her face and neck. Wisps that had teased him to madness.

He'd never seen anyone enjoy something as simple as dancing in the surf so much. Her innocence had beguiled him even more than her beauty had seduced him and left his entire body hungering for hers.

"Keep playing, Xuri!" she'd fussed the instant he'd stopped playing his guitarra to watch her frolicking.

Sadly, the cherished image of her vanished as someone shoved into him. Opening his eyes, he caught Qeenan's fierce glare.

"You could never keep faith with me."

Those words left him aghast and gaping at his brother's audacity. "Faith with *you*? You'd dare throw that in my face?"

Qeenan curled his lip. "Aye, you futtocking bastard! Because of you and your vanity, we're both cursed."

Nibo ground his teeth at Qeenan's irrational stupidity. The rank bastard would never see truth. Not even when it was held up in front of his face.

Or bashed against his head.

"This fight is tiresome, brother."

Qeenan's nostrils flared. "And so's your need to always show off. Look at me," he mocked in a nasal falsetto. "I'm so futtocking special. I'm the best at all I do!"

Nibo was sick of being misjudged. "Don't lay your hate on me. Or your sins. That be your mirror, Qee. Not mine. All I ever wanted was to play me music and be left alone to tend my flock and love me wife. Just like now. You're the one seeking glory and to lead the fools what will listen to you into a quest that will be the death of all. Not I."

"That's what you say. But I see more than you think."

"Nay, that you do not. You see nothing save your own stupid opinions that are colored by an ego so large it blots out the very sun above and casts a shadow over the entire world."

Qeenan's eyes turned bright red as the demon inside him rose up.

Nibo tensed and lowered his voice. "Go ahead, brother. Attack. This time, me back's not turned. Just remember that when you do, I will defend myself."

It was so eerie to see that amount of hatred in his own eyes. To stare at it in a face that was so close to his own. While Nibo held a healthy dose of self-loathing, Qeenan took it to a whole new level.

Right down to arguing over who'd had the prettier identical twin sister.

"You were ever a brat, you rank, filthy bastard. Maman should have drowned you in infancy."

"Too bad she didn't drown you first."

Or leave him to strangle himself with that umbilical cord.

Qeenan exploded into fire. He rushed toward Nibo with a burst of energy and would have engulfed him had he not countered the attack with a wave of his crook. Instead, Nibo caught him with the edge of it and swatted him off like an annoying fly. The blow caused his brother to rebound off the nearest building with a resounding smack that was so loud it caused every spirit near them to turn and stare.

And Papa Legba to burst into laughter.

That did nothing to calm Qeenan's fury. Rather it spurred it ever onward and made him cuss Nibo like a slow-walking dog. Which was fine by him, as he'd called his brother far worse things.

This was, after all, their own personal hell for their crimes against each other. Qeenan for the fact that he'd killed him and caused Aclima's suicide, and Nibo's for his well-noted arrogance that had made Qeenan hate him. He had been a selfish sonofabitch when he'd lived, and he had rubbed Qeenan's nose in the fact that

Aclima was more outgoing than her sister. Truth was, he could still be that prick.

He just tried to hide that sin a little more these days. But his brother continued to revel in his violence and wrapped himself up in the proud cloak of self-indulgent gore and mayhem.

Qeenan peeled himself from the wall and returned to his more human form. "One day, brother—"

"We had that fight already. You won, remember?" His brother had left him with nothing. Nibo glanced to Qeenan's sleeves that were marked with red handprints. The signs of Nibo's murder, and those that marked Qeenan as Baron Kriminal, the hit man for their nanchon. He was the one summoned to do their dirty work in the human realm. If they wanted someone killed, or worse, his brother was more than happy to do it.

No questions asked.

Qeenan spat at his feet. "You should have been left to wander in limbo forever. A forgotten shade."

"Couldn't agree more," he said under his breath as his brother walked off. He'd never asked for either life. This one or his first. He damn sure hadn't wanted to be tied to Qeenan in either of them.

But that was the way of things. Life was ever a gift. And never the one you'd really wanted and had hoped to get. Worse? It always came with a no-return policy.

Take it or leave it.

Disgusted, Nibo headed for the gates. He wasn't sure where he was going. But he didn't want to be here any longer. If he had to listen to fools bitch and moan, he might as well be among the humans. At least they had a reason for their blind stupidity and unhappiness. They were the pawns of the real assholes.

Qeenan watched as his brother walked off, and narrowed his gaze. He grabbed his right hand, Joseph Danger, the loa of justice who traveled with him. They were inseparable, as Joseph was the one charged with righting injustices of the righteous who'd been wronged, and he was the one who wouldn't hesitate to shed blood in their name.

Indeed, he lived for such.

Unlike him and his twin, whom he loathed, he and Joseph were a perfect team. Joseph didn't shirk at what needed to be done to balance the scales. He understood payback and hell-wrath. That not everyone deserved to live.

Or to be happy.

Nibo was pathetic in his sympathy for others and Qeenan cursed his twin's bleeding heart. While Qeenan knew when to cull the herd, his brother was all about coddling the weak and wasting resources on those unworthy.

Nibo's devotion to his pathetic human bitch was a prime example. Rather than cut her loose, he'd bargained to save her.

Futtocking fool.

His human tart would be the death of him. Again. Just like Aclima had been when she'd refused Qeenan's advances.

You're not your brother. And I won't have you. . . .

Her death had been no suicide. He'd kill her again if he could. Just as he'd killed Nibo's latest whore.

"Nibo will gut you if he ever learns what you did."

Qeenan hissed at the fool who spoke too loudly. "He would have risked us all for her. A slag whore."

Joseph's gaze went to Erzulie as she walked past and gave them a covert glance. "There are many who risk more for things they shouldn't covet."

Qeenan grabbed him by the throat. "Remember, I have the power to take out a loa as much as I do a mortal."

Joseph placed a searing hand to his wrist that caused him to gasp and let go instantly. "You're not the only one, Qee. Just because you enjoy the killing and they indulge your hunger for it doesn't mean no one else here can rise to the occasion."

His fury simmering, Qeenan blew cool air across his burning wrist to soothe it as Joseph vanished.

"Go ahead," he breathed. "All of you. Mock me, if you will. But you'll regret your actions."

He'd make sure of it.

Adarian respected him. He understood the future better than these troglodytes. There was a new day dawning. And it wasn't for the bleeding-heart radas who clung to their outmoded traditions and useless ways.

This was the age of division. The age of conquest and fury. Of grudges and hatred.

The Malachai was rising and he and his loyal followers were going to make sure the world paid for everything it had done to them. For all the ill it'd made them swallow.

He was tired of walking in his brother's shadow. Tired of eating scraps and being treated like the dog sent out as a last resort, after all the others had been called for first.

Just once, Qeenan wanted to be the chosen one. His days of being cursed were over.

It was his name they would cheer, and he would be second to no one, especially not the brother he hated.

"Burn, bitches, burn."

And it would be his brother's precious Valynda and the crew of the *Sea Witch* he'd offer up as his first sacrifices to the Malachai to prove his loyalty.

MICHAEL'S
KEY

7

"You should call for your Nibo."

Valynda tensed as she heard Belle's voice behind her. Clearing her throat, she finished knotting the ropes she'd been mending and tried not to be annoyed at the sound of yet another person meddling in her life. After all, when had *that* ever gone wrong for her? "Why would I do that?"

"Because you're weeping."

She scoffed at the very idea. "I can't weep." She had no tear ducts.

Coming around her side, Belle placed her hand on Valynda's chin and forced her to meet her gaze. The beauty of Belle's features never ceased to amaze Valynda. Today, she'd painted an intricate pattern of blue and white dots around her eyes and down the bridge of her nose. The paint glistened against her dark skin and complemented the darker blue and red beads that were braided into the hair she kept held back from her face with a red kerchief that was knotted at the nape of her neck.

Because she was a rigger, charged with climbing up and down the masts, she wore breeches and tunics like the men, and yet she was as regal and graceful as any queen. Indeed, there was something innately feminine and deadly about Belle Morte. Gentle and cutthroat.

That dichotomy was what had drawn Valynda and everyone else to her and kept them all intrigued.

Not to mention the fact that Belle, in spite of her ferocity, tended to act as motherly toward them as the Lady Marcelina, who guarded the entire crew like a fierce lioness. And it was the maternal Belle staring at her right now. "Don't be lying to me, child. I know you better. I see all that's unseen."

And that she did. No one could hide from the powerful sorceress. Valynda knew that. Belle's powers were extraordinary. The only one who came close to them was Janice, the Trini Dark-Huntress who traveled with them and who could only come out from belowdecks after the sun went down.

"I want nothing to do with him, Belle. We're done." Except for the small matter of her needing to seduce him for the Malachai, but it seemed like a bad idea to mention that to the one person who could rat her out and see her gutted for it.

"'Tis a pity, that."

"Why?"

Shaking her head, Belle sighed and released her. She fetched a length of the rope Valynda had been working on for the rigging and headed off.

At first, Valynda assumed she was done with her and was going to carry it to the mast to repair something. Since it was Belle's job, it made sense.

But, in a grand huff, Belle came back to her.

"You know how I died?"

Of course not. How Belle had died was one of the best-kept secrets on board the ship, which, given the grand secrets of this crew, said a lot, as most of them weren't too keen on sharing much of anything, other than a few random shoves, and blows to the egos whenever someone got to thinking too much of themselves. Not even the captain knew what had happened to Belle to bring on her damnation.

The woman kept a lid on that tighter than Sallie kept the cork on his rum bottle where he stored his soul.

Valynda shook her head.

Her eyes turned as stormy as the seas right before a tempest. "I had a family I loved more than anything on this earth or beyond. Husband and a daughter so beautiful that even the angels above wept in envy of her." Belle's voice cracked with the weight of her heartache and pain. "They were the pride of me life, they were, and maybe that was me mistake. I took too much pride in caring for them. In loving them and being loyal to them before even meself. In putting them above and beyond everything else, and thinking nothing and no one could ever divide us. Because I truly believed that—that nothing and no one could ever get between me husband and me. That we had that rare love that comes along once in a fairy-tale dream."

Closing her eyes, Belle visibly winced. "Until the day me husband hired a new barmaid for his tavern. Plain and homely, she was, and I thought nothing of her at first. But it didn't take long to see that she was all kinds of evil. It was evident in the way she talked to others. How she put them down whenever me husband wasn't around and how smug she acted, as if she owned the place. I tried me best to tell him exactly who and what she was. I saw the devil in that one, clear as I stand here before you. She was evil incarnate, and it bled from her tongue with every honey-coated barb and well-practiced, left-handed compliment she dropped every time she opened her fetid mouth. But he refused to listen to me. He told me over and over that I was being ridiculous and that we needed her. I couldn't believe it. He hired her as a servant, and before I knew it, he had her even living with us as if she was a member of our family! He'd even go off a-gallivanting with her in the middle of the day to frolic while I'd be left alone to work by meself to support our family and watch our daughter! 'Twas so bad, some even began to think her his wife instead of me. Instead of being ashamed for what he did and how he behaved, the beast that he became began to throw his thoughtless acts in me face and to blame me for it. And I grew physically sick and weak from the stress of having to work all the time to pick up the slack as he played more and more with this stranger who divided him from his family and duties."

Valynda was stunned on multitudinous levels. One, she hadn't known Belle was ever married. Hadn't known she'd been a mother. Nor that their petite sorceress had owned a tavern.

Indeed, it was all she could do to keep from gaping at all the facts her friend had kept secret.

Twisting the rope in her hands, Belle paused as if the memories were more than she could bear. "And me husband wasn't the only one she toyed with. That horrible slag bitch caused trouble between everyone she came into contact with. 'Twas as if she fed from the very turmoil she fostered, like some gluttonous maggot what couldn't get its fill. Every night 'twas a brawl between patrons caused by her and that rancid tongue that hid its venom beneath disguised insults and doublespeak."

Belle curled her lip. "She had a way of getting into someone's mind and twisting it around until they turned on even their very best friend to the point of murder. And it wasn't just the patrons she went against. Workers we'd had for years quit without warning, and all because of the mischief she'd put in their weak-willed minds where she'd played on their fears and turned their thoughts against me, as if I was the cause of it. For no reason other than she was a mean, petty she-bitch, bent on the utter destruction of all those around her. And that was nothing compared to what she'd done to me poor, pathetic husband."

Valynda held her breath at the venom in Belle's voice. That was a new tone for the tiny woman, especially since Belle never talked badly about anyone. The fact that she didn't like this woman told her all she needed to know.

She had to be evil for Belle not to like her, and her husband to be a true idiot not to know that one basic fact about Belle. If he knew nothing else about his wife, he should have known that. There was an innate kindness in her that radiated out from her like the warm glow of sunlight after a fierce storm.

Belle got along with everyone. She loved everyone and no one could be around her for five heartbeats and not feel it. Everyone was drawn to her. While she might be a bit verbally caustic, she was compassion incarnate. There was no one she wouldn't help. No one she wouldn't reach out to if they were in need.

And if Belle didn't like someone . . . they were rotten to their very core and should be avoided like a poisonous viper in the Garden of Eden.

How could the man who married her not know that?

"What did he say when you tried to tell him about the woman he'd let in?"

Belle ground her teeth. "That she was only trying to help."

Valynda grimaced at the stupidity of that answer. How could anyone be so blind as to not see through something so obvious? Especially if he'd been married to Belle for any length of time. Or known her at all?

With a bitter laugh, Belle shook her head. "I was too sick to argue against them both. Besides, he'd always been my hero. We did everything together. Until that trollop showed up, we'd seldom ever had an argument. We were best friends in all things . . . or so I thought. And never had I known him to be weak-minded, yet she took control of him like a marionette. Pathetic fool thought himself in charge, but she played him for everything he wasn't worth. Before I knew it, he turned on me and our daughter in ways I couldn't fathom. No longer were those his words coming from his mouth, but hers. He let that monstrous whore torture *ma petite fille* and me like she was the mistress of his home and I the tart in the tavern he'd hired off the street. Nothing I could say or do would get through to his mind. 'Twas as if she'd removed his brains and replaced them with mush. I couldn't understand how he could just stand there and bear witness to her evil and say nothing. How he couldn't see what was right before him and blame us for her wickedness. Whatever I said, or *ma petite* Shara, that wench turned around and mutated. She made even the most innocuous comment sinister with her wicked machinations, and never once did he doubt her lies."

Belle's eyes glistened with unshed tears. "As long as I live, I'll never understand how it was my Robbie turned on me the way he did. We'd known each other since we were children. Never did I say or do anything to make him doubt me. I gave him all I had and more, and I loved him more than me life. Had he simply come to me and said he wanted to leave with her, I'd have been fine with that and wished him well. Truly, I'd have packed his bags meself. But nay, rather he stood by and let that slag whore poison me and *ma fille.*"

Wait . . .

What?

Shocked, it took Valynda a moment to grasp the magnitude of what she said.

Then she gasped in horror. "Nay!"

A single tear fell from Belle's eye. "Indeed. Unbeknownst to me at the time, the stress wasn't what had been making me ill. I simply thought myself overworked and overtaxed as I sat there, day after day, watching *ma petite fille* grow weaker with every rattling breath she struggled to take, ne'er really knowing what was wrong with us both, while he knew what that bitch was doing, and said nothing to me about it. How could any man ever do such a thing to the family he'd sworn before God to love and protect? How?"

The agony in her eyes flooded Valynda's with tears for the pain it wrought through her soul.

Her mind reeled at the horror of it all. Belle's husband was worse than the very demons they fought against. What father, or husband, could do something so monstrous? So cruel? How could anyone betray another human in such a cold, brutal fashion? She couldn't understand it any more than Belle did.

There were some lines no one should ever cross. And this level of insidious cruelty was definitely one of them.

Belle shook her head. "Shara was in so much pain, every day, and I was so concerned for her that it didn't even dawn on me that we shared the same symptoms. I actually thought my maternal instincts caused me to feel her ailments in sympathy because *ma petite* cried all the time from it. Poor babe could barely walk. If she managed to eat, she threw it all up. Her body was failing and there was nothing I could do to stop it. I tried every potion I could think of to make her better. Prayed to every spirit I knew. Lit every candle. Nothing worked. Not even Nibo could help her. 'Twas as if all had abandoned me with feckless disregard."

Curling her lip, Belle laughed bitterly. "And would you believe that slag bitchling had the audacity to come into *my room*"—she slapped herself on her chest to emphasize those words—"every day and ask me how *ma petite fille* was feeling? How Shara was doing! Knowing that bitchtress was killing her and that the sole reason my baby suffered? That both me and me daughter were dying from what she was serving us! And all the while me husband would come to check on us and say *nothing*! Just come and look at us with a stoic expression on his vile face."

Sick to her stomach, Valynda couldn't wrap her mind around the harsh cruelty of what Belle described. This was madness on a true sadistic level. Nay, she couldn't imagine a greater betrayal than to know the man she thought she loved was standing there, watching her die. No wonder Belle was barely sane most days. It all made sense now. All the woman's weird idiosyncrasies.

Why she couldn't trust anyone. Who could blame her?

How could anyone be so cold to his own family? His own child?

And for what?

Money? Ego? What in the world could get into anyone's head to make them turn against their family for a stranger and to cause them harm? It just didn't make sense. Why throw so much away?

Another tear fell quietly down Belle's cheek. "To this day, I can still feel the last wisp of her breath on me skin as it left Shara's frail body and she went limp in me arms." Belle broke off into wrenching sobs.

Pulling her against her chest, Valynda wished she could join her tears as she felt Belle's pain deep in her heart and soul. Dear God, no one should bear witness to such a thing. She could imagine no greater horror than holding her daughter as she died. To be betrayed so badly by the man she loved.

It made what Nibo had done to her pale in comparison, because the truth was, she'd rather die a thousand times than see her own child perish before her.

That had to be the cruelest blow life had to give to anyone. Pressing her hand to her stomach, Belle gave her an agonized stare that pierced her like a hot needle. She pulled away from Valynda to wipe at her eyes. "You cannot imagine the scream I let out when Shara left this mortal coil. And the rage that came upon me then. With it was born me clairvoyance and cunning. In that one fatal moment of losing *ma belle* Shara, I heard her whispering to me what had been done to her and by whom. The why of it all— that the slag had come in and wanted what I had for her own and wanted us gone and me Robbie was too stupid to see it for what it was. Then I saw the brightest light shine down upon us. It damn near blinded me. So, I lay *ma fille*'s body back on her bed, and seized me herb knife, then went to find the ones what had harmed *ma petite fille de cœur*."

Her breathing turned ragged as if she were reliving that moment. As if the rage had come back just as fresh now as it'd been the day her daughter had died. "As calm and cool as you please, I found them in the crowded tavern we owned. And the minute I saw that whore slag there, me mind took on the visions of her drugging *ma petite fille* and me, of her actually humming, singing, and smiling as she tainted our food and drink, and of her laughing while she fed her concoctions to us that had killed me daughter. To actually think in her twisted, sick mind that she deserved what I'd worked so hard for! Next thing I knew, I was on them, stabbing and slashing with everything I had and more."

Belle looked up as tears streamed down her beautiful face, leaving streaks behind to mark the pain that was seared into her soul, and now Valynda's in indignation for her. "When all was said and done, I'd ripped them to shreds and cut the throats of two innocent watchmen who'd tried to stop me from gutting them." She met Valynda's gaze without flinching. "Sadly, I wasn't sorry then and I'm not sorry now. Not one little bit. My only regret was not protecting me girl from that bitchling who preyed on her and turned me husband from the loving father he'd been into the beast I no longer recognized. I only wish I'd caught on to them sooner so that I could have saved *ma petite fille*'s life."

"So, you were hanged?"

"Eventually."

Valynda cocked her head. "Pardon?"

Belle's laughter was cold and sinister. "Oh, I ran for it, I did. Like the devil and all his servants. As I said, I wasn't a bit sorry for what I took from the trollop or the rank bastard betrayer. I grabbed a sword, hit the door, and lived for a couple of years on me root work before the law caught up to me."

Sniffing, she wiped the moisture from her cheeks. "I told you, Lady Doll, I earned my damnation. Every what day of it. While I'm not proud of what I did to them and I am sorry for the deaths of the watchmen, I don't deny it. I was about as worthless a person as whatever was born, and I shouldn't have taken the innocent lives that I did. But to get the guilty and to make them pay, I'd do it all again, without hesitation. To pay that debt, it was worth it." She shrugged. "I still don't know why Thorn and the captain agreed to bring me back to serve on this crew and give me a shot to win back me blackened soul. I'm just glad they did, for there's nothing more I want than to see me girl again. To hold her wee little hand one more time and tell her that I'm sorry I failed to keep her safe. Even from her own father."

Her eyes still shining from her tears, Belle turned to leave.

Valynda caught her hand as she started away, and pulled her back to her side. "I know why they chose you, Belle. You've a good heart. The best I've seen. Don't ever let anyone else tell you differently. Not even you."

Smiling, Belle kissed her cheek. "And Nibo loves you, miss. Never doubt that. I don't know the how of what brought you into your death, but I know the mountains he moved to bring you back from the other side and to get you on this ship. That was no easy feat, there."

"How do you mean?"

Belle arched her brow. "Don't you know?"

"Thorn and the captain bargained." That was how everyone had been chosen for the crew.

Belle shook her head. "Valynda, they didn't choose you. Didn't you ever wonder why you're the only one on board who wasn't a trained fighter or brawler?"

"Sancha—"

"Was given fencing and shooting lessons every day of her life. A lady she might have been, but she was more than able to stand on her own."

Valynda hadn't known that. She'd assumed that as a noble

lady Sancha would have had others do everything for her. Janice, she knew, had been trained by the Dark-Hunter leader Acheron to become the fierce fighter she was. Belle had grown up with her father, who'd been a trader and hunter, so she knew that Belle was well versed on how to protect herself. And as an orphan on her own, Cameron Jack had been forced to live and pass herself off as a man for most of her life while her brother was off at sea so that she wouldn't fall prey to others while he was away. So, Cameron knew well how to fight and scrap.

Mara's ancient race had been at war with the captain's and she'd been well versed in warfare, and the captain had trained his sister himself on how to fight.

But Valynda hadn't known how to hold a sword or even load a flintlock.

Her mind reeled at something she hadn't thought about before. Scowling, she thought back to the day when she'd awakened in her straw body to find Belle and the captain standing over her, with Thorn, their unofficial boss who'd assembled their crew and charged Captain Bane with the task of driving the escaping demons back through the fractured Carian Gate.

Disoriented and confused, she'd been too grateful to be away from her hell realm of torture to ask too many questions, for fear of it angering them and having them cast her back to that nightmare hole.

Once that had passed, she'd assumed that her story had been similar to everyone else's. That Bane had gone through her dimension with Thorn and seen something promising in her that he thought would benefit their crew.

But if what Belle was saying was true . . .

Valynda left her immediately and headed to the captain's cabin. She had to have an answer for this.

Why was she on board this ship?

She had to know what had happened when they brought her back. There were so many questions and so few answers.

Suddenly, she felt lied to by everyone. Thorn. The captain. Adarian.

Most of all, Xuri.

No longer did she know who or what she could trust. And that was the worst feeling of all. To be betrayed by those closest to her. To lose all moorings and be cast adrift with no direction in the world. She hadn't felt this way since her parents had found out about Nibo, and they'd lost their ever-loving minds over it.

Valynda froze as those nightmares tore through her with fresh talons and left her ravaged anew.

"You've taken up with a native boy?" She could still hear that strident, deafening tone.

She'd just come home to find her parents clustered in the front of their tiny three-room cottage. A place so small, she had to leave it in order to have room enough to change her mind.

The instant the door had closed, she'd seen the stern look upon her father's face, the taut grimace on her mother's plump brow, and had known she was in trouble.

Serious trouble.

"What is it?"

"Tell us it's not true." Her father had stood by the hearth with a sneer while her mother sat near the window in a chair, wringing her hands and feigning a fainting spell.

"Fine. It's not true. I have no idea of what matter we're speaking, but if it solaces your mind, I'm happy to reassure you, Father."

He'd backhanded her then. A blow so hard it'd split her lip and sent her to the floor. "You've been seen cavorting with an islander in a disgusting, filthy manner. Tell me it's not true."

Her heart had stopped instantly as she tried to imagine who could have seen her with Nibo. They'd been so careful, meeting late at night and in remote areas where her people never ventured.

With her ears ringing from the blow, she'd wiped away the blood. Her hands had trembled as she'd rolled over to deal with them.

"Valynda?" Her mother's voice had cracked. "Answer your father."

Licking more blood from her lips, she'd searched her mind for something plausible to say, but it wasn't in her nature to lie.

"My God, it's true." Her father had stumbled back as her mother began crying hysterically.

"It's not what you think, Father. Xuri's—"

"What kind of name is that?" His roar had cut off her words as he'd seized her arm and yanked her from the floor.

She couldn't remember anything past that. His words had been too cruel and biting for her to commit them to memory. The violence too horrific.

And for no reason other than Nibo had been different from what her father deemed "acceptable." He wasn't what her father had wanted for her.

So, he'd shown up the next day with a man his age and demanded she marry him to take the taint away from their family name. As if her father hadn't done them more harm by his own actions of damning them to a life of bitter, cruel poverty for his own selfish ego that craved respectability from others. Not for anything he'd achieved or done with his life. But for what he'd deprived her and her mother of having.

After all, it was her fault that others whispered and gossiped about them behind their backs and while they were in church. God forbid her father accept the blame for anything, ever. He'd always pushed that off on her mother or her. It was why Valynda hated him. Why she'd never wanted to be around her father. He liked to paint himself as a noble bastard or hapless martyr to all. Some self-sacrificing family man to be admired by the entire world and held up as an example of what everyone should strive to be. Yet that was only a sham. A lie he professed for admiration he didn't deserve.

There was nothing benevolent in her father's heart. Everything he did was for show, so that others would speak kindly about him, because he couldn't stand to be criticized. It was for his own self-glorification and he didn't care how it affected her mother or her. How it damaged their futures. So long as he got what he wanted in the here and now, that was all that mattered. Their only reason to exist was to serve him and his needs and ego. So long as she was a bragging right, he loved her. When she disappointed him, she was nothing to him. Just an object to be cast aside, mocked and ridiculed.

Herbert Moore was a disgusting dog she'd learned to hate

early in life, and she resented her mother, Lizzie, for never standing up to him. But then her mother had always been a weak, selfish woman, more concerned with her own needs than anyone else's.

So here Valynda was. Trapped between worlds.

Soulless and in the body of a doll.

Pain choked her. "I have no place in this world." Truth was, she never had. Even when she'd been human, she'd felt that way. Unwanted. Unloved.

Unnecessary. She was so done with this cold world.

Heartbroken and disgusted, Valynda clutched her fist and drew it back, changing her mind about bothering the captain. There was no need. She didn't want to hear his answer, lest it be something that would only hurt her more.

As everything did.

She couldn't take another kick in her teeth. Even if they were only made of straw.

But before she could leave, the door opened.

Captain Bane drew up short as he saw her. "Miss Moore? To what do I owe the honor?"

Leave it to the Devyl Bane to be so kind and formal. Then again, he was ever a creature of contradictions. He shared that trait with Nibo.

"I . . . um . . ." Why couldn't she ever think of something plausible to say? Really, it was frustrating.

"Aye?"

No reasonable lie manifested. Just once, couldn't she think of something?

What do you expect? Even your brains are straw . . .

And before she could stop herself, the truth came tumbling out of her mouth. "Why did you pick me for the crew?"

The captain leaned against the door frame and arched one incredibly handsome brow. "Interesting way to start the conversation." He rubbed his thumb along his bottom lip.

A distracting gesture, no doubt. But sadly, as handsome as he was, he wasn't the one who made her swoon. "I'm not stupid, Captain. I'm not like your wife. I can't fashion a ship from me body. Nor am I like Sallie, who has his soul stored in a bottle that he can unleash to become a superhuman with incredible strength. I'm not Will or Bart, who are great sorcerers. Or Lady Belle. So why did you choose a woman with so little to offer?"

He scowled at her words. "You're too hard on yourself, my lady."

"And you're avoiding my question."

He let out a fierce, resigned sigh. "Very well, Miss Moore. The truth is, I didn't pick you."

Her heart sank over the fact that Belle hadn't been lying. Not that she'd believed that. Not really. Just that the confirmation burned more than she wanted to admit. It was hard to hear a harsh truth, but she'd much rather hear that than a lie.

In that moment, standing outside his cabin, Valynda felt so unwanted. Again. It seemed ever her lot in life. She was forced on everyone, like some hapless, wandering beggar. "I see."

"Don't be getting that tone, Miss Moore." He cleared his deep voice, then stepped back and glared up. "Thorn, you evil bastard, tuck it in and get here, now. I summon you forth from your infernal lair."

A bright flash appeared just behind her left shoulder. Tall and handsome as the devil himself, Thorn was always a bit of a dandy in fashion and yet he was unmistakably masculine. Dangerously so, point of fact. She wasn't quite sure how he managed to pull it off, and yet there was an aura about him that let everyone know he'd be more than happy to gut anyone or anything who annoyed him, and that he'd do it without wrinkling or mussing his elegantly pressed lace cuffs.

His eyes burned with an intelligence and were tainted with a bit of cruelty beneath them.

"Really, Duel. That's the best you can do? How 'bout a nice 'Thorn, you got a minute? Would you mind?' Or better yet . . . '*Please*'? Would that kill you?"

"Definitely stick in me craw. Probably choke me to death. So aye, I'd say it'd be fatal to even attempt such niceties with you. Therefore, I'll stick to me ways, if you don't mind."

"I do mind," Thorn said, more forcefully. "Not that you'll change. Just feel the need to continue to put my head through the wall that is your obstinate stupidity." He smiled coldly. "So, what can I do you for?"

The captain gestured toward her. "Miss Moore wants to know why you chose her for this grand misadventure. Figured I'd let you have the honors of explaining it."

"Oh."

There was so much hidden by that one consonant that it sent a shiver over her. "Oh?"

"Did I say oh?" His tone was gruff and defensive.

"You did, sir, aye." Valynda couldn't understand why he was being so evasive. "Why?"

"It seemed appropriate."

Rather, it seemed annoying. She gave him a droll stare.

He didn't appear to appreciate that either. So, he pulled her away from the captain to a more secluded area of the deck, though that was a bit hard to manage, as privacy on a ship wasn't the easiest thing to find. He glanced about to the others and waited until he was sure he'd have a moment where they wouldn't be overheard. "Miss Moore, there are things in the world best not asked."

How sick she was of being told that. It wasn't as if she'd just asked her father where babies came from. He might as well have poked her in the eye and told her that she stank and that her hair was made of flea turds while he was at it. "You sound like my father."

He snorted. "Better than sounding like mine. Believe me."

There was no way to miss the bitterness in his tone. Which made her curious, given that it was said his father was the darkest power in existence. However, with those relations, she decided to let it go. "Please, sir . . . I'm trying to understand what happened with me."

Thorn let out a tired breath. "I made a promise."

Ah, now she understood. "To Nibo."

He shook his head to correct her assumption. "Someone who means a lot more to me than that. Not that that says much, since he means nothing to me at all. Suffice it to say that a lot of people moved a lot of bodies to get you this chance. You should be grateful."

"I'm not *un*grateful."

He arched a brow at her that questioned her sincerity.

"What's that supposed mean?"

Could he sense the treachery she plotted? Not that she had acted on it, but to hear her father and pastor speak, a thought was as good as an action. And in that case, she was guilty through and through. There was barely a minute that passed that she didn't think about that damnable crook and what she was supposed to be doing to get it.

Of course, it was followed next by her desire to take said crook and shove it up a place of Nibo's anatomy that would make Vlad the Impaler happy.

Two warring desires that both disgusted her. Because honestly, she just wanted to be left alone.

Nay, not true. She just wanted to be whole and loved. To be human again.

Just for one minute.

Thorn reached out and placed a sympathetic hand on her arm. His gaze turned gentle. "What was done to you, Miss Moore, was wrong. No one should ever seek to control another. Believe me, I had my own daddy issues that make yours pale in comparison. And like you, I ran from the destiny my father tried to iron-fist me into. I ran to the farthest hill I could find, stood on top of it, and defiantly dared him to try and knock me from it."

"And what happened?"

"He kicked my ass and dragged me around the hill a few times."

Not the answer she was hoping for.

"But," he said slowly, "once I picked my teeth up from the ground, and I could breathe again, I eventually learned to walk on my own. Then I learned to attack. The trick is learning when not to."

Her stomach sank at his words, as she definitely had a feeling that he knew about her bargain. "I just want my body back."

"We all want to be human, Valynda. Just make sure that in your quest to regain your body, you don't lose your humanity. Or more to the point, your soul. For that would be the greatest tragedy of all."

He was right. But it was so hard to remember that when others turned against her. "Have you made any progress on when I might have a body again?"

Thorn shook his head. "Sadly, you're asking me for powers I lack. To make flesh and blood . . . that is something reserved for very few."

"Captain! Ship avast!"

Valynda scowled at the sharp cry that rang out from the crow's nest.

Bart went running past so that he could grab a spyglass and try to see what they were looking at. "Colors, Mr. Devereaux?"

There was a brief pause as he looked out to see. "An English frigate. Pirate hunters."

Valynda's heart sped up as her gaze went to the red Roger flying proudly over their black sails, which would draw such beasts like a magnet.

Worse than a black flag, the field of solid red around the *Sea*

Witch's skull-and-crossed-dagger emblem told those they went against that they gave no quarter. No mercy.

No prey. No pay.

To a pirate hunter, that flag meant bank.

To them, it meant trouble.

Bart passed a sick grimace toward their captain, Devyl Bane. "Strike our colors, Captain?"

Ever true to his warring nature that had once set him against the best and worst the world of man and demons had to offer, Bane shook his head. "Turn us about, Mr. Meers. Let the bitches catch up."

8

Her knees weak, Valynda took position as they made ready for battle. This was the part she always dreaded most about being a member of the *Sea Witch*'s crew. Having already survived one sinking, she wasn't eager to repeat the experience. Something not helped as she saw their resident merman pause beside his wife to help her hike up her skirts and secure them so that she could fight with her legs unfettered by the material. Fret etched itself across Cameron's face as she cupped Kalder's cheek. "Careful with you, husband. I'd hate to replace you."

Laughing, he kissed her. "No fears, me fearse. You take care, as you're fighting for two. Don't make me mourn either of you." And with that, he jumped over the side of the ship, into the waves, so that he could lend a hand from where he was the strongest.

Valynda listened to the rumble of the long nines as the cannons were rolled into place belowdecks. Smoke choked her as the linstocks were made ready to light their wicks.

The air became thick with anticipation. Few spoke anything more than orders to the others. Not that any here could die. Still, battle was a serious matter, whether you were alive or dead.

And everyone here was a warring lot who looked forward to what they were about to do, hence why they'd been picked for the crew. All save her. Growing up the daughter of a cobbler, fighting a battle was something she'd never thought she'd participate in.

But she was glad to have a chance to regain her soul.

And her body.

Which meant doing what she didn't want to on this day, and probably the morrow. Valynda took up her staff and made ready for what was to come. Completely focused on the horizon, where the enemy ship grew larger by the heartbeat, she let out a scream as someone appeared behind her and drew her against a hard chest.

Cameron stared at her with a gaping expression as Valynda turned to find Nibo grinning at her.

"Devil step on your tail, cat?"

She popped him on the arm. "You scared the bejesus from me! Why would you do that?" Especially right then!

"Thought you heard me when I popped in."

Drawing a ragged breath, she glared at him. "Didn't know you were here. I should put a bell on you!"

Completely unabashed, he tsked. "I'm not exactly quiet." Holding up his bangle-bedecked arms that jingled mightily, he illustrated the point nicely. Still . . .

"I was preoccupied."

He winked at her. "So I see." Glancing toward the approaching ship, he narrowed his gaze on the ominous crew that wanted to bring them in. "What are you doing, Bane?"

"Dancing with the devil, Nibo. You?"

"Doubting your sanity. That's Jonathan Barnet. Why are you letting him get this close?"

The captain shrugged. "Haven't had a headache in the last two months. Figured it was time. After all, everyone needs at least one good brain tumor once in their lifetime." He jerked his chin toward the ship. "This one comes with friends."

Nibo laughed. "That he does. Weapons, too. Big ones, I'm told."

"Good. It's no fun to attack those who can't defend themselves. More the merrier, I say."

"Then you ought to be deliriously happy right now."

Bane flashed him a most uncharacteristic smile that was actually frightening. Both in its eagerness and the fact that it was such an unnatural look on the handsome man's face that it was downright terrifying.

Valynda groaned at their inappropriate bantering. Men! She'd never understand them. Aggravated at Nibo for his timing, she grimaced at him. "Thought you told me you weren't a fighter."

Nibo shrugged. "Not a runner, either, *ma chère*. I will hold me own in a fight."

"And why are you here?"

"You were calling for me."

Had he gone daft? "Nay, I was not."

He scowled at her. "Pretty sure I heard my name on your sweet lips. 'Tis a most unmistakable sound." He lowered his voice so that only she could hear him. "That does unmistakable things to me body."

Clearing her throat, she glanced about nervously to make sure no one else had heard that. "Pretty sure you didn't."

He looked over at Thorn.

"You've gone senile, old man. And don't be casting those eyes at me. God knows I didn't call for your sorry arse. I've no use for you whatsoever. And especially not for those two trolls you usually travel with. Have to say I'm glad you left their rotten souls at home for once."

"Captain! They're hoisting up the white flag!"

Bane actually looked deflated by the news. "Well, bugger me that." Grinding his teeth, Captain Bane glared at Thorn.

"What? I had nothing to do with it. Why you looking at me with those downcast eyes?"

"Something this disappointing feels like it should have your name engraved upon it."

"Seriously?"

Before anyone could speak, Captain Barnet requested permission to come aboard.

Both Will and Bart turned toward Bane with looks that said

they couldn't wait to see what he had to say about that. And honestly, neither could Valynda, given the captain's behavior thus far.

"Sure. Why not?" Captain Bane said in a sullen tone that conveyed just how unenthusiastic he was about it.

With a deep growl and grand show of irritation, he sheathed his sword, then looked to Strixa, their resident water witch. "Could you at least sink their ship to make me feel better?"

She actually laughed at his beleaguered tone.

Lady Marcelina tsked at her irritable husband before she kissed his cheek. "There, there, my warring love. I'm sure you'll have the chance to gut something before nightfall. Cheer up."

"So say you. Haven't had a good gutting in days. Beheading either." Bane crossed his arms and stood aside as Barnet swung over from his ship to their main deck so that he could talk to them.

Valynda started forward, but Nibo kept her by his side, silently reminding her that Barnet, as a human, wasn't supposed to interact her. While she had a spell over her that kept most humans from seeing her true straw form, it didn't work on all of them. Those who were sensitive or special, such as Cameron and her brother Paden, saw through the spell. Therefore, it wasn't worth the risk for her to mix with humans any more than was necessary, lest they think her a monster.

Nibo had the same problem as a psychopomp. His form was nebulous. To those with a good heart, he appeared as he did to Valynda—beautiful beyond description. Handsome and young. A man in the prime of his vigor.

To those who were corrupt, however, he was a monstrous,

hideous beast who was known to send them into screaming fits of madness.

While she'd never glimpsed that side of him, she'd heard others scream in all-out terror when they looked upon him. Xuri had tried to explain it to her, but she couldn't imagine the demonic horror he described that showed up like some skeletal beast intent to drive all reason from the damned.

It was why her friends had run the night he'd appeared. They hadn't seen him the way she had. Their hearts were blackened by their conceit and petty jealousies. By their inability to see the beauty of others. They were too caught up in their own pomp and self-importance.

For that, she was sorry, because he was a creature of absolute grace. Every part of him. From his broad, sculpted shoulders to the riot of curls that framed the most perfectly formed face ever made. She could spend eternity in silent worship of his body alone.

If only he hadn't betrayed her.

Every time she thought of it, it tore her heart out anew. Who could be so cold?

"Captain Bane." Barnet held his arm out for their captain to take it.

It was obvious Captain Bane would rather not, but after an elbowing from his wife, he did. "Have to say I'm rather surprised by the chance you took, Barnet."

"Not as much as I am by the fact you didn't open fire on me. Grateful, too, that you're still a man of honor."

For it was well known that Captain Bane never fired the first shot. But he rather made a point to always fire the last one.

And, in the end, he left none standing.

Bane inclined his head to him. "So, to what do I owe this . . . chance encounter?"

"I came looking for you as a favor for Rafael Santiago."

That got everyone's attention, as they owed a debt to the infamous pirate who'd helped them out more than once.

"What about him?"

"St. Noir was killed."

A ripple went through the Deadmen crew. Jean-Luc Tessier had been a legend among the pirates they knew. Acting and raiding as Captain St. Noir, Jean-Luc had taken more than his share of treasure, but always with a style and sense of fairness that was uniquely his own.

Yet the one thing he was known for was being Rafael's best friend.

Bane winced. "How?"

Turning sheepish, Barnet swallowed before he answered. "I . . ." He sighed. "I went after Calico Jack, not knowing that St. Noir had sent Bonny and Read back to him for protection while he took on the Spanish. I stupidly thought the ladies were still with St. Noir and under his protection."

"Why would you do that?"

Barnet held his hands up. "Thought it fair for a debt I owed the rank bastard, especially since the women were supposed to be off with St. Noir and clear of Calico's crew." He let out a long sigh. "It was bad timing that I deeply regret."

Valynda exchanged a pained grimace with Nibo as she told him just how bad it really was.

For everyone.

"Anne Bonny was pregnant with St. Noir's child," she explained in a whisper.

Barnet looked as disgusted as Nibo did. "I would *never* have gone after Jack had I known the women were there."

Bane let out a weary sigh. "I take it that they're in custody?"

His features even more tortured, Barnet nodded. "Bound for the gallows as soon as their babes are born. The instant St. Noir heard the news, he made plans to go after them, but before he could, his quartermaster betrayed him and his crew to the Spanish. St. Noir stayed behind to delay them from reaching his men and to give them time to escape . . . bastard dogs slaughtered him where he stood."

Bane winced again in sympathetic pain. Most of them did, point of fact, as loyalty was something every Deadman understood and respected. That was what made them a family—their willingness to sacrifice their souls for each other. "I take it that Rafe is going after Anne."

Barnet nodded. "He feels he owes it to St. Noir, and I offered to help. But it's more than the two of us can do on our own. Since you're such good friends with Santiago, and I knew you frequented the waters here, I thought I'd ask for a sword to help him. Last thing I want to do is send another man to the Locker."

Before the captain could answer, something roared out from far below. Deep and guttural, it shook the boards beneath Valynda's feet. Nibo grabbed her arm and pulled her against his body as the ship tipped sharply to its side. Will went skidding across the deck, as did Cameron until her brother caught her. Both of them transformed from their human bodies into Seraphs—their angel-like state that allowed them to fight demons in a stronger-than-human body. Cameron's white wings exploded out from her back, as did Paden's.

"What is that?" Valynda gasped.

Nibo used his staff to pin them to the deck. "You don't want to know, *chère*. Suffice it to say, it's not something you want to make angry. Rather, it'll come for us and make us a little nubby treat, eh?"

"Not amused."

He grinned, and charmed her in spite of her protestations. Damn, why did he have to be so alluring?

Black clouds rolled in overhead like billowing smoke from a massive fire. Screams rang out from Barnet's ship. As a human crew, they had no idea what was happening. Indeed, Barnet was pale and shaken by the sight of the changes in the men and women around him.

"What are you people?"

Bane didn't answer as he raised his flintlock and took aim for a demon rising up and over Barnet. Barnet barely ducked out of the way before Bane shot it in the head and caused it to explode all over the deck in a grisly, besmirched stain that befouled the air she attempted to breathe. More came up from the sea, flying in wave after angry wave to attack with claws and fangs.

Nibo shielded her, batting them away with his crook. "Get below!"

Valynda hesitated.

The demons grabbed on to the sides of the ship in an attempt to pry off boards. Something that made it hard to blast them, since any blow could go through the demons and damage the hull that was part of Mara's body.

This was terrible. They were about to go down and there was nothing she could do to stop it.

"If we sink, it's a bad idea to be below."

"You're not going down."

She started to ask him what he meant, but before she could, lightning flashed, dividing the dark clouds. The sky turned a sickly green. Around them, the sea began to churn. Kalder was thrown from the waves up to the deck, where he landed near Cameron. Disoriented and obviously confused, he glanced about at them.

Valynda was as confounded as he was while the ship continued to pitch and roll. The wood shrieked in protest as it seemed determined to splinter and leave them to drown.

At least until a tidal wave rose straight up before them.

Nibo raised his crook. The moment he did, the wave exploded into a thousand skeletons and bodies that rained down upon the demons.

The human crew screamed out as the Deadmen scrambled to get out of the way.

Nibo's eyes turned bright orange. He used his crook to control the souls of those he'd just summoned from the bowels of the sea to go after the demons and protect her and her friends. With stunned expressions, Thorn and Bane turned to gape at him.

Nibo ignored them while his army of the dead engaged the demons and fought them down. Valynda scurried to stand beside him as one of the demons came toward her, intent on biting her.

She'd fight them, but she'd learned the hard way that these were coated with a thick, tar-like membrane that would infect any who touched them. Even her.

And it burned like the dickens.

More than that, it bonded to the skin and caused it to rot and smell for eternity. Even straw bodies. So rather than fight, the best course of action was to flee and let someone else risk that kind of infection.

Nibo caught the demon and kicked it back into the arms of a partially decomposed corpse that wrapped itself around the demon, then carried the screaming ugly thing overboard and plunged them both into the turgid sea.

Within a few minutes, the demons were gone and the sea calmed down. The clouds above rolled away and parted to reveal a perfect blue sky.

Barnet opened and closed his mouth like a carp that had been hauled to land. He was even bug-eyed. After a few seconds, he shook his head. "You are a crew of the damned, aren't you?"

Will Death gave him a bedeviled grin. "More like the un-damned, if you will."

"Pardon?"

"Long story, mate," Bane said, coming between them. "You should probably return to your ship and calm them. As for Santiago, count us in." The captain rushed Barnet over to swing to his boat, then turned to Bart.

"I know, Captain. One spell of forgetfulness for the humans on its way. No need in letting them have a single memory of that nonsense." Bart passed an aggravated grimace toward Nibo.

"The correct phrase is, 'Thank you, Nibo, for saving me sorry arse.' And you're not welcome."

Bane ignored that as he approached Nibo. "How did you do that?"

He shrugged. "How does one breathe? Same principle. It's an automatic thing that's such a part of me I don't even have to think about it."

"Well, thank you."

Nibo inclined his head.

Valynda narrowed her gaze on his crook as she finally understood why the Malachai wanted it and what he intended to do with it once he had it under his control. That was a new power that she hadn't known about before, but given that Nibo had dominion over those who'd been lost at sea, it made sense. In the hands of the Malachai, that crook would be dangerous indeed.

She waited until the others had drifted off to leave them alone before she spoke to Nibo.

Amazed by him and his trinket, she reached out to touch his staff. He had the same feathers attached to the loop at the end that were braided into his hair. Strange how she'd never really noticed that before. "Where did you get this from?"

Nibo watched as she ran her fingers over the pale, hand-carved wood that was older than time.

He knew she'd asked him something, probably important, but honestly, he couldn't remember it. Not while she stood this close to him and all he could think about was the endless nights when she'd stroked him with the same tenderness that she was using on his staff. Damn, it'd been so long since he last really held her in his arms.

Had felt her soft hands caressing his body as he lost himself inside her.

How he missed that. Missed the scent of lavender and roses in her hair, mixed with sea and sand. The salty taste of her skin on his lips. No woman had ever held his heart the way his Vala did.

After Aclima's death and until the night he'd met Valynda, he'd always been afraid of any woman laying claim to him. He'd run from them as if they were lepers.

But something about her had lured him in even against his will. Now . . .

"Xuri?"

"Hmmm?"

She shook her head. "Your staff. Where did you get it?"

"I carved it, long ago."

"Really? That's all there is to it? You made it?"

He nodded. Of course, the wood he'd used for the crook had come from the Tree of Life that his father had salvaged from the time before Xuri had been born, something he hadn't known until the first time he'd lost one of his lambs to a ravenous wolf. Heartbroken, he'd used his staff to help gather part of the remains from where they'd been dragged out of his reach.

On his hands and knees, he'd been covered in sweat and thorns as he struggled to do right by the poor lost creature. Then, the moment his staff had touched his lamb's leg, a strange glow had emanated over it.

An instant later, the tiny lamb had bleated and sprang back to life before rushing into his arms.

Nibo had been so stunned that for several minutes he'd been unable to move or even breathe.

When he'd rushed to tell Qeenan what magic had happened, his brother had laughed in his face. "You're such a liar!"

"Nay, 'tis truth!"

Qeenan had slaughtered another lamb to make him prove it. That had been the first time that Nibo had realized something wasn't quite right with his brother. That he enjoyed the killing aspect a little too much and was a little too quick to resort to violence as an answer for any of his volatile mood swings.

More to the point, that Qeenan didn't care who or what he hurt to illustrate an issue or to get what he wanted.

That had made Nibo more determined than ever to cut his brother a wide berth, as such people were seldom reasonable. God knew that he'd never understand the cruelty of the man he'd been born with. Such things were forever beyond his comprehension. Why hurt someone when you didn't have to? Why break their heart when it was so much easier to make them smile?

All he'd ever wanted was peace and a small corner of the earth to call his own.

Live and let live.

'Twas his nature to create and his brother's to destroy.

"I've lost you, haven't I?"

He smiled at Vala's question. "Nay, my love. You're the one who found me." Kissing her scratchy straw cheek, he shrank his staff and tucked it away. "Why are you so curious?"

"Didn't know you could do such a thing. It was quite impressive."

He shrugged. "Necromancy isn't as impressive as it is scary. Best to leave such things alone." As her current plight showed.

Damn them all for what they'd done to her. Had they left her body intact, he could have saved her.

But nay, they'd burned her flesh and left him nothing to work with. No way to save her, which was why they'd done what they had. They'd been that determined to keep them apart and make sure that he couldn't have what he wanted most.

If only he knew the correct god or creature to save her. Why was there no one who could make this right? It was so unfair.

Out of all the magic in the universe, there should have been something.

But that was the thing about injustice and cruelty. They respected no one and left no one out. Sooner or later, those bitches shit on everyone, with equal disdain.

And some days they seemed to go out of their way to cross the street, hunt him down, and take special care to make sure that they shoved a double dose of their venom down his throat.

"Nibo?"

He paused at the sound of Sancha's voice. The tall Spanish lady was always grace and elegance, wrapped in a blanket of ever-present sorrow. Since the day he'd first met her, he'd recognized her as a kindred spirit on this earth.

"Aye, my lady?"

She glanced to Valynda and swallowed. Her eyes turned bright and glassy before she spoke in the lowest of tones. "Might I ask a bit of something?"

In his mind, he already knew her query. He saw it in the back of her eyes like a mirror playing out the horror of her past. The night the lady had come home to find her world ripped apart by its own cruelty.

Her pain reached out to him and tore a jagged hole straight through him. It was the one thing he hated most about his powers—that he could feel someone else's anguish as much as he felt his own. That no matter how much he tried not to care, he did. He couldn't stop it.

With a deep breath, he placed a kind hand on her shoulder. "She didn't suffer, Sancha. Malene knows how much you loved her. She plays in a beautiful garden where she waits for the day where she may see you again so that the two of you can laugh and dance as you did when she used to cry until you picked flowers to make her a crown for her hair."

She choked on a sob before she drew him into a tight hug. *"Muchas gracias!"*

Nibo rubbed her back before he nudged her toward Jake Devereaux, where her future waited, yet she had no idea just how important he would be to her, nor what their future generations would mean to the world. "Think nothing of it."

He bit back a smile as Jake bashfully approached her to check and make sure the lady was fine.

"What are you up to?"

He caught the suspicion in Vala's tone as she eyed him warily. "Why must I be up to anything?"

"Because you have that look about you that makes me nervous."

"I'd rather have that look about you where you stared at me as if I were your favorite dinner."

"Nibo . . ."

Before he could answer her chiding tone, Thorn joined them.

Nibo growled deep in his throat at the creature's annoying timing. "Is there no privacy on this damn boat?"

"Not really." Thorn slapped him on the shoulder. "One of the reasons I'm not fond of traveling by sea."

He growled out loud. "What do *you* want?"

"The Malachai in chains. My father's head on a platter and a willing woman in my bed. But at the moment, I'd settle for something as easy as you telling me what the hell are those?"

Nibo didn't understand at first what he meant. Or that unwarranted hostile tone.

Until he looked up to see what had caused the stress in Thorn's voice.

"Oh my God," Valynda breathed.

"Not exactly." Nibo cursed the sight of a million seagulls headed for them.

Granted, that was a bit of an exaggeration, but from his vantage point . . .

It looked like a million.

Maybe more.

As in a million had a million babies and brought their cousins, along with a few dozen friends.

"Thorn!" Bane called.

"Yeah," he said in a dry, cold tone. "I got nothing for this, old man."

Nibo was feeling that emotion. Especially as he saw their condition and realized that those birds weren't alive or "normal." These were Carrion Gulls let loose from Agiwe's personal closet. More than that, they were soldiers in the petro army and used to frighten their enemies and those they wanted to drive toward madness.

Or those they wanted to destroy utterly.

Inside and out.

"Strixa!" Nibo summoned the water witch as a thought came to him. "Simon!" The Exú priest would be every bit as helpful as Nibo moved forward.

He turned to the water witch first. "Can you summon your Strykyn?" Black war owls, they were her children who served the god Apollo in his army. "Keep them distracted."

"To what purpose?"

"Long enough for me and Simon to summon Exú and get a strong enough wind to drive them back and us forward."

While they made ready for his spell, the rest of the crew threw what they had at the birds . . . fireballs, spears, even shoes.

Nothing daunted the skeletal gulls. Not until Simon and Nibo were able to get their chanting fired into high gear. The Strykyn appeared as bursts of lightning, out of the blue, to attack each of the gulls. They would swoop in and grab one, but for every one they took, it seemed as if there were at least four more.

Valynda watched in horror as there was nothing to be done for the mounting terror that was quickly descending on them.

Nibo's and Simon's deep voices circled around and around, lifting up toward the birds that shrieked as if they were in agony.

Thorn breathed in relief, as it looked like between the Strykyn owls and chanting they might be safe.

Until the chanting opened a glowing portal over the ship's mainmast.

Nibo glanced up and winced. "Shit," he breathed.

Valynda's stomach churned at the sound of that single syllable.

"Shit?" Thorn repeated. "Oh hell no, Nibo, there better be no shit in this!"

"Aye," Bane agreed. "Not unless you want to be seeking the ground for your teeth."

He cast them both a dry, annoyed look. "Brace yourselves. There's a lot of shit coming."

He wasn't exaggerating for dramatic effect, or wrong. Nibo cringed as he saw the next wave of fun that was gearing up to descend upon them. Lowering his arms, he stepped away and shook his head. "Well, that finishes me. Anyone else with any ideas? I'm quitting while I'm behind."

Marcelina and Belle gaped at the large shadow he'd accidentally freed that moved toward them at an unholy speed. "What is *that*?"

Sick to his stomach, Nibo wished he didn't know what it was he knew. More than that, he wanted to put this particular genie back in its bottle and send it home on a tidal wave. Or put them in another dimension far from it. "The *Flying Dutchman*."

"The ghost ship?" Their voices assaulted him as a single unit.

"Sort of." Nibo turned even greener around his gills as he watched it closing in on them with a speed he knew he couldn't outrun.

"What does he mean, *sort of*?" Simon asked Thorn.

Kalder, still wet from his dousing and covered in his strange Myrcian markings, stepped forward to answer. "That it's not crewed by men who were damned for their deeds. That would be us." He jerked his chin toward the ship making fast for them. "That be crewed by the women who've died on the open seas who are hell-bent to make pirates pay for what was done to them. It's why you can hear them screaming out so in the night. For they come for flesh and blood and will be satisfied with nothing less."

He was right about that. Unholy tribute was what they were after. And not just any kind . . . "They feed the goddess Tiamat, who survives on violence and blood." Nibo sighed. "She's unleashed them on us because I opened the gate."

Thorn applauded sarcastically. "Good job, man. Want to disembowel us while you're at it?"

Nibo smirked at the bastard. "Well, I didn't see you helping! And I don't have to, since they're here to do it for me."

Bane whistled loudly to get their attention. "Enough! Beat each other's arses later. Right now, we have a much more harrowing problem to solve, and I'm open to solutions."

Bart gestured to Kalder. "Feed them a mermaid and hope that satisfies their bloodlust."

Cameron gaped before she shielded her husband with her wings. "I think not!"

Nibo smirked. "Wouldn't work anyway. He's not large enough to satisfy them. He'd only whet their appetites."

Valynda went still as she heard the voices of the crew calling out to her.

"Sister, sister, is it true?

"Tell us the name of he who betrayed you."

Those words enchanted her like a siren's lure. They were warm and sweet, and wrapped around her. Over and over they were repeated until they lulled her into a peculiar fog. Her entire body was numb and needing.

Valynda wanted to join them where they were. It was as if someone or something pulled her toward the sea, physically. The urge to jump in was so compelling that it was almost impossible to resist.

"Watch the women!"

Nibo looked up as he saw that Valynda wasn't the only one being lured. Sancha, Belle, and Elyzabel, Bane's sister, all were suddenly glassy-eyed. None seemed to have control of themselves as the *Flying Dutchman*'s crew sang to them, wanting them to join them for their unholy quest.

Worse? The Dark-Huntress tried to come up from belowdecks. Thankfully, Thorn saw her and rushed forward just as Janice would have stepped onto the deck and burst into flames.

Screaming, Janice fought against Thorn's hold as she tried to get to the others. Bart captured Belle while the captain grabbed his sister. Jake picked up Sancha and Will also helped with Belle, but it was no easy feat to keep them from jumping overboard.

As was evidenced when Valynda sank her straw teeth into Nibo's arm and drew blood. Pain exploded through his body. Damn it all!

Nothing had hurt so much since the day his brother had blindsided him with a club. Who would have thought straw teeth could be so miserable?

Yet there was no denying this!

All of a sudden, Strixa began to whine. An instant later, her Strykyn began to fall from the sky. As the war owls landed on board the ship, they turned into men.

"What the hell?"

Nibo didn't get a chance to respond. One of the "birds" fell on top of him, knocking him away from Valynda. The moment it did, Valynda dodged to the railing and jumped overboard before anyone could stop her.

"Vala! No!"

Nibo scrambled after her, but it was too late.

She was already being picked up by the ghostly crew and added to their murderous number.

9

Valynda floated above the planks as if she were in a dream. She hadn't felt so disconnected from her body since the night she'd been murdered.

Bitter memories burned as she recalled that day so vividly. When she'd felt her will bend not to her own desires, but to those of another. One who'd held no love or care for her whatsoever. No regard. He'd only cared about himself and his selfish wants. It'd been the sickest kind of cruelty. To have another person seek to take away her free will and to force his desires on her. He'd been determined to make her his poppet.

Fury rose up inside her as she remembered trying to fight against it but having no ability to do so. No words could describe the helpless, hapless feeling of it. To know something was wrong and to have no one believe her, not even her own parents. No way to let others know what was going on.

She'd felt voiceless. Powerless.

Dehumanized. Even more so then than she did now as a straw doll. No one had seen her, even though she'd been right in front of them. Her soul had screamed out into the abyss and no one had heard or bothered to listen. To this day, she still didn't know how it was that no one had noticed. How such pain could go unobserved by everyone around her when it was so blatantly obvious.

Yet it did.

Was the world really that self-absorbed?

That uncaring?

The truth was as scary as it was scarring.

And she wished to God she was as ignorant to the answer now as she'd been as an innocent, oblivious child, because the truth was that it was so much easier to pretend that the world and that people were what they should be. Fair, kind, and decent. That evil was always punished for the wrongs it did, and that good would win. She liked to pretend that that was how the universe worked. That the light would always prevail over the dark. Order would forever be restored.

Perhaps that more than anything was what marked the end of

everyone's childhood. The day when you realized that might was what made right.

That evil more often than not triumphed over good and that it never got what it should, and that karma didn't go after the people it was supposed to. More often than not, life chose its personal whipping boys and girls for no reason and they were beat down at random, over and over again, without any justification whatsoever.

There really was no sense in the world. It was all chaos.

Because God knew that she'd done nothing to deserve her fate. Nothing more than fall in love with a man she shouldn't have and believed in him, even while he lied to her. That she'd been a good friend to women who'd been bad ones to her.

Now . . .

She found herself standing on board this enchanted ship full of forsaken and damned women like her. Dressed in everything from gowns to breeches, they came from all walks of life and from every culture, it seemed. The only thing they had in common was their gender.

And the mutual mistrust and pain that glowed deep in their eyes that said each of them had been hurt one time too many. Just like the crew of the *Sea Witch II* who had also been wronged by those they trusted. Abandoned by fate and kicked in their teeth by life. It was a chilling sight that was probably the nightmare of many a man, as well it should be, as hell hath no fury as a woman wronged. They were even more frightening than a woman scorned.

After all, there was a reason why wrathful vengeance and the Furies were all women.

"Welcome, sister," a tall, shapely blonde said as she neared Valynda. Dressed in breeches and an ornate brocade coat, she stepped down from the upper deck and moved across the rough planks to meet her near the mainmast.

Other crewmembers encircled Valynda like she was some kind of prized trophy. Their piercing gazes left her feeling uncertain, and it gave her a prickling sensation that crawled over her body like vermin.

Still, there was something eerily familiar about their captain. Valynda felt as if she should know her. "Who are you?"

"Circe."

She sucked her breath in sharply at the name of the Greek goddess who'd saved Odysseus on his way home from the Trojan war during his ill-fated voyage after he'd upset the god Poseidon. The goddess had borne him three children, and after caring for the man, how had he repaid her? He'd turned the gods against her for her kindness and set them upon her and their children with no regard for what it would do to them. Or what their futures would hold. He'd cheated on his wife, Penelope, who had stayed true to him at home in Ithaca for the entire twenty years he'd been gone, even though her fealty had cost her much as she stuggled to keep his kingdom intact and prosperous during his absence. And he'd broken the heart of the goddess now standing before her.

Faithless Odysseus, so lauded as a hero by the world and praised for his cunning, had stolen all Circe had lavished on him, and forgetting that he'd fathered three sons with her, left like a thief in the night, stealing treasure on his way out the door, without so much as a thank-you for all she'd done to save his life. Just as he'd conveniently forgotten his wife and son who had pined for him in Ithaca while he dallied with Circe and Io during his twenty-year hiatus from his responsibilities as king, husband, and father, leaving it all for brave Penelope to contend with on her own.

Of course, that hadn't been his lies, or his story when he'd told it, but it'd been the truth, nonetheless.

No wonder Circe had been chosen to captain this beleaguered crew. "I see."

Dressed as a buccaneer, Circe had eyes as dark as coal, yet there was an innate kindness to them. One that made Valynda want to trust her.

"Tell me, little sister, do you want to join my crew?"

It might be tempting, as they had much in common, however she was already part of a family. "I just want my body back." Those anguished words were out before she could stop them.

After all, it was her ever quest.

Circe arched her brow at words that had become rote, but even so were still emotionally charged. "And what would you give me for such a thing?"

The truth scared her. For there was nothing she wouldn't do. "What do *you* want?"

Circe smiled, as she no doubt could smell the desperation. "Rather bold for you to ask, given that you've already sold your soul."

"If you know that, then why am I here?"

"That is always the question, isn't it?"

A chill went down Valynda's spine as she realized the truth of that simple, yet extremely complex question. No one ever knew their real purpose. Just when they thought they might have an inkling, life had a way of yanking the ground out from beneath their feet and leaving them with nothing on which to stand.

That was why she hated Nibo so much right now. She'd believed in him. Had thought that she could depend on him, and rather than stand fast and remain at her side, he'd allowed her to be cast out on her own and left adrift with no moorings.

One moment they'd been happy. The next . . .

Her throat was still raw from her screams as she'd begged him for help, and he'd turned a deaf ear. Had ignored her. How could anyone claim to love someone and ignore their pain?

Watch them die, and say nothing?

Do nothing?

It burned so raw inside her that some days she was convinced she was no longer sane from it. "What do you want from me?"

"You don't belong with Thorn's Deadmen and you know it. You should be here, among my crew. This should be your home . . . with kindred spirits who understand your pain, Valynda. Join us."

How simple she made that sound.

Just pick up everything, wave good-bye, and go. But . . .

Valynda glanced down at the Deadman's mark burned into her straw wrist. It was the same one that all members of Captain Bane's crew bore. The moment they'd agreed to hunt demons for Thorn for a chance to earn their way out of their damnation, the mark had appeared, and as each one was closer to freedom, the mark became fainter. Once they'd redeemed their souls and were free and clear, the mark vanished.

So far, Captain Bane, Kalder, and a handful of others had already erased the slate and earned back their souls. Belle, Will, Bart, and Sancha were close.

Hers hadn't lightened at all.

Not even a bit.

Because you haven't killed many demons.

Not that she hadn't tried, it was just more difficult for her. Unlike the others, she wasn't trained at fighting. She'd been thrown into a life she barely understood.

Which caused her even more despair, as she feared that she'd never go free.

"Poor Valynda. You don't know whom to trust, do you?"

She stiffened at Circe's astute question. "Pardon?"

"So many offers. So many promises. But none are a guarantee."

And all could be lying.

How could she trust anyone? Especially given the fact that her own parents had betrayed her. The very people who were supposed to love and keep her safe above all others. They had been the first to sell her out. And for what?

Her father's vanity? The man who'd spent his whole life professing to have no vanity whatsoever had possessed more than any man she knew. He'd given up his noble-class ranking and lifestyle in order to appear meek and humble when he was the furthest thing from it. Had chosen to live in miserable penury and condemned his entire family to a bitter, horrid life that had sent her sister to an early grave from illness and exposure because he didn't want to be mocked or called out for being a snob or rich man's son, only to find that he was the worst sort of hypocrite. To spare himself a bit of mockery, he'd dumped twice as much on her and her sister and had killed Rachel in the process.

Because in the end, everything had been about him and how he wanted others to see him. Not reality, but how he'd wanted to appear to the community. A sick form of anti-vanity vanity. Her father wanted to appear a victim to garner sympathy from others and had used them as his tools.

That need to maintain his "standing" and sympathy in the eyes of others was what had led him to destroy his two daughters. Rather than do the right and decent thing for his family that he'd always preached to her and her mother, he'd betrayed them. When she'd needed her father most, he'd turned his back on her and sold her out for his own reputation and sick form of respectability.

"You will marry, or I will see you dead!"

And so he had.

He hadn't even bothered to attend her funeral. So much for his lies about how concerned he was over what others thought of him, and public expectation. In that moment, she'd learned exactly how much her mother loved her. For the first time in her life, Lizzie O'Dell Moore had defied him and gone against his orders to be the sole attendee at Valynda's burial, even though nothing save ashes had remained of her.

If only her mother had defied him sooner, when it'd mattered, and she could have helped her daughter. Then Valynda might not have died and might have survived her father's stupidity. And Rachel might have grown up, too.

Now . . .

Her mother had killed herself two weeks later out of grief over what she let happen to both her girls. The guilt of what she'd done to them and had allowed her husband to do had been more than she could live with.

After that, her father had been shunned by the islanders and forced to endure the mockery of everyone knowing he'd ruined his entire family with his selfish cruelty. So maybe in the end, there had been some form of karma after all. By trying to avoid everyone's mockery by denying his family's money, her father had brought on his worst fears by his own actions.

Too bad he'd destroyed three innocent lives in the process.

Nibo was right. Never run from a fight or from your problems. You'd only die tired if you tried. Better to turn and face them while you had your full strength than to tuck in your tail and try to avoid the inevitable.

Lightning flickered in Circe's eyes. "So tell me, Miss Moore . . . do you continue with Thorn, trusting him to keep his word and find a way to restore your body? Or betray your precious, betraying Nibo and help the Malachai so that he can destroy this world that's never done you any favors? Or join us for our crew where we all understand you and why you don't care about the others? Not really, and who can blame you? Hmm? It's a hard decision, my lady. And I need an answer. What will you do?"

Wyñeria

10

Valynda had no answer for Circe's question. Her life was ever a perplexing mess, out of her control, and had been for a long, long time. Every time she tried to fix it, it seemed to only worsen.

Then worsen more.

Circe leaned forward and blew a fine golden powder over her. It literally spun and danced about in the air like a group of tiny fairies. Enchanting and beguiling, it made her head spin. Faster and faster it turned. She swore she could even hear it laughing. With a faint apple scent, it warmed her.

A sudden gasp went through Circe's crew. They clambered forward as if they were staring at some freakish thing.

Tears blurred her gaze as the memory of insults and the screams of horror rang in her ears. It was just like that first day when Thorn had brought her back before he'd perfected his shield around her straw body and everyone who'd encountered her had seen her freakish poppet form. People were so unkind. So cruel.

And that cruelty resonated inside her now and made it almost impossible to see humanity in any other light. For, once having tasted the bitterest part of it, it was hard to ever remember the sweet. Something not helped by the fact that, rather than do the right thing, so many chose to do the wrong.

Instead of helping her get past what had been done to her by others, they seemed to rush to reinforce in her mind why the Malachai was right and the world needed to end.

It was indeed a struggle to hold on to a belief that there was good in anyone these days. That people could be helpful and kind. Adarian was right. There were far more reasons to end the world than save it.

Circe held up a hand mirror to Valynda's face. Like the others, she gasped at what she saw.

Nay . . .

She must be dreaming. Or else this was another cruel joke being played on her. Aye, that was it. They were beginning to take pleasure in doing this to her.

Damn them for their futtocking cruelty.

Angry tears filled her eyes that had tearducts again as she reached to gently finger her now supple cheek.

"You're human!" Circe was proud of herself for her work.

But Valynda wasn't a fool. She knew well the story of how this witch had transformed men into pigs. Why not turn a pig into a woman? No one did kindness for free. So, it begged the question as to what would the witch want for this? Since she couldn't have her soul, there must be a steeper price to be paid. "Indeed."

Even so, she cupped her cheeks with her hands so that she could savor the sensation of feeling her own flesh. Unlike what Thorn had promised her, this wasn't just any body, it was hers. A body she'd never thought to have or see again. "How did you do this?"

Circe shrugged nonchalantly. "I'm a sorceress, milady. Transmutation is one of my many gifts . . . like the Malachai. But as with him, there are rules to what I do, and there is a price."

As she'd feared. Raw dread made her stomach shrink over what fee she'd exact for it. Would it be even worse than what the Malachai had asked? "And that is?"

"I want my son back. You make Thorn release Agrios, and I'll make sure that you stay as you are."

Stunned, she scowled at her. That seemed eerily easy compared to the fee the others demanded. "And if he refuses?"

Circe sighed. "Then you'll revert back to straw."

Valynda rubbed her hands down her arms that once again tingled with goose bumps. God, how she'd missed that sensation! It was so surreal to have true feeling again, on flesh that could sense something as light as the breeze touching it. "I will make sure he agrees!"

"Good."

Valynda glanced over to the *Sea Witch*. It seemed strangely tranquil . . . almost deserted.

"There's one more thing."

Of course there was. Her stomach shrinking, Valynda hesitated at the odd note in her voice. Wasn't there always one more dreaded thing? "That is?"

Circe handed her a small round bottle of something that looked like blood and herbs mixed together. It strangely reminded her of a darker version of the rum Xuri carried with him. The top was sealed tight with black wax and covered by a hexagram. A piece of twine was wound around it, with a small hagstone and bone charm tied to it. "This is the spell that binds your flesh and maintains you as you are. Keep this bottle safe and undamaged. Should anything ever happen to it, you will again be as you were and become separated from your flesh."

Well, that wasn't creepy at all. What was it with witches and their bottles? Sallie had his, where one had placed his soul as punishment, and now she had hers.

Still, Valynda was grateful enough not to complain. Anything to be human again.

Inclining her head, she clutched the bottle in her palm. "Thank you!"

Circe bowed her head respectfully. "You have until the next full moon to complete your task. If my son returns to me, the spell will hold. If he doesn't, you'll turn back to what you were."

"Thank you, Lady Circe."

"Don't thank me yet. If you fail, this will be a far worse curse, for there is nothing crueler in life than having a glimpse of what you want most and then having it ripped from your hands when there's nothing you can do to stop it."

She was right about that. Valynda had never been one to believe in the old adage that it was far better to have known love and to have lost it than to have not known it at all. Because the truth was, you couldn't miss what you didn't know. And having had her life ripped apart so very viciously for no reason whatsoever, she was here to say that it was much, much better to not know than to watch as those animals who had nothing better to do than play with someone's life tore it apart for their own selfish reasons.

"If I can't have you, no one will. . . ."

Benjamin's psychotic words still chilled her. That was what her father had consigned her to. Two men caught up in their own greed and pride, playing with her life.

And now you're playing with the fate of the world.

That thought sobered her as she realized that she hadn't thought of that before. Maybe that made her even worse than those men.

Terrified, she met Circe's gaze. "You're sure this will hold?"

"Positive. But if you cross the Malachai, he will be after you, and he makes a potent enemy."

Life was a risk and it was one she was willing to take. Besides, this way she already had her body. Everyone else was making promises she wasn't sure they could keep. The Malachai wasn't known for playing well with others. He was a liar and a thief. The worst sort of scoundrel. How could she ever trust someone like him?

Not to mention, she wasn't sure she could separate Nibo from his crook.

A bird in the hand is worth two in the tree. . . .

All the others had done was make unfulfilled promises to her. Circe was the first to actually give Valynda her body and show her that it was possible. Give her a feasible outcome.

This was doable!

"Very well. I will do what I must."

Circe clapped her hands.

In that instant, a huge windstorm began. It blew in from the water to arc up and over onto the deck. There the water formed hands that lifted her and carried her from Circe's ship back to the deck of the *Sea Witch II*, where it set her down gently in front of the captain.

The reaction there was much more animated.

First, they rushed to attack her, as they assumed she was an enemy in their midst.

Valynda ran toward the aft to escape their frenzied madness. Nibo manifested between her and the others and brought up a wall of magenta smoke. He lifted his staff to hold them back. "Stop!"

They drew up short.

Only then did Nibo turn around to stare at her in awe. "Vala?"

She nodded.

Nibo couldn't believe what he was seeing. It *was* Valynda. Whole and restored. Not the poppet monstrosity they'd made, but the beauty he'd fallen in love with. He felt tears stinging his eyes as so many emotions flooded him at once that he couldn't even begin to sort through them. Before he could even think better of it, he pulled her into his arms and kissed her.

When he lifted his head, he saw that familiar blush on her pale cheeks that he'd missed so much. The one that had always made her eyes sparkle and glow. Dear heavens, how he'd missed it.

"How?"

"Circe."

"Her ship's gone."

They looked over to Bart, who had his spyglass trained on where the ship had been.

"What do you mean, her ship's gone?" Captain Bane asked.

Bart handed his spyglass over. "See for yourself, Captain. They vanished as eerily as they'd appeared."

The captain scowled at Valynda. "Did she say anything to you?"

"Not to trust the Malachai."

"You think? Because that's always such a great idea, yeah?"

She glared at William for his unwarranted sarcasm, then returned her attention to the captain. "And she wants her son back if I'm to remain human."

Thorn's eyes widened at those words.

Then he burst out laughing. At least until he realized she wasn't joking. "Question, my little lamb. Did she happen perchance to tell you anything about him?"

Valynda shook her head.

Thorn let out a disgusted sigh. "Well, that's something, I guess."

"How so?" Nibo mirrored her curiosity, especially given the odd note in Thorn's voice.

When Thorn finally spoke, he understood. "Oh, 'twas nothing too serious, mind you. Just that he happened to lead his army against the gods. As you can imagine, they were a little miffed, shall we say, about the whole affair, and being that they're what we call *gods*"—he overemphasized the word—"he's being punished eternally for his blatant and rampant stupidity. Because when in the whole history of the universe has that ever worked out well for anyone, I ask you? So, I'm going to postulate a theory here, children, that getting someone from them after they've been so crossed isn't exactly the easiest thing to do." He blinked and smiled. "What do you think? Huh?"

Ignoring his sarcasm, Nibo gave him a pointed stare. "But you're going to try and get her son back for us, aren't you, Thorn?"

"Ah hell n . . ." His voice trailed off as he looked past Nibo to Valynda. Then back again. "Now here's a thought, what with sonny-boy being dead and all, and you being a psychopomp and all, why don't *you* take a trip down there for once, and do the heavy lifting? How about those pineapples? Huh?"

He gave Thorn a peeved glare. "I would do it in a heartbeat were I able. Sadly, this one's on you as it's someplace I can't venture."

"'Course it is. It always is." Grinding his teeth, he curled his lip and glared down at the sea. "Hate you, Father. Would say I was hoping you were roasting your nuts over an open flame, but I know you're not, you worthless piece of shit." Growling in the back of his throat, he finally stopped, then sighed. "Fine. I'll go, but you know you owe me."

Nibo took her hand. "Knew you were a good demon cackle-berry."

Thorn rolled his eyes. "I hate you so much, Nibo."

"Hate you more."

"Really, not possible."

"And on that note, we needs be underway." Captain Bane stepped back to issue orders. "Stay on the tail of Barnet, Lady Dolorosa. Make sure we watch for any others to attack."

Sancha took up the wheel. "Aye, aye, Captain."

While they began to return to their duties, Nibo pulled Valynda toward the ladder that led belowdecks. His heart pounded as her scent infiltrated every part of his being. Worse, her presence made him harder than he'd ever been. He couldn't remember the last time he'd wanted any woman this badly. But then she'd always had that effect on him. No one had ever commanded him the way his Vala did.

That was what made her dangerous.

Which was why it was a good thing that she had no idea just how much power she wielded over him.

Valynda pulled Nibo to a stop. "What are you doing?"

"I just want to be alone with you."

"Why?"

The heated look in his amber eyes told her exactly what he had on his mind, and while she wasn't opposed to the thought, there was more to it than just that. "Xuri . . . is that all I am to you?"

He looked as if she'd struck him. "You have to know better than that by now."

Did she?

"Then why did you walk away from me when you had a chance to keep me?"

He gaped at her accusation. "Pardon?"

"What is it you said? We have a spiritual marriage? That means you need nothing more from me than that. I'm just a plaything to you when you want release. Something to be used and then cast aside and forgotten as soon as you're done. You told me that I was a fool for ever thinking we could have anything more."

For once, he appeared ashamed and wounded. "Vala, I was trying to protect you."

"From what?"

Nibo fisted his hand in her silken hair as he tried to explain to her that words said to others weren't always what was meant. They damn sure weren't what was felt. Had his nanchon known what she was to him, they would have attacked her and killed her where she stood. As a human, she had no protection, and he had no way to protect her because he couldn't get to her without them releasing him from his dimension.

As they'd proven in the most brutal way.

They'd mocked his best intentions. Just as he'd feared. But he'd done his best to keep her safe. Because she was so important to him.

"From what happened to you. Didn't it ever occur to you that your fate had nothing to do with you, and everything to do with punishing me?"

"I don't understand."

Nibo cupped her cheek in his palm. "I love you, Vala. You have to know that by now." He placed his cheek to hers, and the moment their skin touched, it took her back to the first time they'd been together as lovers.

It'd been a cool night on the beach not very long after they'd met. Valynda had thought of them really as friends, and while she'd been growing fonder of him night by night, she'd done her best to keep her distance.

But Nibo had made it so difficult. He was unlike anyone she'd ever met. There was such a carefree air about him as he frolicked in the moonlight, showing her the wonders of her island caverns. Showing her how brilliant the stars looked while he played his guitarra and made her laugh at silly jokes and puns.

Especially that night on the beach when he'd handed her a small pouch to open while they sat before a small fire he'd made for them. "What is it?"

He'd set aside his guitarra. "Open it," he urged.

With a frown, she'd loosened the strings of the bag until she dug out a gold ring encrusted with tiny, sparkling emeralds. Tears had filled her eyes as she looked from her small treasure to her much larger one. "A ring?" Her voice had been tight and hoarse.

His gaze had warmed her even more than the fire as he nodded. "I consider you mine, Vala. That is my pledge to you."

There, for a moment, she'd felt so incredibly special. For the first time in her whole life, she hadn't felt alone in the world. She'd been a part of someone else. Her heart pounding, she'd pressed her trembling lips together as she rolled the ring around and around in her palm to look it over and appreciate just how exquisite a gift it was. No one had ever given her anything like it. The emeralds had winked at her in the firelight as if they knew some jest that had escaped her notice. As if they were possessed of some ancient spirit themselves.

Never had she expected such a gift from anyone, especially not her loa, who didn't appear to value anything so extravagant or expensive. Rather, he was more akin to her father, even to the point that Nibo usually walked about barefoot.

Though it seemed foolish, his gift made her wonder if it were possible that they might have a life together after all. Dare she even hope for it? Yet why else would he have given her such a costly present, especially when such things didn't seem to be part of his world?

With a devilish glint in his eyes, Nibo took the ring from her shaking fingers, kissed it, then placed it on her hand. He looked up at her, a small, timid smile on his lips. "Like your presence in my life, *ma petite,* it fits."

She closed her eyes, savoring his words that brought so much joy to her heart because no one had ever valued her before. She was nothing, and she knew that. God knew that others were so quick to remind her of that, in so many ways. Indeed, they took pleasure in telling her how unimportant she was. For a minute, she thought that maybe, just maybe, if he saw her as something more, perhaps she wasn't as worthless as they all made her feel. She wanted to be the lady of beauty that he seemed to see whenever he looked at her with those sparkling amber eyes. Not the ugly thing that made the others curl their lips when they looked at her in daylight. The girl who made them jeer and make snide comments about her lowly birth or pity her because of her parentage or penury.

This night, she felt beautiful and special. Not pathetic.

Yet even so, she knew that Nibo was a loa not known for being faithful, and that she was a mere human.

How could they have any kind of future together?

Valynda wanted desperately to ask him what he meant by giving her such a present, but no matter how hard she tried to bring that question to her lips, she couldn't. It was as if she knew better.

As if her heart feared the real truth and so it forced her to remain silent as he claimed her lips for a scorching kiss under the bright moonlight.

Valynda drew him to her so that she could taste him fully. His rich, masculine scent filled her head and set her to trembling. Aye, this was what she wanted.

All she would ever want, even though a part of her was terrified on so many levels. If anyone ever learned of this, it would be the end of her. Somehow that didn't seem to matter. How could it? Her life was absolute misery. She'd never really wanted it, and in truth, she hated every second of it.

The only happiness she had were these little moments with Nibo. He, alone, didn't judge her or look at her as if something was missing. He made her laugh instead of cry. Whenever she spoke her mind, he didn't censor it. It was as if she were a ghost flitting about in a pseudo existence until he came along and awakened her into her real body to make her truly live and breathe.

Her body burned for his touch. Burned for him.

Wanting to feel every inch of his lush body, she ran her hands over his back, delighting in the dips and curves of his muscles. He buried his hand in her hair, cupping the nape of her neck in a way that made her scalp tingle. Moaning against his lips, she ached for him in a way she barely understood.

While she'd never had a man of her own before, she understood from her girlfriends and the bawdy talk she'd overheard on the island the mechanics of coupling. What she wasn't quite ready for was this onslaught of heat that suffused her, nor the demand that her body flooded her with. What was this warm wickedness? No wonder they preached so vehemently against it.

She felt alive and on fire. Molten, even.

The very next thing she knew, Nibo picked her up in his arms and carried her a small distance away to a secluded area of the beach so that no one would be able to see them. He laid her against a bed of soft moss on the sand.

Valynda tried to understand the fire in her blood and the strange aching that defied anything she'd ever known or experienced. Every part of her felt as if it were engulfed by flames. As if it were aching for something she couldn't explain or describe.

Nibo stared at her like a starving man eyeing a governor's banquet. The raw hunger in his eyes sent even more ribbons of heat through her.

She wanted him to devour her and she longed to taste the rich, salty dips and ridges of his muscles until she'd had her fill. But part of her heart told her that she would never be sated with him. Nay, she would always want him and yearn for his touch. How could she not? He was too inviting. Too much fun.

Too delectable.

Licking her lips, she offered him a hesitant smile. "What can I do to please you?"

Nibo closed his eyes at her words, savoring each and every syllable. No woman had ever asked him such a question before. It was such a sweet dream. But then, so was she.

Maybe he was damning both of them to an eternity of rumors and hostility, but for his life he couldn't stop himself from seizing this one moment, this one woman, even though he knew it was a bad idea from every which way he looked at it. He needed her, and the only way he could let her go would be to cut his own heart from his chest. It made no sense. He knew that.

This was absolute madness.

But he couldn't leave. She would be worth each and every torment ever delivered, every bit of wrath he evoked, and he would gladly relive all of it for this one instant in time. To him, she was worth it all and more.

Because she was that precious to him. That unique.

Valynda, who didn't cater to his ego. Who made him laugh when he felt bad and who saw things that others missed. In no time at all, she had become a vital part of his world.

She wrapped her arms about him and he shivered from the tenderness of her silken limbs sliding against his flesh. Lying next to her in the sandy moss, he tasted her sweet lips, her neck where he inhaled her divine, lavender-rose scent. His lips tingled from the saltiness of her skin and he drank of it deeply. This was the only food he needed, the nourishment he had been starving for the whole of his life. She filled a hole in him that he hadn't known was there until the night he'd found her on the beach with her lunatic friends.

Heated fire replaced the coldness in his heart. Every color and scent seemed amplified and more vibrant to him, as if he'd opened his eyes for the very first time ever.

As if he'd been reborn into the world.

Her hesitant touches as she removed his clothes and explored each inch of his body echoed through his soul, crashing through every barrier he'd ever erected to protect himself from harm while he lay there scared and trembling like a naked babe on the edge of a cliff.

Never had he felt so exposed. So very vulnerable. Indeed, one word of rejection from her right then could destroy him. Because he was hers.

She pulled his tunic from him, her hands eagerly exploring each dip and curve of his flesh. Nibo closed his eyes, his body burning.

"Do these hurt?" she'd asked as she saw the faint cuts along his ribs where he'd fought his brother and occasionally scraped himself coming through the gates to reach the human realm.

Nibo shook his head, his throat tight. Truthfully, all his wounds, past and present, seemed healed whenever she was near. And for his life, he couldn't fathom the peace she brought to his heart. "All I feel is you, *ma petite,* and you could never bring me pain."

Valynda's breath faltered at his tender words. She smiled, her body afire with her need for him. No man would ever mean so much. Nor could he ever be such a part of her.

Her head reeled with the masculine sandalwood scent of him. With the gentle pressure of his strong hands roaming over her flesh. Everywhere he touched, hot chills sprang up in their wake.

Valynda brushed her lips over the hard stubble of his neck, delighting in the salty taste of his skin. His throaty moan reverberated under her lips and thrilled her.

"I need you, Vala," he whispered against her cheek as he loosened the stays in her gown and corset.

Valynda pulled him closer. "I will always be here for you."

She shivered as he pulled her gown from her and heat stole up her cheeks. Deep embarrassment filled her heart. Never before had any man seen her so bare. She felt so incredibly exposed, and completely vulnerable to his gaze, his touch.

Worse, she knew her father would kill her if he ever learned of what she was doing.

And yet she didn't want to stop. She wanted to share herself with Nibo. Sooner or later, she would have a husband. Better to be with someone she wanted than someone she didn't.

Honestly, she couldn't imagine ever wanting anyone else the way she wanted this man. She had never been a fickle woman. Never been the kind to do anything without a lot of thought.

Until now.

But he was special, and she didn't want to regret not having this with him.

His eyes burned with an intensity that stole her breath as he moved again to claim her lips.

Nibo savored the rich taste of his Vala. Nibbling a path to her throat, he nipped at her tender flesh. She was sweeter than any rum and could make him twice as drunk, thrice as fast. Sharp, pulsing fires burned inside him. It seemed as if he'd waited the whole of his life for this moment, as if the first time with her was his first time all over again.

More experienced than anyone had a right to be, he still found himself shaking from expectation. Nervous almost beyond endurance. The other loas would laugh and mock him if they could see him like this. He acted like some callow youth, not the spirit of fertility.

But he couldn't help it.

Her lips brushed the flesh just below his ear and he shook from the boiling desire that pitched inside him. "I will always be yours, my brave Nibo," she whispered, her husky voice urging him further.

He separated her thighs.

Valynda shivered in expectation of the pain she knew would come. Even so, she reveled in the feel of him lying against the entire length of her body. A deep part of her soul was absolutely terrified of this and begged her to shove him away before it was too late.

But she couldn't do that. She was already gone.

Because the truth was, Nibo was her life, her breath.

Everything. She couldn't imagine not having him with her.

His body heat reached out to her and she raised her hips to him to let him know that she was ready. With a groan, he buried his face in her neck and slid inside her.

All of a sudden, a horrible, body-wrenching pain tore through her and she buried her nails into his flesh. It seemed as if she were being cleaved in two. Her stomach lurched and burned as she gasped from the agony of it all.

"Are you all right, *ma petite?*"

Sinking her hand in Nibo's hair, she nodded, though honestly, she didn't really feel that way.

As if he could sense it, he smiled down at her and fingered her cheek. It was the most intimate moment of her life to have him looking at her like that while she could feel him buried deep within her body.

And when he began to slowly thrust against her hips, she bit her bottom lip as her pain gave way to spiraling waves of pleasure. Nibo's lips teased her with a knowing grin. "That's it, *mon ange.*"

Nibo froze an instant as he watched the heated look in Vala's eyes. There was something in her innocence that captivated him in a way nothing ever had before. It was as if it reached out and pulled a vital part of him out of his body, or perhaps it was a vital piece of his soul.

He couldn't really explain it. It was just something he felt. In that moment, he knew he'd never again be the same.

And he knew the instant he was completely lost to her, because with his lovers, he was always in control. He always had restraint.

It wasn't like that with her. Quicker than ever before, he came in a blinding white-hot moment of ecstasy, and there was nothing he could do to stop or delay it.

Panting and weak, he felt her stiffen the instant he filled her. It was as if she were in utter agony.

Valynda lay there on the edge of screaming as she struggled to understand what had just happened to her.

"Vala?" Nibo pulled out so that he could look down at her.

His voice sounded so far away that she longed to ask him where he'd gone.

Yet her head spun as if she were the one down a hole. Strange lights and images spiraled around her, stealing her breath. A hundred foreign voices spoke simultaneously, some accusing, some in pity. Her chest tight, she tried to focus her thoughts, but like someone drowning at sea, she couldn't find anything solid to grasp on to.

Then, in the fury of her mind, she clearly saw Nibo in his field, the day his brother killed him.

There was no missing the blood and the anger in his brother's eyes as he'd beat him again and again, without mercy.

Then she saw Qeenan's shame as he tried to hide Nibo's body so that no one could find it. So that no one would ever know what he'd done to his own twin . . .

And that wasn't the only vision in her head.

"Nay!" Scrambling away from him, she grabbed her discarded gown to cover herself with as she wept in near hysterical panic. She cowered next to a fallen tree, too horrified by the images and feelings inside her to think. "What have I done?"

Nibo looked at her as if she'd struck him, and he slowly moved to her side and retrieved his breeches. The pain in his eyes told her that he thought her rejection was of him.

Wiping away her tears, Valynda swallowed the painful knot in her throat and stiffened her spine against the terrible, unbelievable truth she must deliver to him.

"It's not you, Nibo," she whispered. She glanced up but

couldn't bring herself to face the bitter rejection that burned in his eyes.

Why? she wanted to scream. What had just happened? Why had she seen all those horrific images?

Of the past. Of a future that made no sense to her.

But no answer came, only more pain, more regret . . .

More guilt.

And of one thing she couldn't seem to deny. "I—I have damned us both."

A frown lined his brow as he moved to touch her, and though he appeared calm, she could sense some roiling anger inside him. "How so?"

Valynda closed her eyes in an effort to banish the warmth of his hand against her bare shoulder that she didn't feel like she deserved.

And shunning Nibo was the last thing she wanted to do. But she had to keep him safe. But if what she saw was the truth, she had to keep away from him. For both their sakes.

Yet, she needed this man with her, and that need was what would cause his damnation! It was what would eventually cause her own.

How could she tell him that? He'd never believe her. Worse, he might think her mad and have her committed. Honestly, she found it impossible to believe, and she was the one who'd seen the visions.

Maybe they're not premonitions.

Maybe they were dreams. A hallucination of some kind.

Aye, maybe I just ate bad clams.

She knew better.

"Vala, what has caused you such distress?"

Why couldn't she tell him? It should be easy, and yet nothing would come out.

How could she tell him that if he stayed with her they would both be damned to that future?

"You will think me mad."

He brushed her hair away from her shoulder. "I will never think that of you."

She shook her head, refusing his reassurance. She must maintain distance between them to avoid her nightmare.

Nibo gently took her chin. "Tell me, *mon ange*."

Valynda bit her lip. She owed him an explanation for her hysterics. In his eyes she saw his fear that she had rejected him, and his earlier anger no longer seemed important to her. Pain coiled inside her and she knew she couldn't allow him to believe that she had spurned him when he was her very life.

Before she could think, the truth tumbled from her lips. "I see a future where you die."

Nibo laughed. "I can't die, Vala. I'm already dead."

She sighed and reached for him, but her hand stopped just inches from his cheek. She lowered her arm to her side and cast her gaze to the beach around them. "I know you don't believe me, but I swear 'tis the truth. You are hell bound."

Nibo looked away as he heard her words, his heart strangely blank. It was as if his body didn't know how to react and so decided to feel nothing.

She was right. He did think her insane. There was no other explanation for that.

Of all the women alive, he had finally found one who warmed his life, one who filled the emptiness of his heart, and one who was obviously deranged.

"I am not mad!" She glared at him. "I know you don't believe me, but you must! I saw it, Nibo. I did."

He just stared at her. Not even the urge to curse came to him. He had no rational response for this, as it was a totally new experience for him, which, given the wide range of things that had happened to him over the centuries, said a lot.

"It'll be all right, Vala."

Yet it hadn't been. It had been so far from all right as to be ludicrous.

Most had the gift of foresight at birth and lost it with their virginity. Leave it to her to get her powers in reverse. Somehow, Nibo had bestowed them on her inadvertently when he first slept with her.

If only she'd known how to channel them. Or if those powers had been better tuned so that she could have seen more clearly what they entailed. But by the time she realized what it was that she'd seen and how to use those powers, it'd been too late.

She'd been dead.

And damned—just as she'd predicted.

Because she'd fought against who and what she was, too ashamed and too embarrassed by herself to embrace it, she'd let the mores of others dictate her life for her. She'd been so focused on trying to be like others that she'd let it ruin her life, and what had it gotten her?

Her friends still hadn't accepted her into their elite social circles. Not fully. She was their friend only when others weren't around or available. When it was convenient for them and when it wouldn't embarrass them.

Her parents she'd spent her life trying to please had betrayed her and sold her out. And in the end, what had it gotten them? Her mother had killed herself and her father was ruined.

She'd died alone at the hands of a selfish bastard who hated her. Given all that, Valynda should have been true to herself and stayed with Nibo. The world be damned. She would have been better off.

At least she wouldn't have been any worse off. Dead was dead.

Then again, Xuri had been just as bad. Too afraid to stand up to his own friends and family, he'd hidden their relationship just as much as she did. His friends and family knew no more about his real nature than those around her had known hers.

He kept himself every bit as hidden.

The two of them were shadow people moving around, barely seen and vaguely known by the people who interacted with them. No one could be bothered to learn anything about them. For in the end, the heart was ever deceitful above all things, and desperately wicked. Who could ever know it?

Be careful the chosen path and the webs of practiced deceit, for where they led, all were responsible for the outcome of their fate.

Good or bad, no one could be blamed save the person who brought favor or destruction down upon their own head.

Life was ever a complicated tapestry woven by those decisions, large and small, made every day.

"I don't want to be your shadow person anymore, Xuri."

He'd scowled at her. "Pardon?"

Valynda sighed as she reached up and cupped his cheek. Her heart ached for what he'd never been able to give her. While he was loyal and he loved her, he just hadn't been there in the way that mattered most.

He kept denying her in front of his nanchon. That wasn't what she wanted. Not for her and not for him.

They both deserved more.

They both deserved better.

"Xuri—"

"Don't push me away, Vala. Please."

God, how she wanted to. But that simple plea undid her. Mostly because she knew it wasn't in him to utter such a thing. Such platitudes and niceties weren't a part of his nature. He didn't have to deign to such, and she hated herself for the weakness.

You hate him! He betrayed you!

Words so easily spoken, but emotions weren't so easy to manipulate, and the head had nothing to do with her heart, as that stupid organ didn't listen to reason, for it had no ears.

Damn them for it! Why couldn't anyone ever reason with emotions?

Wouldn't the world be better off if fear and hate and love and betrayal could be reasoned with? Why was it so damn hard to make them listen!

Yet the moment his lips touched hers, she was undone by them.

And before she knew it, he was pulling her into the hold of her ship, and into a darkened corner where she was his willing captive in a madness that she knew would have an even worse ending.

Her heart quickened with every kiss and caress. It'd been so long since anyone had touched her. Since she'd been able to really touch another. She was overwhelmed by the sensations of nerve endings.

And when Nibo entered her, she cried out in pure bliss, especially as he licked and teased her breasts in time to his strokes. Damn the man for being so flexible and talented. But then he was known for his skills in this department.

There was no way of denying this part of him. She should have known that.

He was a creature of sex. More so than any other. It fueled his powers and invigorated him.

"I've missed you so much, Vala!" His tone was so deep and throaty that it sent a chill over her.

"And I you."

His arms tightened around her. When he held her like this, it was easy to pretend that he wasn't a loa. That he was just a man who loved her—and maybe that was the problem.

She'd lied to herself so many times. Filled her own head with dreams of what she'd wanted him to be and made him into someone he wasn't. Instead of allowing him to be who and what he was, she had fancied him as someone else, and that wasn't his fault. He'd never once lied to her about who and what he was.

I'm to blame.

"I'm sorry, Xuri."

He pulled back with a frown. "For what?"

"For being the one who didn't see you."

He frowned at her. "I don't understand."

Valynda kissed his lips as she felt her heart breaking at a truth she should have realized sooner. "I asked for more than you could give me."

Nibo froze as he heard the pain in her voice. That was the last thing he wanted while he made love to her. "Nay, Vala. You never asked that. I've given you everything I have."

She placed her hand over the opening in his shirt that he hadn't bothered to remove. "Nay, love, you didn't."

Biting his lip, he swept his shirt off over his head to show her a small red vèvè of roses and skulls he'd tattooed over his heart. Similar in design to his own personal vèvè, this one was different. Taking her hand, he ran her fingertips over the design. "I merged us, Vala. Don't you understand?"

Tears welled in her eyes as she saw what he'd done and realized its significance. "But you didn't defend me to the others."

"Because they would have gone after you. And they did." He swallowed hard. "They kept me locked out so that I couldn't help you."

In that moment, she saw him desperate at the gates while she'd been killed. Heard his screams as he tried to break through so that he could help her.

He was inconsolable in his grief and rage.

And then she saw what no one had told her about that night. Thorn.

The two of them had met in Thorn's hall on the Nether Realm of Azmodea. Nibo had been uncomfortable but determined. What he did was against all the rules. Had he been found there, he could have been destroyed.

For her, he'd risked the wrath of multiple gods. He'd risked his own existence.

"You know there's nothing I can do."

"I don't give a fuck, Leucious. And I know better."

Thorn had grimaced at his real name that he despised, as it gave Nibo as much control over him as it did whenever someone used Xuri for Nibo. "Well, Xuri, I have nothing with which to bargain, and how can I bring back someone who has no physical remains? Of all creatures, you know what you're asking is impossible."

Nibo's eyes had flickered red in the darkness of Thorn's office, where a bright fire burned in a black fireplace. "Maman can fix that."

"Brig?" Thorn had burst into laughter as he sat in his throne-like chair, watching Nibo pace before his hearth. "You'd have me negotiate with *her*?"

He paused to arch a brow. "That a problem for you?"

"Little bit, aye."

"How so?"

His eyes haunted, Thorn had clutched at a peculiar pendant he wore about his neck. One of a three-headed dragon. "We have a past I'd rather not discuss. Suffice it to say, we're not friendly . . . unless you plan to offer her my testicles. And for the record, those I'm not willing to give up."

Nibo's eyes widened. "You're the husband she speaks of?"

Laughing bitterly, he shook his head. "Nay. I'm the one she *never* speaks of."

"Yet you will do me this favor." Not a question. Nibo had demanded it.

Valynda saw that now. He hadn't betrayed her or forgotten her, after all. For her, he'd defied them all.

She felt terrible for ever doubting him. For allowing others to put such treachery in her heart. But it was easy to let others plant those seeds of doubt. Especially given her past, when she'd been told repeatedly that she was unworthy of love or affection from anyone. When not even her own parents had cared what happened to her. How could she believe someone as wonderful as Nibo could want or love her when they didn't?

It still didn't seem possible. Yet it was unfair of her to judge him because they were lacking.

"I'm sorry I doubted you. That I let others divide us." Something too easy to do, as they had agendas of their own. Agendas that weren't in Valynda's and Nibo's best interests.

But it was easy to get caught up in other people's drama and to let them fill her head and heart with their lies and misconceptions. Belle had been right.

She should have gone to Nibo sooner and should have never sought out others to validate her own insecurities.

She should have trusted in Nibo.

"I don't give my loyalty lightly, Vala. But when I do, it's true and unyielding. You know this."

She did. "But the others . . ."

"Are against us still."

That was what made it hard.

"You will always be *mon ange*." Kissing her, he deepened his strokes, and this time, she swore she could feel him all the way to her soul.

212

Sighing, she dug her nails into his back as she met him as an equal.

And this time, they came together.

Valynda held Nibo as she felt his heart racing in time to hers and his breathing began to slow in her ear.

"I love you, Xuri."

"*Et tu.*"

She reveled in the warmth of him. If she could, she'd stay like this for all eternity. But unfortunately, they had to get dressed and return to the real world. To deal with problems that wouldn't cease.

And drive evil back all the way back to Death's Door.

Sadness gripped her as she toyed with the feathers in his hair and his curls that locked themselves around her fingers. Her beautiful Xuri.

After he fastened his breeches, he helped her straighten her gown. Then he kissed her shoulder and smoothed down her hair. "You are the most magnificent woman I've ever seen."

Valynda smiled. "And I love that you lie to me like that."

He tsked at her. "Why do you say such things?"

"Because I've seen Erzuli and Belle and Marcelina, so I know for a fact that you've seen far more beautiful women, but I will take that compliment and run with it."

Nibo started to laugh, until he noticed something moving near them.

Instinctively, he pulled Valynda behind him to protect her, then used his powers to blast at what appeared to be a stain moving along the wall.

Shrieking, it transformed into a demon, then vanished.

Valynda gasped. "What was that?"

"Not sure."

"Where do you think it went?"

He gave her a droll stare. "Having the same amount of information you do, I can honestly say I have no idea."

"That's not a good thing, is it?"

"Again, same information, but based on past experience, I can practically guarantee that it won't be good."

Lovely.

"We should probably tell the captain?"

Xuri frowned. "About our having sex? I should think he wouldn't care."

Valynda groaned at his off-beat sense of humor. Popping his arm, she growled at him. "That shadow stain dancing about his boat, you daft loon."

"Ah, that. Aye. You're right. He'd most likely want to know about the demon, as opposed to me getting handsy with his crewmate." Nibo led the way toward the ladder.

Adarian growled at the trollop on his crotch as she started to pull away the instant the demon appeared in his room. "Keep about your business if you want to be paid!"

And if she wanted to live.

Grabbing her hair, he held her in place and shifted his hips slightly as she returned her lips to his cock.

Then he slid his gaze to the demon. "What?" he snapped.

"As you feared, my lord, she has betrayed you."

He arched a brow at that. "What?"

The demon's glowing eyes turned deep black. "Valynda. She is back with Nibo and someone made her human again."

Adarian grew still at those words as he realized what the demon was saying.

Damn it. He needed that staff and the power it held.

Furious, he shoved the prostitute away, then fastened his pants. "Summon the others."

If Valynda had turned on them, then he would sink that ship and reunite Bane with his first wife at the bottom of the ocean.

It was time for the Deadmen to earn their name and become so dead that not even Thorn could reanimate them.

Wyñeria

11

"Ah, bloody hell and all their handmaidens and hairbows!" Will took a deep breath, then, louder, shouted to the crew. "Avast! Demon to port bow!"

"Demonssss," Bart corrected with an exaggerated *s* to make sure the crew understood they were under siege from a large group of those beasts headed straight for them.

"And they don't look happy to see us."

Bart snorted at Jake's additional comment. "Beg to differ, mate. They look deliriously happy to see us."

"And hungry," Will added. "They look exceedingly hungry."

"Would that make us seafood, then?"

Will scoffed at Bart. "Seriously, mate? You had to go there?"

"It's that or piss me britches. Which would you rather?"

Will moved away from him and put Jake next to him. Just in case he was voicing a prediction about his bladder. Then took an additional three steps more. "That should do. Anyone seen Sallie? Uncork your bottle, man! We need your better half to come kick demon arse! Armor up!"

Valynda ignored them as she saw what was coming. "Xuri!" she called, grabbing a sword. They could definitely use his crook and reinforcements.

She felt the air behind her stir. But as she turned toward it, her smile faded.

That wasn't Nibo.

Identical in looks he might be, but he was definitely not her lover. This one held a sinister air and aura about him that wasn't quite right, and it wasn't just the black overcoat and breeches he wore. Or the black tricorne that was decorated in red and gold.

This man didn't carry himself the same. He bled pure malice and discontent. While Xuri drew her in like a beacon in a storm, this man repelled her more than Benjamin had. Her very flesh crawled in his presence.

"Who are you?"

"Don't you know?"

"Qeenan," she breathed the obvious answer. Baron Kriminal. The man who'd killed Nibo out of petty jealousy.

Her blood ran cold.

"What are you doing here?" He'd never been interested in meeting with her before. Indeed, he'd gone out of his way to avoid her entirely.

And now she was grateful that he'd never shown her any interest, except for the fact that she was now meeting him.

Why?

"I heard a rumor that you were back and I was curious. What is it about *you* that my brother finds so damn intriguing that he can't stay away? But then I've never understood his mind or his taste." He raked her with an offensive sneer.

Valynda scowled at the ogre. *Now? He had to ask about this now?*

"As you can see, I'm a little busy." She started to leave.

Qeenan grabbed her arm. "It's just a few demons. Surely you're not afraid."

She twisted away from him. "Not afraid. The word is *busy,* as in my hands are full." To illustrate the point, she held out her right hand that had a sword and the left one that held her skirt. *"Literally."*

Valynda took a step back and gave him a cold smile. "Now if you don't mind, I think you can understand why I don't want to turn my back on you. So . . . if you'll leave?"

His gaze turned cold at her dig against him for his unwarranted attack on Nibo. "You should be careful who you insult, little girl."

"Don't call me little girl." She tsked. "You asked what it was Xuri saw in me, Mr. Kriminal. That's it. It's my fearlessness and audacity. The fact that I'm willing to call things like I see them."

"And you see me as a killer?"

"That is who and what you are, is it not? A creature who struck his brother when his back was turned and he was unarmed?"

He actually smiled at that. "That I am. Killing is the one thing I'm good at."

"Then perhaps you should pursue new hobbies. Not sure that's much of a bragging point, but very well. Take your win where you can."

"Ah, *chère*," he said in a tone that was so close to Nibo's it made the hairs on the back of her neck rise. "Be glad that I don't take your head."

And with that he vanished, an instant before a demon attacked her so fast that she barely had time to defend herself. Valynda caught the demon with her sword. Forcing it back, she realized how much harder it was to fight as a human than in her straw form. For one thing, she could now feel every blow rattle through her body. For another, her center of balance was off, as were her senses. Not to mention her hair kept getting in her eyes.

Ugh! This was impossible. Well, not impossible. Just harder.

Valynda finally caught her footing and stabilized, then stabbed the beast through his left eye. She took a moment to glance around the ship. Demons were all over, and not just one kind.

Some could fly. Some stayed to the shadows. Others were locked to the ground. Dramonks and sea cronks. It was as if the Malachai had summoned every kind he could think of.

Which meant he must be furious over what she'd done.

I'm the reason for this. . . .

Her stomach shrank as she realized why there were so many what had been unleashed against them. While it wasn't unusual for their crew to be attacked, and viciously so, even this was excessive.

He knows.

She had no idea how that could be other than he was the Malachai and those beasts had unique powers unlike any others. Damn him for it.

And damn her. At least now she understood what the stain on the wall had been earlier. It must have been a Malachai spy.

Guilty over what she'd done, Valynda glanced about. Belle was fighting off two more demons while Captain Bane held off three. Will used his flintlock to shoot one between the eyes before he went after another with his sword. More gunfire rang out as others fought with whatever they could. Her friends were in such grave danger because of Adarian's wrath.

Nay, because of her stupidity and gullibility where none should have existed.

The sea around them churned as Marcelina struggled to keep the ship as level as possible against the waves. Kalder was in the sea below, fighting against a giant squid.

This looked hopeless. And she felt that deep in her heart.

How were they to take down all the forces of evil with just a single vessel? With just this meager crew? What had Thorn been thinking? Why would he ever send so few on such an important mission?

Had this been its own form of cruelty?

Stop that!

Had she learned nothing from her doubt of Xuri? Those thoughts came from a deep, dark place in the mind. An unsettled place. Thorn, like Xuri, had never done anything to make her doubt him or his motives. While his words could be caustic, his actions were true.

Actions speak louder than words.

Of all people, she knew that. And until he gave her reasons to doubt, then she would give Thorn her faith. True and unyielding.

See, I can be taught!

Suddenly, a new rumbling began. One that came from deep below. Crisp and clopping. Gurgling and churning. It sounded vaguely like running horses and it caused a rushing funnel in the sea that began to twist the ship about. The wooden boards creaked and moaned in protest.

"What fresh bloody hell is this?" Bart grabbed a rope before he was thrown overboard.

Kalder reached for the anchor ropes and quickly climbed to the deck before he was harmed. And still the rushing came. Thick and steady.

Unrelenting.

Valynda caught herself against the rigging as her stomach heaved and she feared she'd be sick from the rocking motion— another thing she hadn't missed about not having a human body.

A dark, gargantuan shadow rose up from the sea. Blue fire lit up the sky. Thunderous claps resonated as the demons began to scream and vanish.

More demons ran for cover, only to be vaporized.

"Ah shite." Will's tone was laden with disgust. "You know it's a bad omen when the scariest of things be heading for cover at the appearance of this and then get eaten. Be damned we are now, mates."

And that was how it felt as these new beasts turned out to be two dozen dragons. Gigantic beasts that rolled through the blue fire, circling through the air in a beautiful dance as they devoured the demons.

Except for the blood and entrails that rained down on them. That she could have done without.

Especially some of the grislier bits that fell around her. But at least it got their enemies off them. None of the demons cared about them at all. They were too busy trying to escape the dragons and their talons or fire. Trying to evade becoming a part of their menu.

Not that she blamed them. It wasn't something she'd want either. Which wasn't her concern until all the demons were gone.

Then the dragons began to whistle and turn their attention toward them.

Bart glanced to the captain. "Should we run?"

"Where to, Mr. Meers?" he asked simply. "The ocean's all yours." He gestured toward the open sea.

Valynda would laugh, but this wasn't funny. As noted, they had nowhere to flee.

The dragons swooped in and her stomach shrank. This was it. . . .

They were sitting Deadmen.

One by one, the dragons rushed down from the sky, heading straight for their main deck. She knew they were coming for them as there was no doubt. Their eyes remained focused and unwavering. They kept their wings wide open.

But instead of eating them or attacking, they landed gracefully on deck, then turned into men and women.

Near the mainmast, they formed a small circle with their backs to each other so that they faced the crew.

Confused by their actions, Valynda exchanged a scowl with Belle, who seemed every bit as perplexed by them as she was. How weird was this? Never had she seen the like.

They stared out at the Deadmen as the Deadmen stared at them.

All of a sudden, a hand touched Valynda's shoulder.

She spun about to attack.

Nibo ducked her blow with a charming grin. "Easy, me love. It's just me. I heard your call and brought a few reinforcements." He kissed her cheek, then took her hand and stepped forward. "Bane, you bastard, come and meet my friends. They're sea dragons and should be keeping you afloat for a bit longer."

The tallest of the male dragons moved toward the captain as Nibo made the introductions.

"Nazar, meet Captain Devyl Bane."

There was something ethereal and otherworldly about Nazar. He seemed more elfin than dragon. His eyes were the strangest shade of green Valynda had ever seen. And like an elf, he had pointed ears and shoulder-length brown hair that fell around a handsome, masculine face.

"Pleasure to have you on board." Bane extended his hand.

Nazar inclined his head and shook the captain's arm.

"Don't be insulted if they don't speak much. It's part of their nature, as they don't trust humans or former humans much. It's what drove them to the sea." Nibo jerked his chin at the small group that continued to eye the crew warily. "Luckily, they owe me a favor, and will stay with you until you see this hell-bent venture finished."

Nazar stepped over to whisper in Nibo's ear.

"Nay, you won't have to sleep on board the ship. You can follow after them, if you'd rather. Just keep the Malachai and his spies away from them. Whatever it takes." Nibo looked back at Bane. "Adarian isn't playing by the rules. So, we won't either."

Nazar used his hands to signal to his people. All but two jumped from the ship, into the waves, where they vanished.

Nibo smiled at Valynda. "Two of them will remain among the crew and they'll rotate out. The rest will be nearby should they be needed. Try not to panic or attack if you see the others. Remember that they're friends and they'll take it rather personally should one of them be harpooned."

Bane let out a low whistle as he watched one of the dragons skim the surface, twist, and then spiral back below the waves in a shimmery show of red scales. "Would have loved to have had some of those in me army back in the day."

"Aye, you would." Nibo winked.

Thorn nodded in agreement. "As would I. How old are they?"

"Older than you, demon," Nazar said in a voice so deep, it seemed to rumble. "And we don't serve your kind."

By the captain's face, he understood the dragon's sentiment. "What can we do to make your stay among us comfortable?"

"Nothing. We'll sleep on deck and stay out of your way." And with that, Nazar gestured at the younger of the two to leave, but the young dragon gestured back in a most animated way.

Valynda smiled at Nibo. "Brother, son, or something more intimate?"

"Brother who doesn't listen." Nibo laughed at Nazar, who was quickly losing his patience. "You might as well send Flaxen back. Karawan isn't going to give on this and you know it."

Nazar let out a sound of deep aggravation. "Fine." He gestured for the woman to leave them. Then made several harsh, erratic gestures toward his brother.

The gesture back must have been profane, judging by the tenseness of Nazar's expression and Nibo's increased laughter.

But Karawan didn't say a word. Whereas his brother was tall and lean, he was bulkier in muscle tone and had dark curly hair and amber eyes. Something about him almost reminded her of Nibo.

Which sent a bad feeling over her.

"Just how close are you to them?"

"Get your mind away from that. Not at all what you're thinking, love. We are friends. Nothing more."

Nazar scowled at her as he raked a curious stare over her body. "This is your Vala?"

Nibo nodded.

"Ah."

She wasn't sure what to make of that. "Ah?"

Karawan came over to eye her as if she were the most curious specimen he'd ever beheld in his life. So much so that Nibo pushed him back.

Laughing, Karawan took it in stride. "We're both older than Nibo, my lady."

That made her feel better. Sort of.

As did the fact that Nibo hadn't abandoned her. "Thank you, Xuri."

"For what?"

"Bringing them to us."

His features softened. "Of course. I'm only sorry it took so long to reach you. We came as soon as we could. But with dragons, they often drag their wings." His gaze went past her to Thorn. "There's a storm brewing."

"We know."

"Nay, not the one you're thinking, old man. This one is much darker and deeper. The petro are defecting to the Malachai."

Thorn's expression turned to stone. "Beg pardon?"

Nibo nodded. "It's why I summoned me friends. Qeenan and the others plan to raise up Apollymi the Destroyer. They're after the world and intend to take it over."

"With Adarian? Are they out of their minds?"

Now Nibo had the attention of the captain and the rest of the crew.

"Not with Adarian. They plan to replace him."

Thorn shook his head. "This plan gets dumber and dumber. Have they any idea what they're asking?"

"They think they do."

"And how do they plan to do it?" Bane asked. "Apollymi isn't exactly known for her people skills or her great sense of cooperation."

"Kill the Dark-Hunter leader, Acheron."

Thorn scowled at his words. "How are they going to do that? No one knows where he is. He travels all the time and seldom stays in one place for more than a day or two."

"That's normally true, except for when he's training a new Dark-Hunter."

Thorn lost color in his cheeks. "Come again."

Nibo sighed as he glanced toward Valynda. "Qeenan learned that Acheron is here and that he's been training Jean-Luc Tessier. Captain St. Noir. So, his plan is to kill him and raise the Destroyer."

Thorn sat down and then spread out on his back. "That's it. I quit. Take me, Bane. Pierce me heart and have done with it."

"Get your arse up, Leucious, I'm in no mood. You're the one what got me into this with your stupidity. Be damned if you're going to quit on me now."

Thorn looked up at him. "You are a contrary bastard. For centuries you tried to kill me. I finally lie down to let you do it and you refuse."

"Because you brought me back for a mission. And I know you better than that." He kicked Thorn's feet. "Up with you. You're embarrassing me."

"Fine, but only because if I quit it would make my father happy." Thorn stood up and sighed. "All right. New game plan. To our deaths!"

The crew grumbled in protest.

Nibo shook his head. "New game plan. Reach Acheron. Stop the Apocalypse. Club me brother in the head and lock Adarian down."

"For the record," Will said, "we like that one better."

Thorn scoffed. "You say that like it's easy."

"Your father had him neutralized. I'm thinking that means you know how to do it, too."

"Maybe."

"Maybe isn't going to cut this, Leucious. You better go find us something better than a maybe."

Thorn mumbled under his breath before he let out a begrudging "All right."

But even as he said that, Valynda heard the doubt in his tone. More than that, she felt it in her heart. Worse, she saw it on the beloved faces of those around her.

Please, don't let this be a mistake.

Because now that she was human again, she had so much more to lose. Not just her life, but a heart that could break again, and that was the last thing she wanted. This was no longer about her, and it wasn't just about Nibo.

This was about the crew that had become her family, and it was about the survival of the entire world.

"We won't fail."

They couldn't afford to.

12

There was much that Nibo had in common with Acheron, who sat outside a rundown brothel, drinking alone while ignoring the women and even a few men who were trying to entice his business.

A twin brother he couldn't stand who wanted to kill him. A past he tried not to think about. People who were always trying to bargain with him, and not just for sex, even though those lined up for blocks to the point it was more tiresome than flattering. And more responsibilities than he'd ever signed up for.

More than that, Nibo was intimately acquainted with that expression of supreme disgust etched on the Atlantean god's face as he saw him approaching, because there were so few either of them could trust that they both had an instinctive need to pat down anyone who dared to come near to ensure they weren't packing one of the few weapons that could kill them. Not that they really cared, as death would be a welcome respite from the misery that served as their pseudo-existence.

It was so ingrained, Acheron's hand actually headed for the sword he had strapped underneath his plain black buccaneer coat. Though Nibo had to admit, those clothes looked good on the ancient being, right down to the red scarf over his waist-length black hair and the gold hoop in his ear. Acheron had a silver ring on each of his fingers that scraped against the hilt of his sword as he gripped it.

Amused, Nibo picked up Acheron's black tricorne hat from the chair and set it on the table between them before he audaciously took a seat. "I know . . . I know. What the fuck do I want, and why the hell am I here?"

That succeeded in shattering the grim expression on Acheron's face as it melted into a rich laugh. Shaking his head, he held his arm out to Nibo. "I would apologize, but . . ."

"You only see me when I need something, so I don't hold the hostility against you. One day, me brother, we need to spend the night doing nothing but swapping nightmares and getting shit-faced." Nibo held his rum out to Acheron, who took it.

"Too good to shake my hand now, eh?"

"Too tired." Nibo winked at him as he toyed with the white

plume feathers that trimmed the edges of Acheron's hat. "Besides, the rum's better."

"That it is." Acheron took another deep draught before he passed it back. "Compliments to the producer."

"Yeah. Damn shame me irritable brother gutted him." Nibo took a drink and sighed. "Where's Tessier?"

Acheron pointed up at the sky and the bright sun shining down on them. "At the moment, not bursting into flames. Why?"

Nibo poured whatever Acheron had in his mug out and confiscated it for his rum, then poured himself some before handing the bottle over to his friend. "There's a crew heading this way who wants to avenge him. But more to the point, we're going to guard your body."

Acheron choked on his drink. "Pardon?"

"You heard me."

"Guard me from whom?"

"Sadly, my idiot brother."

He wiped his mouth with the back of his hand before he removed the small round spectacles with dark lenses he'd been using to conceal his inhuman swirling silver eyes from the mortals. "Is Qeenan out of his mind?"

"All the time, hence my severe concussion."

"Sonofabitch."

Nibo let out a small hiss. "I would agree, but I do love my mother and have no wish to insult her in such a manner."

"Sorry . . . asshole."

"That, I will drink to." Nibo held the mug up for Acheron to clang the bottle against. "May his testicles rot off."

Acheron choked again.

"You've got to stop wasting me rum, Atlantean. It's too good to spew."

"Then stop catching me off guard."

"Didn't think that was possible."

Acheron laughed. "Normally, it isn't. You have unique skills."

"So they tell me."

The wind around them began to stir, and with it came a rhythm that wasn't found in nature. Nibo cocked his head as he heard a faint drumbeat off in the distance.

Acheron tensed as if he heard it too. "Heartmen?"

"That or dupey. But neither should be active this time of day."

Snorting, he handed the bottle back to Nibo. "Freaks come out whenever they want. Haven't you learned anything during all these centuries?"

"Oh, I've learned lots. More than I wanted to, most days, as it was shoved violently down me throat." Nibo stood up and began to scan the horizon for the source of what was tormenting them. The temperature dropped.

A chill ran up his spine. How he hated portents. They were the gods' way of sending an obscene gesture at them all.

He manifested his staff at the same time Acheron did his. The winds picked up a howl that sounded more like a pack of banshees.

That sent the natives packing, and they scrambled for cover, thinking it some kind of tropical storm.

If they only knew. . . .

Nibo exchanged a peeved grimace with Acheron. "I've got the shit-stains on the left."

"I'll toss whatever comes from the right." Acheron rolled his shoulders. "Simi? Human form."

His Charonte demon that existed on his skin in the shape of a dragon tattoo over his heart peeled herself off as a shadow that twisted and twirled in the wind until she became an adorable human teen who stood at his side. Dressed as an islander with dreadlocks that were held back from her face with a purple scarf, Simi smiled the moment she saw Nibo.

"Ooo! Baron Sexy! It's so good to see you!" With an adorable squeal that flashed a bit of her fangs, she ran at him so that she could give him a huge hug. "How you been!" She tugged playfully at the feathers he had braided into his hair.

Only Simi was allowed to do that.

And Vala.

Anyone else would be sent straight to the floor and then their demise.

"Good to see you, Sim. How have you been?"

"Better if akri ever let his Simi eats his heifer goddess, but no he say. Simi no eats the heifer." She shook her head sadly.

"Aye, well, Sim, feel free to eat any of *that*." Acheron pointed with his staff toward the horde of creatures moving toward them.

Gasping, Simi clapped her hands together with glee. Her eyes widened. "Really, akri?"

"Oh, yeah."

With an ear-piercing scream, she manifested a giant bottle of some condiment Nibo could only guess at before she sprouted wings and flew out toward them.

Nibo laughed at her enthusiasm that he definitely appreciated. "We need more of her."

"No, we don't," Acheron said drily. "While I love and adore my girl, trust me, one is enough. Charonte are like piranhas. You really don't want to unleash a murder of them if you don't have to."

Nibo arched a brow at the thick mass of creatures headed for them. There were so many that they blotted out the daylight. He smirked at Acheron. "Really? You think that'd be a bad idea right about now?"

Acheron let out a tired breath. "Yeah, that was a stupid comment, wasn't it?"

"Far be it from me to call you a dumbass, Atlantean, but . . . you're a dumbass."

Acheron caught the first one that reached them. He batted it away and split it in two with his powers. "Definitely resembling that criticism. Not even going to attempt to refute it."

With a growl, Nibo engaged his lovely opponents. For once, he was grateful he was dead. While their bites hurt, there wasn't anything they could do to him.

Other than piss him off. Which they were doing.

Acheron blasted them with a wave of god-bolts . . . lightning-like shock waves that went through the demons and scattered them. Even better, they lit the growing darkness with bright colors that caused their attackers to arc up and flip through the air as they were barbecued for Simi.

"Don't you have any more friends to summon for reinforcements?" Acheron asked in an irritated tone.

"Not really. Don't you have an immortal army to fight these things?"

"At *night*. Hence the whole *dark* in Dark-Hunters. There's a reason why Artemis didn't name them Noonday-Hunters or Morning-Hunters."

"How about Mute-Hunters? Would like a little silence in this fighting, Ash." Nibo grunted as one of the bastards took a bite out of his shoulder.

Growling, he flipped it over and stomped it. "Little concentration goes a long way."

"For you, maybe. For me? Bad idea."

Nibo ducked a blast that came too close to his head. He spun and kicked one back into a nearby wall, where it exploded. "Ooo! Shiny!"

Acheron passed him an irritated glare as he staked another one. "What is it with loas and shiny objects?"

"Ask your demon. Besides, I'm more attracted to rum and other illicit things." Nibo caught two more, flipped them with his staff, and was about to stab them when something caught him hard across his back.

He stumbled.

Then fell hard against the ground. Before he could regain his footing, he was hit again and knocked senseless. His ears rang from the blow.

What the hell? More hard knocks came. So fast and furious that he wasn't able to recover or regain his footing. He hadn't been hit like this since Qeenan killed him.

That memory didn't help, as it caused him to panic as he was struck again and again.

Badly. He was completely unprepared for the surge in emotions this beating caused, especially fear. He couldn't breathe or think. All sanity fled. The only shred of it he had told him to protect his staff. Shrinking it down, he hid it, but that was all he could manage against the onslaught that left him covering his head so that they didn't split it open the way his brother had.

Fire exploded close to him. Nibo held his hands up to deflect it. It didn't work.

An instant later, he was consumed.

13

Valynda was completely unprepared for the sight of a wounded Nibo as Acheron appeared out of the blue by her bed with Xuri in his arms. Until now, she hadn't even known that he could become harmed.

In any way.

Her heart sank and then pounded as she saw him raw and bleeding. "What happened?" She rose from her bunk and pulled the covers back.

Acheron laid him down on her straw mattress.

"We were attacked. He wanted me to bring him here." He met her gaze. "To you."

Those words brought tears to her eyes. "You should have gone to Masaka. She's a real healer." All she could do was bandage him.

Xuri took her hand into his. "She lacks empathy." Then he gave her a weak smile. "And you'll kiss my boo-boos."

Acheron snorted. "Are you saying you don't want me to heal you?"

Nibo turned serious and his eyes flared as he turned his attention back to the Dark-Hunter. "You better heal me, you arse. This shit hurts."

Acheron took the insult in stride. "Just checking. Didn't want to upset you if you were some kind of secret masochist. You know, the gods forbid I should ever interfere with *that*." Acheron pushed the sleeves of his coat back before his hands began to glow.

Xuri let go of Valynda as Acheron placed his hands on the center of his chest. The glow ran over him until it encircled his entire body. With a curse that questioned the legitimacy of Acheron's birth, he grabbed the Dark-Hunter leader's coat. "Last time I share rum with you, asshole!"

Acheron laughed. "And here I was actually beginning to like you."

Xuri shoved him back. "Next time, I'm feeding you to the thing that wants a piece of your sorry ass."

"Sounds about right. I'm only surprised when I don't get shoved into the jowls of whatever is coming at us."

Valynda didn't speak as she caught the pain that backed those words and realized what really bonded both the Dark-Hunters and

Deadmen together. What made them family. The fact that none of them had ever been able to trust anyone in their human lifetimes.

Ever.

Not their families. Their best friends. The people who were supposed to protect them, the ones everyone said they were supposed to be able to put their faith in had all let them down, time and again, in the most brutal of ways.

Never once had they ever come through for them. Not even for the most basic necessity or need. In the end, they'd all been hung out to dry and left to die alone from the worst sort of betrayal.

So in death, they were there for each other. Hell or high water. Because they knew what it was to have no one, they made sure that they never dealt that to those who wore their colors.

It was what had made her love Xuri.

"Call my name, mon amour, and I'll come. Night or day."

He'd never failed her, until the one night when she'd needed him most. The night when her soul had been ripped from her body. When she'd screamed out the loudest.

It was what made forgiving him so hard. Because those screams still burned raw in her throat. Echoed in her head and haunted her nightmares. Both waking and sleeping.

Just as he was haunted by the fact that his own twin had brutally murdered him over so petty a reason as hurt feelings that had nothing to do with anything Nibo had done. He hadn't intended to slight his brother. He'd been utterly innocent in the matter, and it was the fact that he'd been so lackadaisical about the competition, not caring if his brother took the win that he'd have forfeited had Qeenan asked him about it that had angered Qeenan most.

Meanwhile Qeenan had been so intent on victory that Nibo's attitude had driven such a rage inside him that he'd killed him over it. And that had upset Qeenan the most. Because Qeenan had been trying to win and had lost while Nibo hadn't cared at all. . . .

That was the worst rub that had driven Qeenan over the edge and made him feel as if Nibo didn't deserve the praise. Didn't deserve to live.

Rather than strike out at the ones who'd hurt Qeenan and who had made him feel inferior to his brother, he'd attacked the one person who had actually loved him and who would have protected him. The only person who'd been willing to fight and die for him, no matter what.

Qeenan had killed the one true innocent party that he held responsible for his pain for no other reason than Qeenan had been in an unending competition with his brother that Nibo hadn't even known was taking place. Because Nibo had never felt competitive with Qeenan at all. To him, they'd been a single unit, brothers united against the world, and when one succeeded, they both did. In his mind, they were supposed to help each other without question or failure. Nibo had never cared about credit or seeking praise, nor had he cared who got it. He was just as happy for Qeenan to have it as for himself.

To Nibo, the only thing that mattered was getting the job done well and done correctly as quickly as possible. Praise be damned.

Qeenan only cared about taking credit and getting all the glory for having the job done and didn't care who did it or how well. Just so long as he could strut and swagger, and pretend he was the big man in the room, that was all-important to him.

That was why Nibo's gifts had been better received that fateful day when they'd offered them up. Because he took pride in the work he did and sought no fame or fortune for it. Praise was irrelevant to him.

Taking credit had never been his goal. People, and the matter at hand, were all he cared about. The most selfish thing about him was that he liked to have fun. To laugh and enjoy himself while he worked, because he liked his work and was innately happy. A free spirit who sought to make others as happy and carefree as he was.

Unlike his spiteful brother who was given to bouts of extreme depression over the fact that he felt persecuted by the world at large. Rather than make people laugh, Qeenan spent hours ranting about how he'd been done wrong by everyone around him.

Qeenan forever looked to the past.

Nibo to the future.

A single tear fell from her cheek as she realized how badly she'd misjudged Nibo. She'd let her anger and hurt overshadow her common sense that knew his true nature and beautiful spirit. But then, it was sadly too easy to take someone for granted, especially when they didn't bemoan their fate or tell other people what they owed them.

The fact that he'd fought for her meant everything. She just wished that she'd known it sooner. The pain of betrayal stung so deep.

So foul.

No wonder the lowest level of hell was reserved for betrayers and thieves. They deserved it and more. And though she knew in her head that he'd done his best to get to her, she still couldn't shake the memory of being tortured.

The horror of being alone and needing him. She wanted to get past it. She did. But it wasn't that simple. Her heart was broken and bleeding. They had torn her soul into shreds. Valynda had never been all that keen on trust to begin with, and now having given her trust to him and then being left to cope on her own . . .

She wasn't sure she could get past this.

"Akri! Is merpeople on the Simi's menu?"

Acheron's eyes widened. "I'll be back." He vanished as Nibo laughed.

"What was that about?"

"I think his demon daughter is about to have a go at your Mr. Dupree."

Valynda frowned. "Pardon?"

Nibo sat up on the bed. "Simi likes seafood. No doubt she considers the Myrcian a delicacy."

"Oh dear Lord," she gasped as she realized the Charonte might actually try to eat their resident mermaid. "That could be bad." Cameron would be beside herself if her husband got eaten by a demon. No doubt she'd take it quite personally.

"Indeed. I'm just glad loas aren't part of her culinary cravings." He took her hands into his and kissed her left palm and then her right. "But I pray that I'm still on *your* menu."

He was. God help her, against everything else. And that made her ache inside as those words warmed her instantly. Especially when he nudged her closer. Her breathing turned ragged as she pulled the scarf from his hair and freed his lush, wonderful curls.

Damn him for them. They'd always made him so boyish and charming. So irresistible.

She could be on the brink of murdering him and one glimpse of those curls loose about his handsome features would undo her most violent fury where he was concerned. And he knew it, too.

Cupping her hand to his lips, he stared up at her with those delicious eyes that did the most wicked things to her. His whiskers tickled her palm while his tongue teased her flesh.

"You're such a trollop."

He grinned at her teasing insult and nipped her thumb. "I am that. Reprobate, through and through. It's what you love most about me."

"Nay. It most certainly isn't." She tugged playfully at his curls. "Are you sure you're all right? You looked like you were about to die again, a moment ago."

"Were you worried?"

"Petrified."

He pulled her down to sit in his lap so that he could kiss her. "And so, you're scolding me?"

"Someone needs to."

He opened his mouth to continue their argument.

"Shh," she said, placing a finger to his perfect lips. "Don't say anything else." Her gaze raked his sexy body with a hungry frown. "Otherwise my common sense might overtake me again and I'll change my mind."

Nibo arched a brow at that. And his breathing intensified as she reached out and ran her hand over his chest, across his own taut nipple, dragging her nails ever so gently over his tunic.

Damn . . . that couldn't be any more erotic had she been touching his bare flesh, and it made him so hard he swore he could drive nails with his cock.

A thousand chills erupted through him as his body burned from the inside out.

She moved her hand from his lips so that she could loosen the collar of his shirt to expose his chest to her warm hand. He sucked his breath in sharply as he watched her dip her head so that she could draw his nipple into her mouth and suckle him ever so tenderly.

He moaned from the pleasure her lips and tongue gave him. God, it'd been so long since she touched him with this amount of care and tenderness.

And it made him weak for her, especially when she leaned him back on the bed so that she could slowly, torturously trail her hand down between their bodies and dip it beneath the waistband of his breeches until she cupped him in her hand.

Dizzy and on fire, he was past the point of any kind of rational thought. The only thing in the world to him was this woman and the need he had to sate the deep hunger that had gnawed at him incessantly since the moment he'd seen her defying him on that dark beach the night they'd first met.

No matter how many times he had her, it wasn't enough. Forget his rum, Vala was what made his head spin and lifted his spirits to the highest level.

Cupping her face in his hands, he met her lips with the whole of his passion. She moaned into his mouth as she continued to stroke his swollen cock with her hand.

With a need born of desperation, he used his powers to melt their clothes from them. He wanted nothing between them, and he was too impatient to waste time peeling her layers of aggravating fabrics from a body he'd been deprived of for far too long.

Valynda shivered as the cold air rushed against her suddenly bare body. She feared she might faint as her head swam from the taste of him and the blood rush, from the silken feel of his rigidness under her fingers. There was nothing she loved more than when she had him like this and knew how much power she wielded over him. This was the only time she didn't doubt his loyalty or love for her. When she knew that he'd do anything she asked.

Nibo, who was so powerful and who yielded to no one, whose will was absolute, loved her. At least for this one moment. Here, like this, he was hers and hers alone. She shared him with no one.

She wrapped her arms around his neck and pulled his lips to hers for another long, deep, and satisfying kiss.

Nibo didn't disappoint her as he plundered her mouth like a pirate. She sighed in contentment, and ran her hands down his lean, hard back. Oh, how incredible the man felt.

He tasted even better.

Leaving her mouth, he trailed a scorching kiss to her neck, where he suckled and teased her flesh with his tongue and teeth. Valynda arched her back, writhing in pleasure as his hands skimmed over her body. Down her arms, over her waist so that he cupped her hips in his hands.

As he moved toward her breasts, she stopped him. He looked up with a frown.

"Not this day, my sweet, precious loa. You are *my* cheval." She rolled him onto his back and straddled his waist.

Nibo stared up in awe of her as he felt her hairs gently teasing his belly.

Her smile grew wider. She dipped her head toward his and instead of giving him the kiss he expected, she lowered her mouth to his throat. Nibo groaned at the heat of her mouth as she seared him. Her tongue darted over the whiskers of his neck, teasing and tormenting him with wave after wave of pleasure.

She leaned forward so that her breasts were flattened against his chest.

"Sweet Vala," he breathed, running his hands over the smooth, pale skin of her back.

And then she moved her mouth lower. Slowly, thoroughly, she covered his chest and arms with her scorching kisses. Her breasts pounded against him, flaying his chest with pleasure, as her hands explored every inch of his skin.

He couldn't remember a woman ever being quite so bold. One who seemed to derive her own pleasure from giving it to him. It was incredible.

Valynda savored the sounds of Xuri's pleasure filling her ears. Wanting to hear him screaming in ecstasy, she dipped her mouth to the flesh of his hipbone.

He sucked his breath in sharply between his teeth as he quivered beneath her. She laughed deep as she continued her relentless exploration of him.

Nibo buried his hand in her thick, dark hair as he fought the urge to roll her over and take control. He would have his chance to fill her shortly. For the moment, he would content himself with letting her have her way.

But it was hard. And getting harder by the minute. It wasn't in his nature to be passive.

However, when she moved her hand again to cup and stroke him, and then lowered her head to take him fully into her mouth, he was grateful beyond belief for his patience.

Nibo growled out loud as he sank his hand in her hair and trembled from the weight of pleasure that invaded every part of him. More than that, he shook all over as her tongue toyed with his body.

His breathing ragged, he let her lick and tease until he couldn't stand it anymore.

Valynda looked up as Nibo shifted his body.

He flashed a charming smile as he stretched out beside her with his head toward her feet. Then he positioned his hips even with her head.

"Don't stop," he said, his eyes warm and wicked.

Before she could respond, he nudged her thighs apart and buried his lips against the center part of her body.

She closed her eyes and moaned at the feel of his tongue delving deep inside her.

Oh, it was incredulous. She'd forgotten just how talented he was in this department. Though how . . . she couldn't imagine. After all, this was what he was famed for. Needing to feel more of his touch, she opened her legs wider.

She bit her lip in ecstasy, then returned to the tender ministrations she had been giving him.

Nibo's head spun as he again felt her mouth and tongue close around him. He cupped her hips to him as he ran his tongue over her and felt her quiver in his arms.

She was delightful. But then, she'd always been that way. Even before he'd ever touched her, he'd sensed how passionate she was. It'd shown in everything about her. No woman possessed her amount of spirit without it.

Valynda moved to playfully nip at his hipbone. The heat of his mouth seared her as he teased and suckled. And even more incredible was the feel of his fingers plunging inside her. In and out and around. Her body quivered and jerked as her head reeled from the sensations.

She closed her eyes. It was too much for her. And just as she was sure she would die from it, her body exploded.

Grateful, Valynda threw her head back and screamed in release as the world spiraled and careened.

And still his tongue tormented her.

"Xuri," she sighed.

He laughed almost evilly as he kissed her thigh. "I'm not through with you yet." That was a tone of warning and yet somehow it remained playful.

He rose up between her legs and positioned his body over her. Valynda reached up and buried her hands in those irresistible curls as he used his knees to spread her legs wider.

He brought his lips down upon hers, then plunged himself deep inside.

She groaned out loud and dug her nails into his back.

He leaned back ever so slightly and reached his hand down between their bodies until he found her nub so that he could heighten the pleasure even more.

Instinctively, she rubbed herself against him, impaling herself even more deeply than before.

"Aye, *ma petite*." He closed his eyes to savor the warm, tight heat of her body around his. "That's it."

His breathing ragged, he let her take control of the moment as she milked his body with hers. Never had he felt the like. He was more than happy to be her cheval and to let her ride him for as long as she wanted.

Opening his eyes, he saw the look of wonder on her face. Aye, she liked being in charge.

Ever one to please her, he rolled over without withdrawing from her.

Valynda groaned as she found herself on top of him. She stared in awe of him and the sensation of his body inside hers and between her legs.

His eyes dark and gentle, he reached up and cupped her breasts in his hands. She covered his hands with her own, then lifted her body up, drawing herself down his cock.

"Aye," he breathed. "That's it. Faster."

And then his hand returned to cup her between her legs as she rode him hard and fast.

And this time when she came, he joined her.

Sated and exhausted, Valynda stretched out on his chest and simply enjoyed feeling his arms around her as his breath stirred her hair.

Nibo leaned his head back, shaken by what had occurred

between them. Aye, she was indeed his precious firebrand, and he would never grow tired of her passion.

Never would he be sated.

If anything, he wanted her more than he ever had before. His Vala truly had no equal.

And that had always been their problem.

Valynda lifted her head to look down at him. "Is something wrong?" She drew her brows together into a deep V.

"Nay." He ran his hands over her back, savoring the softness of that beautiful skin he'd missed so much while she'd been cursed. It wasn't really a lie.

In truth, things had never been more right.

And likewise, they'd never been more wrong.

Because now that she was intact again, they could both be punished in ways that had made all the others seem like mild bruises.

How could he save her? Why did relationships have to be so damn complicated?

Vala scowled as she gingerly touched his crook. For the first time ever, he didn't flinch or react. He actually allowed her to take it into her hand and toy with it while it lay in the shape of a small necklace in the hollow of his throat. His only reaction was to watch her with a hooded, peaceful smile as he tangled his fingers in her hair. "Why is this so important?"

"How do you mean?"

"The Malachai wanted me to steal it from you."

He went cold at those words and she saw the heat in his eyes as they widened. Still, he didn't pull away, but he was tense now, and on alert. His suspicion permeated the air around them both. "Pardon?"

"You heard me. I want to know why it's so important to him."

"And I want to know if you're still planning to steal it."

She leaned down to press her nose against his. "I should."

He arched a brow at that.

Valynda pressed her hand flat to his neck, cradled it, and smiled, then kissed him. "Relax, my precious. Had I planned to take it, I would have done so and not said anything about it."

Nibo relaxed and snorted. Saddest part? She was the one person in the universe who could have done so and gotten away with it. "Why didn't you?"

Valynda sighed as she nipped his lips with her teeth. "Honestly? I had planned to. The thought was right there when I saw it." She traced the outline of the staff. "But as much as I'd like to think otherwise, I'm not that big a wanker. I could never cause you pain, Xuri. No matter what the Malachai or anyone else promised me. You mean more to me than that." Tears filled her eyes. "You mean more to me than my own body, and I hate you for that most of all."

Cupping her hand in his, he led it to his lips so that he could kiss her fingers, then nibble her knuckles. "The reason why everyone is after me crook, love, it can bring back the dead."

She was glad she was sitting down. "It does what?"

"Brings back the dead."

That went over her like an icy wave as she glared at him. "You could have brought me back?"

He followed her as she pulled away from. "Nay, Vala, it's not what you're thinking. Don't be mad at me." Nibo gently grabbed her arms to keep her by his side. "Your body was gone, *mon ange*. Its powers wouldn't have worked in your case. Believe me. I wouldn't have hesitated to use it for you if I could have. It's why they made sure you had no body left."

Those words chased themselves around her head as she realized exactly the sinister game they'd played with him. The bastards had cruelly marked them both. "Sorry."

With a pained expression, he brushed the hair back from her forehead. "You've got to stop looking for my betrayal at every turn. Trust me, I know it's hard. I'm the one what got binged by me own brother the minute I turned my back on the feckless bastard. But we're not all here to hurt you, and God knows I would never. Having tasted such unwarranted cruelty, I'm the last one who would do that to anyone, especially you."

She leaned against him and nodded.

Nibo closed his eyes as he felt her shivering in his arms. He knew how bad it felt to have the betrayal she'd known. That piece of the heart that never fully healed because it wanted to keep its soul from ever being hurt so badly again. There was nothing worse than to let another person in and to know that they were so cold and unfeeling as to come after you when you'd done nothing to them to cause their betrayal. When you'd loved them and cherished them, and they'd repaid your love with selfish cruelty and calamity.

Especially when they were your family. He'd experienced it with Qeenan and she'd been betrayed by her parents. As bad as it was when friends turned against you, blood should be thicker than that. Family ties should mean more.

They should never be broken.

Once severed, it was so much harder to ever put faith in anything or anyone again. He knew that better than anyone. Because when those were the ones who'd come for your throat, you had no belief in anyone else ever again. How could you?

Trust was hard. Treachery seemed to be too easy for most. How could he make her understand that he was different?

"I will never hurt you, Vala." He just wished that she could believe that. But words were so easy to speak.

And so few people actually followed through on such promises.

He knew that, too. Half his job as a psychopomp was escorting those who'd been killed by those who were supposed to love and protect them forever.

And in the back of his mind, he carried his own doubt. Especially given that she'd just admitted to him that she'd been harboring traitorous thoughts against him. It made it so much harder now to believe in her. Would she be like Qeenan and club him when he turned his back?

Damn. Now that she'd stirred his fears, he wasn't sure if or when he'd ever be able to lay them aside again. Too much betrayal lay in his own past. Too much hurt.

Too much hate.

It was why he lived the way he did. Superficially. Let no one in. Keep everything at a distance. It was easy not to care when you didn't.

Damn him and damn his heart that was far too entangled with her now for his liking.

Her eyes were dark and shiny as she looked up and met his gaze. "How well do you know Thorn?"

That hit him like a fist to his gut. Why was she asking that? Was he planning treachery, too? Or was it something even more sinister?

His stomach cramped at an even worse thought. "Beg pardon?"

"I need to know if I can trust him."

Still not placated by that, he frowned at her. "Vala . . . word of advice, never talk to a man about another one when you're naked in his arms. We don't like that."

She playfully tugged at his curls. "Stop! I'm not interested in him and you know it. I just want to know if he'll do what he said."

Grinning, he kissed her, relieved that it really was what she wanted to know. "Aye, he's as good to his word as any." He scowled at her. "What's this about that has you so upset?"

The teasing died instantly beneath a wave of fret. She dropped her hand to his chest, where she toyed with his necklaces. In particular, she picked up the cross she'd given him so long ago and stroked it between her thumb and forefinger. "Do you think he can release Circe's son?"

"I don't know. Agrios's hubris was extreme. But if you want, we can lend a hand."

Her eyes lit up. "What?"

"I make no promises. It's not my realm and I hold no real negotiating power, but we can try. Being what I am, I can get to him and at least see if there's something we can do."

"You would do that?"

"Vala . . . for you, I would do anything."

"Then why didn't you offer earlier?"

"We were attacked and then we were naked."

"Nibo!"

"What?" he asked innocently. "I was going to tell you. As I said, I can make no promises. This is more Thorn's territory than mine. I drop souls off at such places. Getting them out is not something I ever thought about doing. I've never made such an attempt and have no idea how to really go about it. But for you, *mon ange,* I'll risk angering the great powers of the universe."

Those words made her heart sing.

And he proved them as soon as they were dressed. She watched as he used his powers to paint his face in the loa style so that it bore a skull over his features, and his loose-fitting island clothes changed to his trademark dandy fashion of an ornate black overcoat with a purple sash and shirt. Skulls and crossbones bedecked his black-and-silver tricorne that he wore over a long purple headscarf trimmed with silver coins.

He looked dashing.

Dangerous. Mysterious and haunting. One glance and it was obvious he was a creature born of ethereal things. A man who walked between realms and who feared nothing and no one. While she knew his kindness, he was renowned for his vicious lethality that could come out whenever he sensed someone was in the wrong. He hated injustice and was highly protective of those who fell under his protection. His temper was legendary, and she'd seen him lash out at his own companions at times. Especially if he was in his cups.

Oddly enough, he seldom drank around her. Maybe a few sips, but never to excess. Until now, she'd never given much thought about that.

And that made her smile, for Xuri wasn't known for his restraint. "Why is it you never drink around me?"

He paused checking his pockets to stare at her. A slow, charming grin spread across his face. "Don't you know?"

She shook her head.

Wrinkling his nose, he walked into her arms and kissed her. "Who needs rum when you already make my head spin, *chère*?"

Aye, he was a sexy, incredible beast. Especially when he held her like this and she could feel every inch of his body pressed against hers.

"You are far too charming." She tugged at his feathers.

He flashed a devilish smile. "That I am."

Then he dressed her in a dark burgundy gown with an outrageous feathered headpiece that held a ship in the center, where it appeared to be sailing in a storm of swirling silver-and-black feathers with pearl accents. Using his powers, he painted her face and teased her hair into a bold hedgehog style, with thick curls that fell to her waist.

She smiled at him. "You are ever an outrageous dandy."

"Life is not for the meek, *mon amour*. And neither is fashion. Both always favor the bold. When you enter a room, you should turn heads, not stomachs."

"I don't know. Sometimes restraint is the better form of valor."

"Not when you're going to war. What better place is there to clash and be loud?"

He had a point. They were certainly loud. There was no denying that.

She liked it. "So where are we going?"

His grin turned roguish as he tucked his skeletal cane beneath his arm and pulled on a pair of black gloves. "You know I try to take you to the best places, *chère*. We're going to hell without a handbasket."

And with that, he took her not only to the hell he'd promised, but straight into the lowest, darkest pit of it, where only the most tortured of souls were sent.

14

Valynda glanced around as they emerged from the darkness into a rather pleasant field. "This doesn't look so bad." Especially when compared to the hell realm where she'd been tortured and that Thorn had rescued her from. This one was bright and cheery, point of fact. Children ran about, singing and dancing, chasing each other. Granted, off-key, but still it was a nice, pleasant day.

How could this be anyone's hell?

Nibo snorted. "One man's trash is another's rose."

No sooner had he spoken than she heard the agonized scream of someone in the throes of absolute misery.

The sound sent a chill down her spine and brought her up short. "What the devil is that?"

"What the devil, indeed." He grinned at her as he turned around and spread his arms wide. With true psychopomp flare, he walked backward toward the noise.

More curious than she wanted to admit, she followed after him. What could be going on to cause someone to lament this heavenly place in such a manner? 'Twas obvious the screaming person was in agony. But she couldn't imagine why.

Until she saw it.

Then she was even more befuddled by a sight that made no sense whatsoever. Before them stood a man almost seven feet in height. With blond curls and a face that had been carved to perfection, he wore the ancient battle armor of a Greek god and was covered in . . .

Baby vomit.

And children. A lot of children, who clung to him and climbed on him and did everything they could to get his attention.

Well, on second thought, she could see where that might be rather horrifying, after all. Come to think of it, she'd probably start screaming too.

There were a lot of cloying children. And they weren't exactly in a pristine, unleaking condition. Indeed, they seemed to be having an excess of mucus. Even for small children.

"Sing to me!"

"I need food!"

"Help! Help! I needs go potty!"

There were dozens of children around him, all vying for his attention as they tugged on him. Several pummeled him with their small fists and one . . .

One bit his shin.

"Damn you! Get off me!" He tried to escape them, but they were after him with a tenacity that was as impressive as it was terrifying.

A little angelic girl tripped him, and the moment he was on the ground, the children swarmed him like ants running over a sweetmeat.

"Give me a story! Give me! Give me!"

Another began bouncing on his belly and clapping her hands. "More bounce! More bounce!"

"By Hera's hairy armpits, get off me, you little demonspawn brats!" He screamed even louder as a boy bit his thigh and a girl clamped down on his wrist.

"Oh," Valynda said slowly. "I see."

Nibo chuckled. "Now you know why I'm so glad we don't have a hell in Vilokan." A shadow passed over his face. "Then again, living a mortal life is its own form of torture. Reincarnation back into mortality is as bad a punishment as any hell ever conceived by any god."

He had a point there. One she didn't want to think about.

Cupping his hand around his mouth, Nibo gave a shout. "Agrios!"

He froze, then turned toward them. "Help! For the love of Zeus, help me!"

"Not for the love of Zeus, but . . ." Xuri pulled out his crook and enlarged it. "Demons, demons all around. Careful whose joy you come to drown. Day in and day without, you will learn not to strike out." And with that, he struck the ground.

A shock wave ran over them and sent the "children" flying in all directions. They spun and hissed like a glaring of wild cats. Some even arched their backs.

"Nibo!" One of the larger children bared a mouth full of razor-sharp, serrated teeth.

"You don't belong!"

"What are you doing here?"

"Well, it wasn't for the company, that's for sure." He held the end of his crook out toward Agrios, who gratefully seized it and allowed Nibo to help him to his feet.

"I'm hoping you're more friend than foe."

"To you. For the moment." Nibo cast his gaze around at the others as they nipped and clawed at Agrios, who kicked them back. "Really? Your personal hell is children? Out of all the things you could have picked in the world that are terrifying, you fear small children?"

Agrios passed him a stare that not only questioned his parentage, but also his sanity. "You ever been around any? Not only do they smell, they drool. Some part of them is forever leaking some kind of disgusting gelatinous goo. They ask too many questions that are none of their business. Have no tact. Eat things that make you shudder. Have no sense of boundaries. And the selfish little bastards take you for granted and stab you in the heart when you least expect it."

Nibo arched one eyebrow at his acrimony. "That pretty much summarizes every adult I've ever met, too, and most of my family. As well as my relationship with them. And they're not nearly as cute."

By the expression on the warrior's face, Valynda could tell he'd never thought of that. And Nibo was right. That had proven true in her case as well.

In particular, certain members of the *Sea Witch* fit that category. Not so much the stabbing in the heart, but the drooling . . .

Well, she didn't want to think about that, as most of them, including herself, had been known to do that whenever some of the men came around. Especially when they took their shirts off.

She cast a sheepish glance toward Xuri and felt heat scald her cheeks. It was probably best not to have those thoughts too close to Nibo, who would definitely be offended if he knew.

Squelching the sudden need to whistle innocently, she diverted her gaze.

Another demon came running for them. Nibo caught him with his crook and batted him away.

Valynda was impressed. "So, how are we going to get him out of here?"

Nibo sighed. "Well, a psychopomp led him in . . ."

"You should be able to lead him out."

"That's one theory."

She didn't like where this was heading, and a bad feeling went through her. "You didn't think this through, did you?"

There it was . . . that adorable grin that came with bad, gut-wrenching timing. "You always said that was my weakness."

Aye, she did. Valynda ground her teeth. "I swear, Xuri . . ." He got himself into more disasters by his failure to look ahead. "So, what was your plan, then?"

"Beg. Plead." He winked at her. "Beat the shite out of whatever comes at us."

"Thought you weren't a warrior," she teased. Because she knew better.

"There are times when we all surprise ourselves with what's inside us. Today, I'm more akin to Sallie with me warrior's soul in a bottle that's been uncorked." He slapped Agrios on the shoulder. "Come, good Greek, let's see about getting you home, shall we?"

That made him pause. He appeared stunned, as if he'd heard a promise too good to be believed. "Home?"

Nibo nodded. "Your mother bid us to fetch you to her."

"My mother? Circe?" He spit on the ground and cursed violently. "She's the one who got me cursed here. Why ever would I want to rejoin her anywhere?"

Well there was something neither of them had foreseen. "I beg your pardon?" Valynda looked from Agrios to Nibo and back again.

"Beg all you want. It changes nothing. I don't want to be anywhere near my mother. Ever. She can rot in all of Tartarus for all I care."

"Fair enough." Nibo whistled for the demons. "Here you go, kids. *Bon appetit.*"

Panicking, Agrios looked about and appeared as if he were about to climb someone's leg. "What are you doing?"

"It's us or them, mate. Choose your hell."

Valynda gasped as she finally saw the demonic incarnation of Nibo. No wonder the damned screamed in terror. His skin held a translucent quality that let her see the sinew and muscles beneath. It was macabre and yet strangely beautiful. Monstrously intriguing.

An aura of lethal power permeated the air around him.

Agrios staggered back as the demons surged.

"Playtime!"

"I need to potty!"

"Feed me!"

"Call them off!" Agrios screamed. "For the love of the gods! I'll go! I swear. Just please, send them back to wherever!"

Valynda had to stifle a laugh. Honestly, given the horrifying things they'd encountered, she rather liked these. They looked much more cuddly and cute.

Without thinking, she reached out toward one. Its eyes widened before it opened its ravenous mouth and lunged for her.

Gasping, Valynda smacked the demon on the nose. It bit her forearm.

"You little bastage! How dare you! And here I thought you adorable!"

"You're going to die! All of you!"

"I'm already dead." Frustrated, she felt a peculiar surge within her. One she couldn't explain. The next thing she knew, a bolt of lightning shot from her hands and blasted the demon back.

Both Nibo and Agrios turned to gape at her.

"What did you do?"

She shrugged at Nibo. "No idea. I've never done that before." Amazed, she stared at her hands as if they belonged to a stranger.

As did Nibo. He took them each into his own so that he could study them. Then, he kissed her palm. "We will marvel over this later. For now . . ."

"We need to go before we're eaten."

He winked at her.

This time, Agrios didn't argue. He followed along like a dutiful pup as they made their way through the dark, murky depths of a hell realm where the souls of the damned echoed.

Valynda scowled. "Where are we?"

"Tartarus."

They approached a river made of fire. One that crawled with giant slithering snakes. "Now *that* is what you should have feared." Valynda shivered at the sight of it.

"And spiders," Nibo added.

Valynda drew up short as they turned a corner and found a giant spider's web. "Nay . . ." she breathed as her heart lodged itself in her throat to choke her. There was something you didn't see every day.

Nibo cursed. "Forgot where I was."

"How so?"

Agrios sighed. "You say your fear . . ." He gestured at the web. "You manifest it."

Beautiful. Leave it to Nibo to pick such a lovely terror.

"Spiders?" she asked. Of all the things in the universe to fear, she'd have never put that one on his list.

Nibo gave her a sheepish grin.

The web around them began to shake.

So did her legs. Especially when she could hear the horrendous sound of the arachnid moving from somewhere in the darkness, out of sight, and judging from the echoing clacking and clamor, it wasn't just one great big spider.

It came with friends.

And neighbors.

Probably a few of their friends and family. And some distant relatives.

"Damn you, Nibo!" Valynda pulled out her sword. "Why couldn't you pick a better fear. Like butterflies?"

Agrios grabbed his sword as well.

With a fierce grimace, Nibo chose his throwing daggers.

"Harm one of them and you'll never leave this place. And given that you're all three dead, you might not anyway. But violate the laws here and it will be a certainty that you will become a permanent resident in our merry home."

They turned in unison to find a shadow speaking to them. One Valynda had seen before but didn't know. Not much taller than her, he had eyes that were a peculiar shade of grayish blue and hair pulled back into a neat queue that was neither dark nor light. Rather, it was a mixture of the two, like two kinds of straw bundled together to make a unique shade.

Well built and every bit as handsome as Nibo, there was something about him innately powerful. Innately sexual and cold. She would call him a demon, and yet there seemed something more to him than just their cruelty. While she had no doubt he could be as lethal as any and do whatever it was he needed to, something about him said that he wouldn't relish the vile deed.

Nay, this creature had a conscience.

And it ran as deep as the searing intelligence that burned in those unique eyes.

Most peculiar of all was his overcoat that was made completely of leather, with high brass buttons and a high collar. Unlike the dandies who preferred billowing lace, he wore a plain black tunic that was open at the neck, with tight black breeches and boots.

Aye, he was dangerous. The kind that made the hairs on the nape of one's neck stand up and sent a chill down the spine. She had no doubt he'd left a trail of bodies in his wake.

Along with an untold number of broken hearts of women who couldn't claim this one as their own.

"What are you doing here, Shadow? This isn't your realm."

His features softened into a teasing, roguish grin. "*Au contraire, mon frère.* My domain is anywhere the daylight and moonlight don't reach. That nebulous nothing in between." He moved to stand beside Valynda, which caused the spiders to back up as if they feared him. "You're the ones who don't belong here. Not I."

Nibo narrowed his gaze on the creatures. "Why are they afraid of you?"

"Not afraid. *Respectful.*"

Nibo snorted. "What? Did you eat their leader for dinner?"

"Breakfast." He flashed a debonair and charming grin at Valynda. "Now I'm looking for a tasty morsel for dessert."

A sword point appeared at Shadow's throat, forcing him back

from her as all humor left Nibo. "Well, you won't be having none of that, mate."

With an amused glint in his steely eyes, Shadow tsked at Nibo's sudden distemper and knocked the blade away with his bare hand. "Duly noted, and you can relax, old man. I was only teasing." He jerked his chin toward something past their shoulders. "That was the morsel I came here for. And the dessert I was speaking of, anyway."

Valynda turned to see an incredibly attractive goddess approaching them.

"You're late," she chastised Shadow. With ebony spiraling locks and a body made for long hours in a bedroom, the statuesque beauty commanded attention. And without meaning to, the goddess of blessed death made Valynda feel like a Kewpie doll. Not because the goddess was trying to, but because she was just that stunning and physically perfect.

In fact, Valynda had to fight the urge to go hide.

"Sorry, love. Had to stop and help out my friends. Besides, you know I've never been one to pay close attention to punctuality."

Sheathing his sword, Nibo shook his head. "Damn, boy, you do have giant, whopping bullocks. Makaria? Seriously? Have you lost every bit of your sanity?"

Unrepentant, Shadow shrugged as he went past them to approach the goddess who didn't walk, she glided with grace and beauty. Which made sense given that she was the psychopomp in charge of caring for those who'd lived long, gentle lives and died peacefully in their sleep.

Shadow lifted the goddess's pinkie. "What's Hades going to

do to me that hasn't already been done? Besides, Maka has him wrapped around her most beautiful little finger." He kissed her hand, then her cheek as she preened from his praise.

"Does she now?" Nibo challenged.

Valynda cleared her throat to politely get her favorite psychopomp's attention off the much more beautiful woman before she completely escaped everyone's memory. "Might I ask how it is that you seem to know her?" she asked Nibo quite pointedly.

He laughed. "Rest your jealousy, *mon ange*. She's a psychopomp. I'm a psychopomp. Our paths have crossed a few times over the centuries as we've collected our souls, here and there."

That made sense, she supposed.

Makaria inclined her head to Valynda. "Indeed, we've even fought over a few."

There was something she'd never thought about before. "How so?"

"Territory. Who owns whom. Where they need to go." This time there was no friendliness in Nibo's tone. "Makaria is in charge of those Greeks who die peacefully."

That much she'd known, so how the two of them would be in conflict over the dead made no sense to her. "Yet you're in charge of those who die violently. I should think you'd never be confused by the two."

"Aye, but there are those who are murdered by poison and other means where they seem to pass peacefully in their sleep, and yet didn't. In which case, we sometimes argue as to dominion. Especially if the person is in denial and doesn't want vengeance on the one who killed them."

That made sense. But it left Valynda with one question. "Who wins when that happens?"

Makaria stepped forward and gave a smile that was sweet and bone-chilling. "The one most determined."

A shiver went down her spine at the way the goddess spoke, as she had a feeling that she wasn't just talking about the souls anymore.

With her skin glowing from an ethereal light, Makaria glanced from Nibo to Shadow to Agrios. "I assume since you're here that you wish to take this soul from my father's lands?"

Nibo's smile turned charming. "You'd be correct, and I was hoping you'd be understanding. Even cooperative."

The spiders skittered away as if the mere mention of such a thing terrified them.

"Well, that can't be good," Valynda said under her breath.

Shadow let out a low, evil laugh. "Fear not. Makaria won't let anything happen to Nibo . . . at least."

Oh, like there was nothing sinister in *that*. In fact, those words made her stomach knot up and sink south toward her feet.

Xuri, however, didn't appear the least bit intimidated. "Or to what Nibo cherishes," he said pointedly, taking Valynda's hand and pulling her closer to his side. Grateful, she wrapped her arms around his muscular biceps and let his warmth soothe her. "Which means all three of us need to leave here intact. No tricks."

Makaria considered that. "And what will you offer my father for such a service?"

Nibo cast his gaze about the stalagmites and shrugged. "I'd offer him doom and gloom, but he seems to have that aplenty."

With a withering stare, Makaria was much less amused by that than Valynda. "My father's normal price for such is a soul for a soul."

Valynda gasped as she realized Circe's game. *That* was why she'd made her human. So that she could take her son's place here.

That conniving bitch!

"Nay," Makaria said as if she heard Valynda's thoughts. "Not you, little one. Your soul is already spoken for by others." She held up Valynda's wrist to show her the Deadman mark that made her a member of Captain Bane's crew. "My father will have no use for you."

"Don't look at me. I have no soul whatsoever."

Makaria laughed at Shadow. "Not true, either, my precious demonspawn. But yours is so dark that my father would rather not chance you trying to take over his domain."

Shadow scoffed. "No fear there. I deal with enough dead assholes. Have no use for more."

Nibo ignored his comment as he kept the goddess on point. "Then where does that leave us?"

Makaria shrugged. "Trapped here, apparently."

"Not the rules, Makie." Nibo leaned against his staff with a flourish. He glanced to Valynda and a strange light came into his eyes before he spoke again. "Give me until the full moon and I'll send him a soul."

A light of suspicion turned her dark eyes even darker. "No trickery?"

"None."

"Very well. You have it then. But don't forget or else there will be dire consequences indeed." She vanished.

Folding his arms across his chest, Shadow sighed. "She forgot to warn you about getting out of here."

"Don't look back?" Nibo asked flippantly.

He inclined his head respectfully at Nibo. "Good, you know." He pointed to his left. "Door's that way."

Nibo held his arm out to him. "Thank you."

"I would say it's a pleasure, but I'm off to have that now. Stay safe."

Valynda shook her head at his hasty departure. "He's such a peculiar beast."

"That he is. And if you think he's odd, you should meet his brother."

Agrios kept eyeing the spiderwebs as if waiting for one of the spiders to come and get him. "Can I really go?"

"We're about to find out." Nibo gestured toward the direction Shadow had shown them.

Valynda led the way. "Have you known Shadow long?"

"Long enough."

"For what?"

"To know not to ever fully trust him."

That seemed odd given that he'd helped them without question. "How so?"

"He's the son of Azura."

She stumbled at the last thing she'd ever expected him to say. Dear Lord! Had she really been that close to the spawn of all evil? Could the Queen of All Shadows really have a child? "What?"

"Aye. At one time, he was her lead general and the right hand of Noir. Hence why they call him the Prince of Shadows."

Her jaw dropped. "But he's no longer on their side?"

"That is the question, isn't it? Shadow is a nebulous little bastard, which makes him hard to trust. Especially when one of the reasons he was so quick to kill in the past was his ironclad belief that it's all right to slaughter the innocent, since so many who profess good too often practice evil in its name."

"He's not wrong," Agrios groused.

"No, but it's a slippery slope. Once you begin to justify something, there's no end to it. And when we justify bad behavior as something our innocent victims deserve when we know in our hearts they don't . . . that is when we're truly damned." He paused to look at Valynda. "Can you imagine a world where people tried to help each other up, not kick each other down?"

Nay, she could not. Because she'd been one of those innocents who'd been kicked repeatedly for no reason at all. By far too many.

Nibo shook his head. "As much as it pains me, I have to admit to how sage that little prick is."

"How so?"

"He's also the one who said that we are never punished for the sins we commit, but rather by them."

Valynda flinched at the truth of that statement. "Ouch!"

"Indeed."

And that made her wonder just what had happened in Shadow's past that had made him learn such harsh lessons. That kind of wisdom came with a price. One she wished she'd never been forced to pay.

But then he was the son of Azura.

She could only imagine how much worse his past must have

been. Pity that life was ever so harsh. For everyone who walked it. She only hoped that Shadow found some sort of solace.

Just as she prayed that Nibo and Circe didn't betray her. But it was hard to have faith. Hard to believe in others when so many lashed out.

Which made her curious as to another matter.

"What of this soul you plan to send back?"

Nibo hesitated. "Pardon?"

"Whose soul will you send here to replace Agrios's?"

He turned sheepish as they walked. "Was rather hoping you wouldn't ask."

Her stomach drew tight as fear choked her. "Meaning?"

"Don't get that tone. I'm not going to offer up you. You heard what she said."

Mayhap not, but some would be worse than her. "One of my friends?"

"I don't think so."

"Don't think so?"

He paused to look at her. "I haven't quite figured it out yet."

Failure to think ahead . . . "Xuri!"

He held his hands up in surrender. "What do you want from me, Vala? A lie?"

At the moment? Sort of. Honestly, she wasn't sure, but she really didn't like where this was heading, as it was making her a bit sick to her stomach. "So, what? You just randomly pick a soul and cast it down here?"

"Kind of."

"Kind of?"

"Fine, I'll pick an evil one to send in. Would that make you happy?"

She supposed. "Can you do that?"

"I think so."

"You *think*?"

"Pretty sure."

"Xuri!"

Again, he looked a bit helpless. "I told you before, *mon ange,* that I'm on uncharted territory. I'm not Thorn. This isn't what I do. Bringing souls in should be easy, as that's what I usually do, but this isn't my normal route. So I'll try, *n'est-ce pas?*"

Hands on hips, she shook her head. "I'm beginning to not like you so much."

"I'll let you in on a bit of a secret, Vala. Some days, neither do I." He winked at her.

Growling low in her throat, she followed after the men as they continued on until they neared the door and found the exit cut off by a band of winged creatures who were hideous in form. With forked, serpentine tongues, they hissed at them and flicked long, braided tails.

Nibo pulled her back. "Beware. They spit venom that can bind you here. Kill your soul."

His nostrils flared as one of the beasts flew at them. "Hades!" He called out for the ancient being who ruled this domain.

Instead of the Greek god, Qeenan appeared in front of them. "Hello, brother."

"What are you doing here?"

Qeenan shrugged. "Spoiling your day the same way you've sought to spoil mine. Turn about and all that."

Nibo was aghast. "What the hell, man?"

"You couldn't stay out of my business and so I refuse to stay out of yours." Clapping his hands, Qeenan laughed. "Get them!"

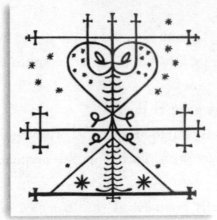

15

"Ever wish you were an only child?"

Nibo gave Valynda a droll stare. "Only every time I get near my brother. I should have drowned that little bastard when we were children in a bath."

Agrios grumbled something behind them.

Nibo pulled a bottle off his belt and slammed it on the ground, shattering it. A dark purple cloud engulfed them.

"For this, we got dressed up." She choked on the smoke.

Ignoring her, he took her elbow and guided her back the way they'd come. He used his crook to grab Agrios to make sure he followed.

"What are we going to do?"

Nibo didn't respond to his question. Turning, he sent a blast at the flying rats after them. Then he pulled another bottle and sent it flying.

Valynda's heart pounded as she struggled to see. She hated this. It was terrifying to hear their pursuers and see nothing. To know they had an enemy out there who wanted them dead.

No sooner had the red mist rolled out than she heard the echoing sound of an outraged god. It shook the walls around them and sent the beasts after them cowering.

Even Qeenan vanished.

But not before the very walls around them turned into giant stone creatures who surrounded them, imprisoning them. They writhed and loomed, rising up to stare down as if intent to trample them into oblivion.

"This isn't good." She stared at Nibo.

"Who dares to breach my domain!"

Valynda froze as lightning shot through Nibo's mists and more thunder shook the room. The screams of the damned went silent as if they were too terrified to draw the ancient god's notice.

Out of the dark, swirling mist emerged a man wearing flowing black robes and walking with the swagger that said he was the sole lord of this land and that no one here had better challenge him.

Though to be honest, she would have thought the ancient Greek god of death would be more . . .

Monstrous.

Hideous.

She was expecting cloven hooves. Some horns.

Honestly, Hades was quite pleasing to the eyes. Other than the fact he was furious at them.

"Not another one of *you*. Do I need to send out for pest control? Or just find out who left the door open and gut them?"

Nibo tsked. "Hades . . . how have you been?"

"It's late summer. Need I say more?"

Valynda winced at words that meant the god had been without sex and his wife for months now. Which put him in an obviously bad mood and them at a great disadvantage.

Nibo flashed him a charming grin. "Well, you're not me type."

Hades crossed his arms over his chest. "Really? You're going to piss me off more? You think that's a wise move to make?"

"Can't seem to help myself."

"You should try."

"Why, when this is so much fun?"

Hades blasted him. "Aye, it is."

Valynda gasped as Nibo was thrown back against the stone creature that held them prisoner. He hit the slab so hard, it was a wonder he hadn't shattered his bones. Blood poured from his nose.

Furious over the god's childish behavior, she glared at him. "That wasn't necessary!"

"You willing to bleed for him?"

"If needs be. Aye. Are you?"

Hades's eyes widened. Then he burst out laughing. "Have you any idea what I could do to you?"

Sadly, she did. And it would most likely hurt. However, it wasn't in her nature to back down or be intimidated.

Even when it was stupid. "But you won't. Last thing you need is me in your own little hell here, leading a rebellion against you, day after day. Year after year."

"You're threatening me?"

Valynda shrugged with a nonchalance she really didn't feel. "Just explaining consequences."

Coughing, Nibo let out a nervous laugh. "She's not jesting. That's me girl, Hades. Believe me, if anyone can lead a rebellion in hell, it's her. You'd be wise to be afraid. The Bondye knows, I am."

He paused to consider it. "I would call you both liars, but Persephone has educated me well on what a woman can do when she sets her mind to something. Truly, it's terrifying. So you're right. I know to be afraid. Sometimes the smallest mouse makes the loudest roar."

Nibo pushed himself to his feet. "And I wasn't breaching your domain. I came to negotiate. It was your daughter who told me I could leave here with Agrios."

"Mel?" he growled. "I don't believe you. And none of my Furies would ever do such a thing."

"Makaria."

Hades rolled his eyes. "Ah, bloody hell. Damn that heart of hers. I'm surprised she hasn't set loose half the souls here for one reason or another." He growled low in his throat. "I'll talk to her later about this." Narrowing his gaze at Agrios, it was obvious he didn't want to honor his daughter's word, and for a moment, Valynda was sure they'd have to battle their way out.

Finally, Hades nodded. "Fine. Take the worthless beast and go."

Nibo inclined his head to him. "Thank you, my lord. And might I ask one more thing?"

Hades arched a dark, irritated brow.

"Makaria said that I'd have to return a soul to you within a month. As I'm not one of your usual messengers, is there someone in particular I should be seeking to fulfill your quota?"

Hades appeared impressed. "Well, at least she remembered that much. I'm surprised it stuck." He passed a speculative look to Agrios, then Nibo. "But this one time, I'll let that pass in lieu of a favor."

Nibo felt his insides shrink with fear at those words. No one ever wanted to be beholden to a god. That never worked out well for anyone. "What kind of favor?"

"No idea. But when I come to you for it, you will remember, and you won't deny me."

Beautiful. That had all kinds of disaster upon it. Yet when Nibo passed a tender look to Valynda, his gut unknotted. Whatever price the god demanded, it would be worth it, and he would pay with a smile on his face. "I will remember."

"Then take your worthless warrior and go."

Hades dissolved all obstacles between them and the stone doorway.

Nibo took her hand and pulled her forward, then grabbed Agrios by his hauberk. "Remember, don't look back."

They headed out.

It wasn't until they were halfway out that Valynda began to understand all the warnings. All around them were the voices of their past. Their loved ones, calling out for them to join them. Insulting them.

Worse, asking for forgiveness.

Pain ripped her apart as she heard her mother's voice for the first time since her death.

"Valynda! I love you. Where are you, my daughter?"

She choked as tears filled her eyes. She wanted to go to her mother in ways she couldn't even begin to explain. But she knew better. As much as she loved her mother, had always wanted her mother to love and approve of her—to praise her—they'd never had that kind of relationship.

Her mother had forever disappointed her. And that burned rawest in the deepest part of her soul. She'd never once put Valynda first, and that had hurt most of all. Valynda had spent her entire life craving that maternal instinct. Wanting, praying that her mother would find some shred of humanity that caused her to reach out and make sure that she was safe against the world.

It'd never come.

Harden yourself.

But it was so difficult. Because deep inside, she was still that little girl who craved her mother's love and approval. Who wanted to see a smile on her mother's face as she wrapped her arms around her and told her how much she meant to her.

"Valynda! Come to me, child!"

It's not real.

Sadly, it could never be real, and had never been. It was only a sick fantasy that she'd tortured herself with when she was young. An image she'd seen from others.

It's not for the likes of you.

Maybe no one had ever really had it.

That was what made her cling all the more to Nibo. He'd been there when no one else had. He had held her when she cried. When her parents had ignored her, he had been there to wipe the tears away. When she needed something, he didn't ask why. He merely gave. Like now.

He was here to ensure that she would maintain her body. No matter what, and he asked nothing in return.

She would never forget that. When everyone else had abandoned her, even her own parents, he had stood by her and protected her.

Yet you sold him out to the Malachai.

Guilt stabbed her heart. How could she have lost sight of what she'd had with him? Of all he'd done for her?

Like this? He hadn't hesitated to walk into hell to help her. How few people would do such a thing?

I've been such a fool.

He was her strength. The better part of her world. *And I will never forget it again.*

Never again would she let anyone in her head to turn her thoughts from him or make her doubt his motives or intentions. Not when his actions spoke so loudly.

People were poison. They sought to destroy what they were jealous of. What they wanted to possess, especially when they didn't have it. It was what had led her to this.

What had made her girlfriends try to come between her and Nibo.

He doesn't love you, Valynda. How could he? He doesn't treat you right.

Their lies had been many as they sought to divide her heart from his.

But she was stronger than that. Just as she knew better than to listen to the voices of the damned trying to lull her to stay in hell with them.

Misery loved company.

"You can wallow on your own!" she called out. "I've better things to do than let you own a piece of my soul." Or her time or thoughts. "Me future's me own."

And they were to have none of it.

With those words shouted out, they suddenly found themselves through the gates of Hades and back in the mortal realm.

Agrios stood by their side with a baffled expression on his face. "I can't believe I'm back!"

"Can't believe it worked." Nibo let go of her hand.

But as he moved away, she caught him and pulled him back to her to kiss him soundly on the lips, grateful beyond belief for what he'd risked.

For her.

When he pulled away, he looked down at her with a frown. "What was that for?"

"Being you, my love. For being wonderful."

"You are me Vala, right? Not some shape-shifter masquerading as my girl?"

She tugged on his curls and feathers. "Don't make me hurt you, Xuri."

"Now there's me threatening *chère*." He kissed her forehead.

Savoring the warmth of his caress, she stepped into his arms and hugged him. "I've never adequately thanked you for all you've done."

"Aye, you have. Every time you look at me like you do right now . . . or like you want to gut me. Sad to say, I relish both."

"Um, people, I hate to break up your tender moment and all, but should I be asking about *that*?"

Valynda pulled away to see what Agrios was talking about. But the moment she could see where he had his attention, she regretted that she'd bothered.

Far off in the distance, there was a black cloud that seemed to be swallowing the sun whole.

"Mother of God, what is that? Is it your brother, too?"

Nibo let out a tired breath. "Nay. That be the Malachai rising. It's his demons."

Agrios ran back to the gate they'd just come through. Only now it was a solid rock wall. He began to pound on it with his fist. "Hades! Let me back in! I love children! I do! They're awesome! Lovable creatures!"

Nibo shoved at him. "Shut it, you big baby. Or else I'll feed you to one."

Still the cloud grew larger. Darker.

More ominous.

Valynda gulped as she felt her own panic rising. "What are we to do?"

Nibo shrugged with a nonchalance she wanted to beat him for. "Judging from the size of that, I'd say we're going to bleed. A lot."

16

Jaden listened as the rumbling of evil grew louder. Stronger. It was absolutely deafening in its zealous squeal. Soon there would be nothing left to hold it back. He knew that better than anyone. His son Xev had just been summoned into action. He could feel it deep inside.

As one of the Malachai's oldest and most powerful generals, Xevikan held a unique essence that was impossible to miss whenever he awakened from his eternal sleep. Not to mention that as a cursed demon-god, Xevikan forever came awake more pissed off than the others, and that resonated through them all. His son still wanted the hearts of all the gods to feast upon for what had been done to his wife.

Especially Jaden's.

I should have stood up for him. There were a lot of things he should have done. But not even he could change the past.

All he could do now was try to save the future. For all of his children. Including Caleb, who was locked into slavery at Adarian's side.

By trying to save them and spare them more harm, he'd failed them all abysmally.

No wonder Savitar stayed on his island in seclusion. It seemed ever the treachery of fate to go out of her way to slap them down every time they tried to help the ones they loved.

"Forgive me," he whispered, knowing that for him, there would never be any such thing. How could there be?

His entire job was to sell people out.

Especially the ones he loved.

"And one day, brother," he sneered at Noir's bedroom door, "I will add you to that list."

And Kadar Noir would be the only one he'd relish doing it to.

For now, he would keep to Cam's plan and they would wear down the Malachai. Weaken him. It was still the best and only plan they had. Neutralize Adarian and the world might survive this.

It had to work. Otherwise . . .

They were all doomed.

Nibo watched as the sky turned as dark as night and the demons boiled out of the ocean. He should probably fight them, but really . . .

Where did one start with a number *that* large? Really. It was so overwhelming, all he could do was stand here and gape.

"You look a bit stunned."

He dropped his gaze to Agrios. "Well, I don't see you jumping in there to take them on, old man. So before you berate me, how's about it then, eh?"

Agrios snorted. "What form of stupid do I appear?"

"The kind that questions the loa who let you out of Tartarus."

Valynda cleared her throat. "Gentlemen, should we not be a bit more focused on the end of the world that's bearing down upon us?"

"I would, but I'm too busy shitting my armor."

Nibo laughed at the Greek's exceptionally dry tone. At least Agrios was honest. And not that he blamed him. He was having his own reservations. The idea of crawling into the nearest crevice and sitting this one out was beginning to appeal to him as well.

But cowardice wasn't his forte.

Stupidity was even less so.

What was left when facing a horde this large?

Tactful retreat? That would be Thorn's answer.

Suddenly, he heard a loud whistle.

Valynda rushed past him toward the sandy beach.

"Rosie!" she shouted, waving her arms over her head. "Oh, thank goodness!"

Nibo dragged his gaze from the swirling demons to see the small rowboat making its way to shore.

Off to the side, way out past the shoreline, the *Sea Witch II* was moored and waiting for them. Leave it to Bane to follow the swirling mass of demons to Death's Door to find them at the gates of Hades.

And Barnet, too, as his ship wasn't far behind.

"I take it they're on our side?"

He nodded at Agrios's question. "While my lady isn't the most circumspect, she doesn't normally rush off to greet her enemies with open arms."

Using his crook to test the shifting surf around his feet, Nibo followed Valynda as she waded out toward her friends. Luckily, the demons were distracted by the ship and began attacking the crews. Thunderous cannon fire rolled out and was punctuated by the screams and curses of the demons as they were struck and fell from the skies.

Which made him wonder where his brother had gotten off to.

Nibo paused to search the sky around them. Agrios rushed past him to climb into the boat. "Where are you, you worthless nithing?" The bastard couldn't be far. It wasn't like him to sit out any fight.

Not for long.

"Nibo?"

He took a deep breath at the sound of Valynda's call. Something about this didn't feel right, and it wasn't just the demon attack on the ships. There was a sinister feel to the air. Something that crawled over his skin like a dead hand.

"Is he all right?"

Valynda paused at Rosie's question as she saw Nibo standing in the water. Her breath caught at the unbelievably sexy image of him there in his tricorne with his curls and feathers, poised so regally while the water lapped against his hips. He was commanding and fierce. His face was painted, and at the same time it didn't detract at all from its unbelievable beauty.

She settled her skirts down and nodded. "He's listening."

"To what?" Hinder asked.

"What we can't hear." She'd seen him do it countless times. Those voices of the dead and damned who told him things. The mysterious language of the ether that floated in the air around the living, unheard, and carried secrets.

After a few seconds more, Nibo blinked and closed the distance between them.

Rosie held his arm out to him to help him into the boat. With a graceful leap, Nibo came aboard and settled himself by her side as more cannons fired.

"Thank you," Nibo said to her crewmates. "Impeccable timing, gentlemen."

"You have the captain to thank there." Rosie sat down to retake his oars.

Valynda watched the fighting. Not even the dragons could drive them off. "How long have the demons been circling?"

Hinder sighed. "Too long. They seem to have taken a liking to us. Wish they'd find another pet to maul."

"I don't like your friends." Agrios eyed them warily.

"Neither do we." Rosie wrinkled his nose. "But they go well with the whole doom-and-gloom atmosphere, don't you think?"

Nibo snorted.

More cannons thundered.

"What's that?"

Nibo glanced off to where Agrios pointed at another ship that was joining the fray. "Not quite sure. Rosie?"

He shrugged.

Valynda couldn't tell either.

It wasn't until they were back on board the *Sea Witch II* that she could finally tell the new ship was Circe's.

With the help of her crew, the three ships and dragons were able to drive the Malachai's demons away.

But there still was no sign of Qeenan. And she could tell that was concerning Nibo by the way he watched the horizon and clutched his crook.

"What do you think your brother's up to?"

He let out a tired sigh. "I wish I knew. Ever have a feeling something is so wrong that nothing is going to make it right?"

"Every day I was in the body of a straw poppet."

He pulled her closer. "Understood."

The two of them fell silent as Circe's ship pulled alongside the *Sea Witch*. Barnet and his men hung back. A tense silence fell over the crew as they watched them cautiously.

Agrios didn't appear much happier.

The pall over all the crews and dragons was tangible and was almost as thick as it'd been while they battled the Malachai's demons.

Circe swung over to the deck of the *Sea Witch*, but instead of rushing toward her son, she approached him slowly, almost cautiously.

Nibo watched the guarded way Agrios met his mother. He'd seen warmer receptions between rabid porcupines.

More affection, too.

Glad I'm not a rabid porcupine.

Or a son of Circe.

Circe passed a cool stare to Nibo. "Thank you for returning him." Her words lacked the gratitude she professed.

Unsure of how to respond to that, Nibo met Valynda's gaze. "Our pleasure." Then he leaned in to whisper in her ear. "But I feel for the boy."

Valynda nodded. She did, too, given this lackluster reunion. She'd expected so much more. Why had his mother been so hellbent on having him back if this was all she wanted from him?

A bad feeling went through her. Was there something more to all this? What could Circe be up to?

Maybe she just wanted a chance to work things out with her son? To fix their broken relationship?

It was too late for her. Her mother was gone and had never had any interest in repairing their shattered hearts. It was a sad lot when a child broke from their parent. Tragic, really, and it still burned in her that she'd cut away from her parents the way she had. But that was on them. She had done nothing to deserve their hatred. And she would never understand how they could have turned on her the way they did.

Perhaps it was the dreamer in her that hoped that maybe, just maybe, they could pull together through this.

It sounded pithy even to her, but she would keep them in her prayers, because she wanted it to work out for them. For someone to have a happy ending. Because that gave her hope that perhaps such things weren't dead.

And hope was something she desperately needed right now.

Circe moved to stand in front of them and held her hand out to Nibo. "I won't forget your kindness."

"What about Valynda's body?"

"It's hers now. But it will still take time for the soul to bind. Until then, she's vulnerable to losing it again. Guard the bottle." And then she and her son were gone.

Valynda hated the sound of that.

Guard the bottle. Great. She glanced over to Sallie and his rugged, weathered face as he grinned at her. It was a terrifying thought that she could lose her soul so easily.

But at least she was whole again.

Thanks to Xuri.

She kissed his cheek. "Have I told you lately how wonderful you are?"

"Not in the last half hour."

She smiled. "Then I've been remiss."

A hungry, dark look entered his eyes. One that was familiar and foreign at the same time. He toyed with the feathers on her headdress. "Me colors and style look good on you."

"Glad you think so."

Bane shook his head at them as he gave orders to weigh anchor and head out.

"Nibo!"

He growled as Masaka popped in behind him with her frantic call. Couldn't he have five minutes without his family interfering?

Well, at least it isn't Qeenan. . . .

Even so it annoyed him. He smirked at her. "I'm a little busy at the moment."

She was having none of it. "Legba needs you."

Nibo gave her a droll stare at the inconvenient timing. "Now?"

Masaka gave them each a peeved glare. "He didn't say to wait, and you know how Papa is."

Nibo stiffened as he caught the note in her voice. Aye, he knew how they all were. Spiteful. Intolerant.

Selfish.

And he was tired of them snapping their fingers and expecting him to come running without question. He wasn't their lapdog, and he'd been doing that since the day he died and they'd taken him in to help others like him cross over and reach their final resting place, or to be reborn.

At first, he'd loved it. Especially guiding others who'd died violently, as he had. To help them understand the myriad of emotions that came with such a horrible passing. Such as betrayal and rage.

But after that came the hurt, the emptiness. That dark place of knowing how little you meant to the world and to the one who'd killed you. Of accepting the fact that others just didn't care and of how little you mattered.

That was what he enjoyed helping them with. Allowing them to find their self-worth again, after it was all over. To get past the betrayal that stayed so long it became its own form of haunting and torture.

So, he'd learned to ignore the others and to play along with them. To focus on what needed to be done and ignore the downside. To let the good outweigh the bad until he'd lost himself to their world. Lost himself to the rum.

That had been easy, because he hadn't cared. As a twin, he'd never really had his own identity anyway. Not really. Not the way other people did. They only saw him as part of something else. Part of a matching set.

He'd never concerned himself with developing his own identity or thinking of his needs above someone else's.

Be a good son. A good twin.

Don't talk back.

And it'd worked, until he'd been clubbed in the back of his head.

Instead of knocking him senseless, it'd knocked sense into him.

He'd spent so much time getting along and going along that he hadn't thought much about anything else.

Everything had been fine until he'd met Valynda. Her rebellious spirit and love for life were infectious. Because of her, he'd wanted more than to be dutiful.

He'd wanted to become the man she saw him as. The hero she needed him to be.

And today, he intended to step up.

Nibo held his hand out to her. "Want to come with?"

Valynda's eyes widened at the unexpected invitation. "Seriously?"

He ignored the shocked gasps and stares of the crew that surrounded them, and in particular the scowl on Bane's face. And the gape on Bane's sister's face. "Time you met them."

Masaka scoffed indignantly. "What are you thinking, man? Have you lost your rum-loving mind? You can't take her with us!"

"Why not?"

"She doesn't belong in Vilokan. No one will welcome her. They'll throw a fit if you bring her there!"

Nibo ignored her anger. He'd never been more sure of anything. "Vala is welcomed wherever I am. And she belongs at me side."

"She's *human*!" Masaka sneered the word as if it were the worst sort of insult. Because to them it was.

Not long ago, he'd have agreed.

But not now. Nibo pulled Valynda to his side. "She's me wife."

Valynda gasped.

So did the crew.

Cursing, Masaka refused to hear it. "Spiritually. And she's not your only one."

The hurt those words wrought on Valynda's face cut through him and made him want to beat Masaka for her cruelty.

"I'll have no disrespect from you." Nibo turned toward Valynda and pulled the ring he'd given her so long ago from her finger, ready to complete the ceremony that he'd begun that night on the beach. "I should have done this a long time ago."

He cupped her chin with his warm fingers and smiled down at

her. "Will you have me, Vala? Faults and all? To keep for yourself, knowing what a surly, selfish bastard I am?"

Valynda was completely stunned by the last thing she expected. "You're not japing?"

"Not about this." He glanced to Bane. "Marry us, Captain?"

"Aye, I will."

Masaka's eyes turned bloodred. "You re-accept that ring, human, and you've no idea what gates will open."

Circe had told her that she needed to make a choice in her life. She didn't want to serve the Malachai and be his general. While the world had never done much for her, she wasn't up to ending it out of simple spite. There was still plenty of good in it.

Still . . .

She glanced to the captain and the other members of the crew, then down to the mark on her arm. "I'm not a free woman, Xuri." She owed them her service until she finished earning back her commitment to Thorn. She had to continue this fight against the Mavromino forces. Not just because of her mark.

Because it was the right thing to do.

Because the Deadmen were her family and she couldn't abandon them.

He inclined his head to her. "We'll worry about that later." That was forever his lackadaisical nature. Take the world in stride.

It had never been hers.

But . . .

Today, she would refuse to look ahead. "Then, aye. I'll have you for every day I'm allowed."

He kissed her, then nipped his own wrist until he drew a bit of blood so that he could coat the silver band in it. Whispering words she couldn't quite understand, he slid the band onto her finger then licked the blood clean. "We are bound together, my Vala. Forever. With this, you can now not only summon me, but cross through the gates between this world and Vilokan."

"Ah, bloody hell!" Masaka threw dirt at both of them, which caused Hinder to give a low whistle and Sancha to suck her breath in sharply. "Have you any idea of what you've done?"

Recalcitrant and unapologetic, he gave her a droll stare that dared her to defy him. "I know."

"You're a fool!"

"Nay. For the first time, I see clearly."

"You see *nothing*." Masaka shook her head. "You've just sold us all out for your human. I hope you're happy!"

"Delirious."

Cursing, she vanished.

Those hate-filled words made Valynda's throat go dry. "Should I be worried?"

"Nay, Vala. Remember, she lives on theatrics. If she's not scaring small children and grown men, she's not happy."

And with that, he carried her through the gate and into the unknown underwater realm of Vilokan.

Stunned and amazed, Valynda drew up short at the perfect island city that glittered like a jewel nestled on rippling turquoise waves.

She wasn't sure what she'd expected, but it definitely hadn't been this treasure. People spoke of paradises. Dreamed of such rich, amazing places. This one actually seemed to be such a realm.

The weather was perfect. The beach a lovely caramel against the most serene seascape. As incredible as Kalder's home had been, it had nothing on this one.

She gaped at Nibo. She didn't understand him at all. "Why would you ever leave this place?"

"Because you weren't here." He gave her a dry stare. "Besides, as with any place, the company here can get a bit stale."

That was sad. Truthfully, she could live forever just watching those perfect waves roll in. In fact, she could imagine the crew of the *Sea Witch* in the harbor here, making jokes and dancing. Kalder in the water, with Cameron yelling down at him to hurry back to her.

She couldn't imagine finding fault with this picture-perfect life.

"Where do you live?"

He pointed to a small rise where a white cottage stood stark against the horizon. "There."

"'Tis beautiful."

"Aye, but it was missing one thing."

"That is?"

He gave her a pointed smirk. "You, *mon ange*."

Those words warmed her, but she didn't believe them for a moment. "You are ever an epic charmer."

"Nibo!" That shout rent the air.

He let out another elongated sigh. "See now why I told you to call me Xuri? 'Tis the only way to get me attention in this godforsaken place, as they wear the other name out."

She stifled a laugh at his put-upon tone.

He let go of her hand and turned toward Papa Legba and two others she didn't recognize as they moved toward them with a gait that said exactly what Masaka had predicted—Valynda wasn't welcome here.

Dressed in purple and with a glare that went straight through her, Papa Legba seemed even more fierce than normal. "What is the meaning of this?"

Nibo took it in stride. "You called for me. I assumed that meant don't dawdle."

"Don't get lippy with me, boy. What is *she* doing here?"

Nibo shrugged nonchalantly as he swept her body with a mischievous grin. "Standing."

The look on Legba's face said that Nibo was one answer away from annihilation.

And Nibo's expression said that he couldn't care less. In fact, he was daring them to do something to remove her. Say something against her.

Valynda held her breath. She'd never seen a standoff quite so impressive. Not even between Kalder and Cameron or the captain and his wife, and those couples had had some extremely impressive ones.

The kind that should be legendary.

For that matter, the captain and his sister. As well as Cameron and her brother.

But even they had nothing on this one.

"We don't let her kind here, and you know that."

Nibo shrugged. "Then you don't need me if you can't accept

me wife." He swept his gaze over the other loas who were drawing near to witness the spectacle. "You've made plenty of accommodations for others. Including Brigitte and the petro. Vala is mine. If she's more than you can handle, then perhaps it's time you assign my duties to another and I find a new pantheon that is more to me tastes. One not so narrow-minded."

Legba arched his brow at the threat. "You know what that would do. What it would cost you."

"Aye. 'Tis a price I'm willing to pay. But are you?"

Valynda couldn't believe what he was doing. For her!

The hair on the back of her neck stood up as she suddenly realized there was a lot more going on than she suspected. What was this?

While she knew that gods could come and go through pantheons, she'd never heard of there being a consequence to it.

However, it must be extreme given the dire expressions around her.

"Are you threatening me, Nibo?"

"I asked a question, Papa. If you no longer wish me to be here, I'll leave."

An elegant, beautiful woman with blond hair and green eyes approached Valynda and hugged her. "Welcome, Vala. I'm Maman Brigitte. It's good to have a new family member." She offered her a dark bottle.

"Brigitte!" That deep, resonate tone echoed around them like thunder.

Yet it didn't faze the beautiful loa whose pale skin glowed like iridescent pearl. She merely passed it off with a wave of her hand. "Stop, Samedi. We don't want to lose Nibo over such a trifling thing. If she makes him happy, what's the harm?"

"She has no powers! She doesn't belong here!"

Brigitte rolled her eyes. "Is that all that concerns you?"

Several of the loas grumbled answers.

She looked over at Nibo. "So, you love her?"

"Aye, Maman."

She met Valynda's gaze. "And you?"

"Aye. He's everything to me."

"Remember that. Never let anything or anyone divide you." There was a note in her voice that said she spoke from experience. But she didn't elaborate. Rather, she plucked a small chain from her belt. At the end of it was a bowl no bigger than a quarter cup. The loa filled it halfway with her rum, then her blood.

She held it out to Valynda. "Drink."

Ew! Valynda felt her stomach heave over the very thought of it. Honestly, she'd rather have her eyes plucked out. "Um . . . no, thank you."

"Drink." The loa was extremely insistent.

Valynda wrinkled her nose. "Really, rather not."

"If you want to stay here and have power, drink."

Do I have to? She barely bit those words back as she cringed at what had to be the most disgusting act on the planet. Who had thought of this? Ick!

Nibo winked at her. "Tastes like chicken."

The hell he said. "You're not funny."

"But I am cute."

Not at the moment. Cringing and revolted, she reached for the concoction she was certain would hit every gag reflex in her entire body. There was no way it would go down and stay. This would be worse than any hangover cure ever invented.

With three deep breaths, she closed her eyes, braced herself, and knocked it back.

And aye, she gagged. Yet somehow managed to keep it down. But not without grabbing Nibo's sleeve and twisting her hand in it.

"You all right?"

Most certainly not! Was he kidding? It was even more revolting than she'd imagined.

Yet she shook her head, then pounded on his arm. "Hate you so much!" Tears leaked from the corners of her eyes as she stuck her tongue out and tried to get rid of the taste.

Nibo handed her his kimen, which she quickly opened and gulped down without a care. He smirked at Legba. "And you thought she wasn't one of us. Bah!"

Legba rolled his eyes. "We have a problem."

"Seems we're having a lot of those lately."

Legba wasn't amused by his sarcasm. Rather, he grabbed Nibo's arm. "Stay focused. I need you to find your brother."

"Why?"

"Notice what's missing?"

Valynda looked around the exquisite town that seemed to have everything imaginable. Gilded buildings. Swans that swam. Singing seagulls. Colorful buildings. No detail appeared missing.

Yet the humor faded from Nibo's amber eyes as he turned a bit pale. "The petro."

Legba nodded slowly. "They've been gone for hours and no one knows where."

Nibo broke off into a round of cursing that left Valynda blushing.

Valynda wanted to ask why that incited such a hostile reaction but figured this probably wasn't the best time to go into it. Especially since everyone else was staring at them with a curiosity that made her want to run and hide.

Nibo ground his teeth and sighed. "I'll find them, and Qeenan."

"Good. Then bring your brother back here and I'll deal with them all."

Inclining his head, he stepped away and took her hand.

As soon as the others had dispersed, she leaned in to whisper in his ear. "What's going on?"

He didn't answer.

Instead, Valynda felt so peculiar. Odd and off. Like the world around her was tilting . . .

She tried to get her bearings, but she felt more like she was at sea in a storm on the main deck. Churning about in the waves as they slammed against her and sent her reeling.

This made no sense.

"Xuri?"

He caught her before she fell.

Everything seemed to fade around her. While she heard their voices, they were at a distance. Like something in a dream or nightmare. She felt Nibo holding her. Smelled his rich rum scent that was mixed with the salty seawater, but even it grew fainter.

And the last words she heard were his, and they were tear-filled.

"She's dead."

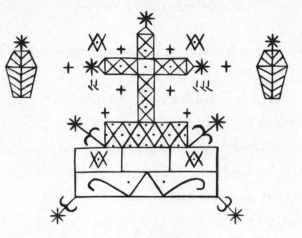

17

Rage darkened Nibo's vision as he held Valynda's lifeless body. Of all the low and dirty tricks that had been done to him, this was the worst.

To poison his Vala . . .

He glared at Brigitte as the urge to rush her throat went through him.

"Calm yourself, Nibo. It's not what you think."

How could it not be? They were treacherous and cold. He'd known better than to trust them. He should never have brought Valynda here. They'd killed her once before.

How could I have trusted them again?

This was all his fault!

Brigitte stepped forward to place her hand on Valynda's forehead. Before he could stop her, she cupped Valynda's chin and held her head before placing a kiss to each of her cheeks.

Nibo curled his lips at her cruelty. He tried to push her away.

Until Valynda gasped as if awaking from a nightmare.

Stunned, he couldn't believe what he was seeing. She was alive! "Vala?"

Opening her eyes, she met Nibo's gaze. "Xuri?"

Tears choked him, especially when she reached up to wipe at the moisture on his cheeks. "Hey, *mon ange.*" He pulled her in and kissed her with all the relief coursing through him. "Never die on me again."

"Um, I'll try not to."

Shaking with relief, he laughed at her confusion, then kissed her forehead. Sobs hung in his throat. He still couldn't believe that Brigitte had saved her life.

Until she pulled away. "I don't feel good."

"What's wrong?"

She began to shiver.

Even more worried, he tightened his arms around her. "Vala?"

"She's fine." Brigitte knelt beside them. "Breathe. Relax. Don't fight what you feel."

Valynda sank her hand into his hair. "What is she talking about?"

He had no idea.

"I gave her some of my powers, and it's her human body trying to adjust to them. If she's to live among us, she'll need them."

Stunned, he gaped at Brigitte. "What?"

She kissed his cheek, then cupped Valynda's. "I'm a sucker for a happy ending." She glanced over to Papa Legba and then to her husband. "My life hasn't always been easy, and I've had several men I've loved. Children I've lost. If I could save you two that pain, I would. Sadly, life has a way of kicking us in the throat when we least expect it. It's why you need my powers."

"Maman—"

"Shh." She placed her finger over his lips to silence his words. "You know I think of you as a son. What happened to her before was wrong. I couldn't stop it then, but I can now. This is my way of making amends."

That was why he loved her so. "Thank you."

"My pleasure. Now go. Kick Malachai ass."

Smiling, he looked at Valynda. "You up to it?"

"Um . . . not quite sure. I'm a little wobbly on me feet, love." She gave him a shaky smile. "Are we sure my new powers aren't projectile vomiting?"

Laughing, he helped her to her feet. "Pretty sure that one's not on our list of powers."

"Pretty sure it might be added soon. Am thinking I could take out a whole city block."

More amused than he wanted to admit, he shook his head. "Fine, let us see about setting this right." And with that, he took her to the gate that led to the mortal realm. Qeenan better run. He was coming and it was time to finish this.

Nibo had a lot to lose now, and he had no intention of losing anything ever again.

On board the *Sea Witch*, the Dark-Hunter leader, Acheron, sat in Captain Bane's chair, staring blankly at Thorn. "Are you futtocking kidding me?"

Thorn shook his head. "Why would I?"

"Because you're an asshole."

He gave him a droll stare, then rolled his eyes and sighed before turning his attention to the other immortal in the room.

Savitar.

Dressed in a white tunic and loose linen breeches, Savitar was a hard immortal creature to miss. Mostly because his exposed flesh was covered in tattoos and his eyes were an eerie violet shade that wasn't always purple. Eyes made more vivid by his dark caramel skin and dark hair and goatee.

That would be sinister enough, but when coupled with his lethal smile-at-me-and-I'll-gut-you-where-you-stand aura, he could easily play the villain role in any Greek tragedy.

Oh wait, he'd already done that.

Several times, and enjoyed it.

Acheron tried not to be amused by his own rambling thoughts. "So, what do you think, Savvy?"

"I think you need to find a new nickname for me before I spank you, Ack-Ack."

And this was why Acheron had banned the Necrodemian Paden Jack from the room. All they needed was one more sarcastic asshole and Acheron would be forced to throat-punch someone. For that matter, he'd also banned a few others. No need to add those temptations, as none of them would have ridden herd on their tongues and he just wasn't in the mood for it. He took enough lip from his own Dark-Hunters. He didn't need to add Thorn's little group to his migraine.

Out of the whole crew, he'd only tolerated Bane, along with Nibo, Valynda, Cameron, Mara, Kalder, Rosie, Will, Bart, and Belle to join them. They, alone, didn't test his nerves.

"So, about the plan." Acheron enunciated each word slowly so that Savitar would follow him.

"I know you meant the plan, Mighty Pain. I just don't like the name."

"Would you answer my question?"

Savitar passed a smirk to Thorn. "It's not as stupid as his last one. The fact that no one is being taken to my island to stay there this time is a plus. I vote for it based on that one fact alone."

Acheron groaned while Bane laughed at the memory of the crew taking refuge there.

"I vote for anything that keeps us away from any more demons," Will said. "Had enough of those buggers for a while."

Bart elbowed him.

Laughing, Nibo shifted his weight to his other leg as he stood in the corner. "So, we're good, then?"

Acheron hedged. "Yes and no. Getting Madoc to comply . . . that's going to be tricky."

Nibo frowned at him. "How so? He has no emotions, right?"

Acheron snorted at what should be a really obvious answer. "Because he has no emotions, he doesn't care. Blow the world up. Or down. No vested interest one way or the other."

Nibo growled as he realized what Acheron had meant. That was definitely a problem. How did one motivate such an ass?

"But if we use him against Adarian . . ." Valynda trailed off into thought.

"It'll definitely be worth it." Nibo stroked his whiskers as he tried to think of some way to coerce a god who had no emotions and no desires to want to do them a favor.

"Yeah," Will groused, "this is a tough one. I've got nothing."

Bart agreed. "I've wasted me two last brain cells. All they're saying is to jump ship while we're able."

"I did that once." Kalder grinned. "Worked well for me, but I can breathe underwater. You poor bastards are screwed."

Acheron ignored his comment. "Are you sure this will weaken him?"

Nibo hesitated as he considered the question in all seriousness. So far, Acheron didn't seem to know that Madoc was Adarian's son, which technically made him Acheron's brother. They needed to keep it that way, as they didn't need the complication or risk that Acheron might decide blood was thicker than water, and defect to Adarian's side without warning. Granted, Acheron had never done that in the past, but why risk it?

Acheron had unbelievable powers. There was no need to put

any temptation there if they didn't need to. So he decided to keep the truth from Acheron. Nibo cleared his throat. "It's his Dream-Hunter powers that we're after. That and his being one of the oldest of their breed and all . . ."

Luckily, Acheron believed him. Which was a miracle, given that Acheron normally could sense a lie three leagues off. Which meant Nibo was getting better at this and learning to hide from other immortals.

Acheron nodded. "I can assign Madoc to my newest Dark-Hunter, Jean-Luc. That might work."

Nibo frowned. "I don't follow."

"Whenever one of my Dark-Hunters is created, I usually have one of the Dream-Hunters assigned to him or her for a few hundred years. It helps to siphon off their excess rage over being betrayed, as well as the pain of being alone in the world and cut off from their family."

Nibo understood that. Since the only way a Dream-Hunter could experience emotion was through someone's dreams, they lived for such tasks and were perfect for it.

Not to mention, he still wasn't over Qeenan's betrayal, and that had been thousands and thousands of years ago. Emotions that intense tended to last. Though he doubted if a Dream-Hunter could handle his.

Acheron scratched his chin. "Madoc won't think it unusual if I make a request for him to be here for that. But I still don't see how you think a simple Dream-Hunter can weaken a Malachai."

Unwilling to share the truth, as it would only lead to somewhere bad, Nibo shrugged. "It's a theory I'm working on.

Something Shadow said about the Primus Bellum and something he observed."

Acheron stood up. "All right, then. Wish you luck with it."

So did he. This would either work, or blow up in their faces. Which his past experience said would be the more likely outcome.

But he was ever an optimist . . . as in absolutely never, yet it didn't keep him from trying while hoping for a better outcome. He just wasn't willing to share that with the group. There were some things they didn't need to know. Near death being the most obvious one.

Acheron pulled out his dark spectacles. "I'll go see Madoc and try to talk him into the human realm. How long do you think it'll take to weaken the Malachai?"

Nibo considered it. "If what Shadow said was true and we can keep him here and get him to help us in the battle, should be rather quick. I hope."

"Then I'll see what I can do." He vanished.

Savitar frowned at Nibo with a sinister glare. "What are you hiding?"

But he refused to be intimidated. "How do you mean?"

"You reek of deception."

"And here I thought it was just me smelling that." Bane retook his chair that Acheron had vacated. "'Course I also thought it could just be Bart, as he hasn't bathed in a few weeks."

"Hey now! 'Tis true, but still! No need getting personal."

Savitar ignored him as he rose to approach Nibo. His lavender gaze narrowed dangerously. "What are you not telling us?"

"I think you know."

"Do I?"

"Don't you?"

Thorn snorted. "So, this is what it's like to witness my conversations with *you*. Fascinating."

Savitar blasted him without taking his gaze from Nibo.

Luckily, Thorn ducked the blast, which made a large black stain in the side of the ship.

"Hey now, watch it! That be me lady you're striking," Bane growled. "Careful with your tempers."

"Forgive me." Yet Savitar's tone was anything other than apologetic.

"Help us bind Adarian."

Savitar shook his head. "I'm not involving myself in the politics of this world. Not anymore. Been there and failed that. My days of being a world protector are over."

"Why is that?" Nibo arched a brow.

"It cost me too much in the past."

"Yet you never elaborate beyond pithy little hints."

Savitar gave him a cruel smile. "And neither do you, Xuri. We all have our secrets." His gaze went meaningfully to Valynda.

Nibo didn't understand where he was going with that. Sometimes trying to follow his line of thought was like watching the flight of a bumblebee, confusing, erratic, and the stuff of nightmares. "What's that supposed to mean?"

"Why do you think you're so drawn to her?"

"She's wonderful," he said without hesitation.

Savitar rolled his eyes. "Think about it, old man. You're not *that* stupid. You've only felt this way about two women in your life. . . ." He glanced to Thorn before he returned his gaze to Nibo. "Or have you?"

A chill went down his spine as he finally caught on. "Aclima?"

Valynda felt a rush of cold go through her at the way he whispered that name. With a loving reverence unlike anything she'd ever heard from anyone before. It stung her with a jealousy so profound that it burned her raw and left her aching. While he'd never mentioned that name to her, it was obvious he had a great deal of affection for this other woman.

Biting her lip, she saw the look on Cameron's face as she stepped toward Kalder and took his hand without speaking.

Savitar nodded. "You felt it the moment you first met. It's why Qeenan tried to keep you two divided. Why he's an even bigger threat to you than you know." He crossed his arms over his chest. "Now, knowing that, do you still want to take on the Malachai?"

Nibo moved to stand behind Valynda so that he could place his hands on her shoulders protectively. "Knowing that, it's imperative that I take him on, and stop him."

And with that, he used his powers to take her from the room and into hers below the deck so that he could speak to her alone.

Valynda's stomach ached in fear of what he had to say. Although she already knew. Aclima was obviously someone important. Someone she couldn't hold a candle to.

"You don't have to say anything, Xuri."

His amber eyes scorched her with the intensity of his emotions. "Aye, I do."

Tears filled her eyes. "Nay. It's probably best—"

He cut her words off with a scorching kiss that made her head spin and left her breathless. "Xuri, what are you doing?"

"I should have known it was you the first time I tasted you."

"What?"

He laughed and kissed her again, then started tugging on her clothes, which was beginning to make her angry.

"What are you doing?"

"I want to be inside you."

"Nay . . . I don't think so."

He looked up, stricken. "What? Why?"

"Because you're thinking of another woman!"

Shaking his head, he smiled at her. "I'm thinking only of you, Vala. There's only ever been you."

"You're thinking of Aclima."

"Who is you."

She scowled at him as she tried to follow his reasoning. "What?"

His features melted into a loving grin. "Oh, *mon ange*. You are Aclima. Don't you get that?" Turning her around, he pulled her toward the looking glass that stood in the corner and held her so that she could see herself there. He pressed his cheek against hers.

"Think back, Vala. To a simpler time and place. We were promised to each other. But Qeenan wanted you for himself. You are the only thing I ever fought my brother for, because I didn't want to live without you."

She started to deny it, but as she stared at the mirror, she began to see images of the past. Images of her and Nibo sitting on a distant mountain . . .

With her long dark hair flowing freely to her waist, and dressed in vibrant red with bare feet, she saw herself so clearly while he sat beside her playing on a lute. The wind tugged at her hair while she laughed in time to his tune.

Suddenly, everything came pouring back. Every memory of their life together. Then, as now, she'd been of humble origins. A simple shepherdess. Unpretentious and quiet, she'd never wanted much of anything in life.

Except Nibo, who had come rushing into her life one day when one of her lambs had been trapped and she'd been unable to free him. The bleating had been so intense, and she'd been so focused on helping the little one that she'd paid attention to nothing else.

"I've got him. Stand back."

Startled, she'd moved away as Nibo had climbed into the dangerous ravine with nothing more than his bare hands and feet and somehow lifted her lamb up to her and set him free.

She'd gathered her lamb to her to hold it and had watched as he lifted himself up and smiled at her. Not smugly, but in pure bashfulness. It'd been the sweetest expression she'd ever seen.

"Is he all right?" he'd asked as he came to check on him.

She'd fallen in love instantly.

How could she ever forget that? "You promised to marry me in the spring."

"Aye," he whispered. "You were to wear baby's breath braided in your hair."

Because he liked it best. He thought it made her look like a fey princess. And it was then she realized that he still wore her ring on his pinkie. He'd kept it all these centuries. Tears filled her eyes.

"I've never stopped loving you, Vala."

Those words toppled her emotionally. How could anyone hold on to that for all this time? Especially Nibo the feckless?

"I know you better."

"Aye, you do. It's why I was never attached to any other woman. They weren't you."

That succeeded in making her cry. This time when Nibo drew her into his arms, she welcomed him with the same passion. Never had she thought a mere kiss could be such a wondrous experience.

And when his warm, calloused hand closed around her breast, she sighed in blissful contentment. Absolute pleasure pierced her as heat pooled itself in the center of her body. She couldn't imagine craving anyone else. It absolutely consumed her. It was electrifying. Tormenting, and it left her wanting more of him.

Nibo left her lips to kiss a trail down her throat to the breast he cupped. Valynda swallowed at the sight of his dark curls brushing against her pale breast, at the feel of his tongue teasing her taut nipple. His tongue was rough and hot, his lips soothing and tender.

She cupped his head to her and let the locks of his hair tease her fingers.

He was so beautiful there, tasting her, teasing her. His beautiful face showed the pleasure he received just from touching her like that, and she sighed in contentment as she let the incredible earthy sensations sweep her away until she was nothing but an extension of the man holding her in his arms.

She would forever be his.

Nibo had never tasted anything like her body. She was so

warm, so inviting. More so because he knew she was sharing with him what she'd never shared with anyone else.

He was her first and only.

In this life and her other.

Why she would choose his worthless arse, he couldn't imagine. He was so unworthy of what she offered. So unworthy of her, period.

She was lightness and joy.

He was darkness and sorrow. Tragedy. Nothing good had ever come from him.

Yet he was glad that, for this one moment and for whatever reason, she was with him now.

Valynda tugged at his shirt. Eager to oblige her, he pulled it off. Biting her lips, she ran her hands over his tense arms. He clenched his teeth as his head reeled from pleasure.

The things her touch did to his body . . .

It was incredible. Invigorating. It made him feel virile and wild. Made him hard and aching. Most of all, he felt vulnerable to her. She was his one and only weakness.

But he couldn't pull back. Nay, he needed more of her. Needed to touch every inch of her body and to claim it as his own.

Forever.

Valynda smiled up at him as he gathered her into his arms and carried her to her bunk, where he threw her playfully and then covered her with his long, languid body. Her thoughts scattered at the glorious feeling of his skin against hers. Of his heavy weight that felt good instead of oppressive.

Nibo took her hand into his and guided it back to him. "I love when you touch me."

Valynda ran her hand down his shaft as the tip of it probed her. It made her even more tender toward him. "I love when you're inside me."

He kissed her again, then drove himself deep inside her.

Nibo whispered sweet endearments in her ear while he used his tongue to toy with the tender flesh of her neck.

She panted in pleasure as he coaxed her. And in this moment, she reveled in the strength of his arms around her and the sound of his deep voice in her ear. Valynda wrapped her arms around his shoulders and buried her face against his muscled neck where she inhaled the warm scent of him. It gave her courage and strength because here, she knew she was home.

This was all she wanted. To share her body and soul with him. If they lost this fight and this was her last peaceful moment, she wanted this memory with him. She needed it.

Nibo wanted her in a way unimaginable. She surrounded him with heat, and her breath against his neck sent a thousand chills over him. She felt wonderful and he never wanted to let her go.

He smiled at her courage and at the sight of her lying underneath him, her body bare and perfect.

It was the most incredible thing he'd ever seen. A wave of fierce possession tore through him then, especially when he looked down to see them joined.

"I love how full you are inside me," she said. "I would give anything to carry your baby."

Nibo laughed at that. He'd never had a woman speak of such things. But then talking was what she did best. From the first night they'd met on the beach and she'd told him off.

"How do I feel?"

"Full and deep. I can feel you all the way to my core."

He sucked his breath in at her words and the image they created. He liked to hear her speak of such things. "Can you now?"

She nodded.

He pulled back, then thrust his hips hard and deep against hers.

They moaned in unison.

"You feel so incredible!" She sighed.

Nibo rolled over with them still joined. He sat her on top of him and watched her in the darkness.

Her smile turned wicked as she realized what he wanted. "I see you liked being my cheval."

"Aye, I did."

Wrinkling her nose, she braced her hands on his muscled chest and began to slowly ride him.

Nibo ran his hands down her thighs and watched the way the moonlight cut across her pale skin.

"May I ask another question?"

His mind was dazed from the feel of her naked body sliding against his, and it took a few seconds before he could respond. "By all means talk, *mon ange,* if it gives you pleasure to do so. Tell me more about how I feel inside you."

"Hard and strong. I can even feel you quivering here." She pointed to her lower abdomen.

The sight of her hand stroking her stomach almost shattered his control. He took her hand into his and led it away before he succumbed too early to the orgasm he longed for.

Nibo lifted his hips up, driving himself deeper into her as she ground herself against him in a way so sublime that he growled in satisfaction.

Valynda felt so strangely free with him. She ran her hands over the hard muscles of his chest and abdomen. It was so odd to see him lying there under her, between her spread thighs. But the truth was, she loved this.

Just as she loved him.

He held her hips in his hands and guided her movements. But what held her transfixed was the bliss on his face. His cheeks were flushed, his eyes dark and unfocused.

She moaned as he ran his hands up from her hips to her breasts, where he toyed with her swollen nipples.

"What do I feel like to you, Xuri?"

"Wet and soft."

"Do you ever think of any of your past lovers when you're with me?"

He scowled at her question. "Nay, love. How could you ask me such a thing when you know you're the only one I've ever loved? In any lifetime."

"Because it worries me." Especially given the numbers of lovers he was reported to have. Many at the same time. How was she supposed to ever measure up?

He shook his head. "All are forgotten, and none ever competed with you."

She smiled at that. It made this moment all the more special to her. "I'm glad. I want to be the only one who occupies your mind."

Nibo cupped her face in his hands. "Believe me, love, you are. And none of them were ever my wife." He pulled her down and kissed her fiercely.

Valynda trembled at the passion she tasted, at the way he teased her lips with his and twined his tongue around hers. His muscles bulged around her, making her tremble.

Nibo pulled back from the kiss, then rolled over with her and took control.

Valynda arched her back as he moved faster. Harder. Every stroke brought more pleasure. Every kiss and touch reverberated through her.

"Make me yours, Xuri."

He claimed her lips again as he slammed himself into her even deeper than he'd been before.

She wrapped her legs around his hips and let his passion sweep her away. After a few minutes, he lowered his head down to her shoulder and growled as he released himself inside her.

Laughing in satisfaction, she drew a ragged breath as he collapsed on top of her and held her tight.

"Thank you, Vala," he whispered in her ear. "For making me whole again." Then, he kissed her lips in a tender caress that sent chills through her.

He withdrew and rolled over onto his back and pulled her against his side.

She assumed he was through with her, so it surprised her a few seconds later when he spread her legs and touched the most private place of her body.

"Still not sated?"

He shook his head. "I was selfish, and I want you to have your pleasure."

"I already had it."

He smiled wickedly at that. "Nay, my innocent dove, you didn't. And I know that."

Valynda swallowed as his long, lean fingers delved deep into her body. She tensed a bit as they burned the tender flesh of her nether lips.

"Don't dry out on me, love." He laid his body between her legs and spread her thighs wide. Then, he ran his long, tapered finger down her cleft. She shivered as he used his fingers to spread her open and dipped his head down.

Valynda jerked as his mouth covered her. Every nerve ending in her body sizzled as he stroked her with his tongue and lips. Dear Lord, he was so incredibly talented.

She moaned as she cupped his head to her. No longer able to speak, all she could do was feel each and every luscious lick he gave her.

His breath was hot against her bared flesh, and when he slid a finger deep inside her and rotated it, she thought she would die.

She looked down to see him staring up at her while he tormented her with ecstasy.

He pulled back but left his finger inside her. A strange sensation of intimacy overwhelmed her. With a mind of its own, her body writhed to his touch and kisses.

"Oh Xuri," she groaned.

And as he continued, she found herself unable to speak anymore. Unable to do anything other than feel him. Feel his tongue sliding around her, his finger swirling.

Her pleasure built to an unimaginable height. Until she was sure that she would explode with the weight of it.

Then, in the span of one heartbeat, she did explode. Her body splintered apart, and she cried out.

Nibo didn't stop. He stayed there, licking and teasing, until she'd come for him twice more.

When he seemed content to tease her more, she begged him for mercy. "Please, Xuri," she whimpered. "If I do that one more time, I fear I shall die of it."

He chuckled at her plea, then turned his face to suckle the tender flesh of her thigh.

Valynda lay there, completely spent and weak. She breathed raggedly as Nibo gathered her into his arms and held her close. He kissed her brow and cradled her head with his hands. "I wish I could stay here with you forever. No war. No Malachai. Just us."

She understood exactly what he meant. She felt the same way. If only they could.

But they had the world to try and save.

First, they needed to get dressed.

As soon as she had her gown in place, Valynda opened the door to find the Dark-Huntress, Janice Smith, outside. Her face heated up as she realized that Janice must have heard them. To her credit, the beautiful Trini didn't say a word. "I left me book."

Valynda gulped. "Ah. I didn't see it."

"I'll look for it . . . later."

Embarrassed to the core of her being, Valynda did her best not to think of it and to wonder how Acheron was faring with his task. . . .

Nibo watched as Valynda rushed off. Her embarrassment about such things had forever amused him. Both in this life and her previous one.

Smiling, he retrieved Janice's book and handed it to her on his way out.

The Dark-Huntress stopped him from leaving. "Don't you think it odd?"

"What?"

"If she is your fiancée returned, why now? After all these centuries? Why was she kept from you and then returned at this particular time and place? From my experience and knowledge, such things are never accidental." And with that Janice walked away.

Nibo sucked his breath in sharply as he realized something that should have occurred to him. But he'd been so happy and caught up in her return that he hadn't thought about it.

Until now.

Janice was right. They'd been reunited for a reason. And his experience was that such things were never done for a good one.

Shit.

What? You have something better to do in your useless, eternal existence?" Acheron still couldn't believe Madoc had refused his request.

But then why was he surprised? Nothing ever came easy to them.

Almost as tall as Acheron, Madoc had jet-black hair and eerie blue eyes like all the Oneroi, or Dream-Hunters, as they were known since they patrolled the sleep of humans and Dark-Hunters to keep them safe from preternatural predators and demons who could prey on them in that unconscious state when they were so vulnerable. Sadly, they'd all been cursed centuries before to have no emotions, after one of them had played a prank on Zeus while he slept.

The head Greek god had never been known for his sense of humor. Instead of punishing just the one who'd done it, he'd taken his wrath out on their entire race.

All of them had been rounded up and stripped of their emotions so that they'd never again want or desire amusement or anything else.

What Zeus hadn't realized was that in the dream realm, they'd be able to bond with those they visited and feel whatever their "host" felt. That some of them would then begin to crave or become addicted to the emotions they lacked and thus turn into their own form of demonic creature who then preyed on humanity, gods, and others. Such creatures were termed Skoti.

And Skoti were hunted by Madoc and his crew of Oneroi, who wanted to make sure that Zeus and the others never rounded them up again for further punishment. Apparently once with the big guy was enough to ensure Madoc never wanted a repeat.

Hence the droll stare on the god's face as he smirked at Acheron. For someone with no emotion, he was doing a good job imitating a look of disgust. "As a matter of fact, I do. There's been a major Skoti uprising with the Malachai. We've been quite busy trying to keep them from driving humanity crazy. Literally."

"And this is just as important. Trust me. Weaken the Malachai and your Skoti will go back to behaving."

"They never behave."

Probably true, as it was true for most creatures when given a choice between doing what was right and what was wrong. Most went left instead of right.

Even Acheron had been known to stray down that path. Sometimes for the right reasons. To his eternal shame, sometimes not.

However . . .

"Do it for me, then, Madoc. I've a Dark-Hunter who could use the release."

Madoc grumbled under his breath, proving he had been spending a lot of time in dreams and that the residual emotions were still with him. "Fine. But you will owe me."

"Don't I always?"

He didn't respond as they headed toward the portal that Madoc needed to take him to the mortal plane.

But once they entered the room and went through the portal, what they realized was that finding the Malachai and his army wasn't as easy as they thought. There was a lot of evil in the world, and the Malachai used it to mask his own. Humanity was so easily corruptible, they were going wild with temptation and making it harder and harder for Acheron and Madoc to find the ones they needed.

Days went by as they did their best to locate the Malachai and his miscreants.

For whatever reason, Adarian had ceased to attack. It was as if he sensed they had something on board that weakened him.

Not even Nibo could locate the petro. They were attacking humans in concentrated waves.

Valynda stood back to watch as Nibo stood at the prow alongside Acheron, Bane, Kalder, and Thorn. Now that was about the sweetest view what any woman could ever hope to see.

Mara and Elf, the captain's sister, moved to stand next to her. "Should I ask what holds your attention so?"

Valynda passed her a knowing smile. "Methinks you are well aware. And that you share it."

Mara cradled her distended belly with her hands. "Aye, but there's only one who holds my fascination."

"Doesn't mean you can't appreciate the views of the others, sweet sister." Elf's eyes twinkled with mischief. "'Tis a pity we can't bronze that and make it a permanent feature for those of us what can't lay claim to any of those fine backsides."

Valynda glanced askance at her. "Well, as one who does claim one of them, so long as you confine yourselves to looking . . ."

Elf grinned. "No fear. I'd never do such a thing to either of me sisters." She kissed Valynda's cheek and danced away to go and tease Sallie as he worked to repair a sail.

Valynda smiled fondly at the girl until her gaze was caught by what held the men's rapt attention. "Lady Mara?"

"I see it."

Slowly, all the Deadmen came up from below to mingle with those on deck so that they could see the ships that had gathered to meet the coming storm.

"What is that?"

"The last gate." Mara sighed. "It's been opened."

Valynda held her breath as she saw the color of two ships she knew well. Captain Barnet's and Rafael Santiago's. There was no mistaking them. They stood still on the water, something easy, given that there was no wind whatsoever. It was as if they'd sailed into a vacuum of some sort.

Silence reigned. The still water didn't move. It was like glass for as far as the eye could see.

The sun hung on the horizon with an eerie beauty. Still and flat. Chills ran up her arms.

This was bad.

Gathering her skirts, she made her way to Nibo's side. "What's going on?"

Captain Bane stood with his spyglass, staring out at the other ships. "I don't see anyone on Barnet's ship." He lowered the spyglass. "Get us closer, Mistress Dolorosa."

"Aye, Captain."

But that was easier said than done, given there was no wind to fill their sails. That meant they'd have to rely on Strixa's powers to move them.

Valynda wrapped her arm around Nibo's. He covered her hand. She could feel the tension inside him. "Is it Adarian?"

"We're not sure."

For the gate to be open, it was so strangely serene. Like the calm before a storm. Valynda had expected fire and brimstone. Lightning. Screaming Furies.

A thousand fighting demons.

Something.

This was far more chilling.

The last time a gate fell, they were battling for their lives. Not staring eye to eye with their friends across a calm sea. The dragons came up from the sea to stand on deck with them.

As they pulled near Rafael's ship, the pirate waved at them, then swung over to speak with Captain Bane. Ever the epitome of a swaggering buccaneer, Rafe had a shaved head with a set of distinctive tattoos that made him look as fierce as his gruesome reputation. There wasn't anyone who sailed in the Caribbean who wasn't familiar with the lethal reputation of Captain Cross and his ship, the *Soucouyant*.

His dark skin set his amber eyes off to perfection, and they were deadly serious. "We've been stuck here for almost two days. No winds. How did you sail in?"

"Magic."

He was unamused by Bane's bland answer.

Will stepped down from the railing. "Where's the rest of your crew, Santiago?"

Before he could answer, a fight broke out between Jake and Sallie.

"Don't touch me!"

"You don't shove me!"

Before Bane could get to them, another fight started between Hinder and Kat. Then another and another.

Valynda gaped as she realized what had happened to the crews of the other ships.

They'd turned on each other.

Nibo realized it, too. "Qeenan!" he shouted. "Show yourself!"

There was no response.

Yanking at one of the necklaces on his chest, he pulled it off and twisted a small coin from it. He handed one to Valynda. "Put this under your tongue. It'll keep you from turning and hearing the voices they'll send." Then he handed one to Bane, Thorn, and Acheron, with the same instructions.

Valynda obeyed.

The moment the coin was in her mouth, she could see the spirits inside their crew. It was as if each one's body was a thick coating over the demonic creatures who were using them like a suit.

"Are they all right like that?"

"Aye, but whatever you do, remember that it's your friends inside and don't harm them. While stabbing one or fighting them will get rid of their demons, it will also kill your friends."

"Noted."

"So, what do we do? How do we get them out?"

Acheron shot a god-bolt into one. The blast instantly knocked the petro loa from the Deadman he was possessing.

"That works." Nibo winked at her. He went off to help.

When Valynda took a step forward, she felt someone at her back. Invisible arms held her in place. Suddenly, a deep, dark voice spoke in her ear. "You didn't get the crook for me."

Her blood ran cold as she realized it was Adarian.

"I know you've had time. Why haven't you done it?" His growl was fierce.

"I refuse to betray him."

"Then you can mourn him instead."

Valynda gasped as Adarian vanished, then appeared behind Nibo in his full Malachai form. With black-and-red-swirling skin, he had black leathery wings and horns. His red eyes glowed with fury and hatred.

Truly there was nothing more terrifying. He reached for Nibo and grabbed him.

Nibo tried to blast the demon, yet it had no effect on the ancient being, who turned around and slashed him with his claws, then hit him with his own surge of energy.

"Don't use your staff!" Acheron called as he saw Nibo reaching for it. "You'll only make him stronger."

"How?"

"It's from the Tree of Life. It will feed his powers."

Nibo's eyes widened. "Now you tell me?"

"Never saw you fight a Malachai before."

There was that. Nibo ducked as Adarian went for his throat and twisted away. As he stepped back, someone tripped him.

He went sprawling to land at the feet of Qeenan.

"Damn you, brother!"

Qeenan curled his lip at Nibo. "You were supposed to be on my side!"

"And you on mine." Nibo flipped himself to his feet.

Valynda froze as she watched the two of them fighting and she remembered their past. Remembered the way Qeenan had once stared after her whenever he saw her with Nibo. It'd been so uncomfortable. And she'd felt so unsafe around him.

He was a treacherous bastard.

There was no worse feeling than to be in the home of your

husband or fiancé and have that skittering sensation of danger. To be terrified of what might happen should he turn his back or you drift too far afield without him.

No one should live in fear. Especially not in their own home or in that of their in-laws. Yet she'd never felt comfortable or safe.

Because of Qeenan. And Nibo's parents.

They'd fostered that competition, thinking it was good for their sons. That it would make them more manly and strive to be better.

In the end, because they'd refused to let their sons be and had forced them into positions unsuited to them, it'd destroyed their family entirely.

Just as it was about to tear them apart again.

"Enough!" She rushed between them and forced Qeenan back. She held her sword at his throat. "No more!"

Qeenan laughed at her. "What are you going to do?" He used his powers to drip blood and appear fierce and frightening.

But it would take more than his parlor tricks to work on her. "Don't push me, Qeenan. You didn't scare me as a girl and you don't scare me now." A bit of a lie, but she wasn't about to give in to that monstrous ego of his.

"What?"

"You heard me."

Scoffing, he pulled something from his pocket and blew it at her.

Valynda choked while he laughed cruelly. Then she staggered back into Nibo's arms.

But she didn't stay there. She caught her footing and righted herself, which instantly stopped his laughter. "Goofer's dirt? Really? What next? A nail in me footprint?"

He gasped.

Until Masaka came up from behind her. "Here, Baron. This is what you need!"

Valynda felt a tug on her gown. An instant later, she saw her bottle fly into the hands of her enemy.

Nibo went cold as he realized what his brother held. "Don't you dare touch that, Qeenan! Give it to us!"

"Why? What is it?"

Masaka smirked. "The girl's soul. Open it and she dies."

Growling, Nibo sent a blast toward his former friend. "Damn you!"

Masaka went flying overboard as he turned back to his brother. "I mean it, Qeenan. Don't you dare harm her."

"Give me your crook and join us in this fight."

Nibo pulled the crook from his neck.

Valynda was horrified at what he was doing, yet flattered that he didn't hesitate. "Nay!" She grabbed his arm. "You can't do this, Xuri. Think of what they'll do with it."

"Don't care. There's no world for me, without you. We'll deal with whatever comes."

Tears blinded her. "I can't lose you again."

"Nor I you."

Qeenan made a sound of supreme disgust. "While this is all stomach churning, no one cares. Give me the staff."

Nibo extended it.

Qeenan reached for it with greedy fingers. But the moment he touched it, Valynda grabbed it and used it to hook him about the waist and jerk him forward. As he fell, she went for her bottle.

Time seemed to slow down as she heard Xuri screaming out her name.

For the merest, tiniest instant, she had the bottle in her hand and was home free.

Until something ripped it from her grasp.

"Nay!"

Then everything went black.

Nibo couldn't breathe as he saw Adarian scoop up Valynda's soul bottle and shatter it against the boards of the deck. An unfathomable hatred rose up inside him and shot out through his crook as he attacked the Malachai and set him on fire.

Adarian screamed in pain and dove for the sea.

The other petro pulled out of their bodies and dove for cover.

Qeenan tried, but he was past that now. Nibo wasn't about to let him escape his wrath. Not after this. Not after what they'd done.

Again!

"You bastard!"

At least his brother had the good sense to be scared. Qeenan backed away from him. "I was going through with the bargain."

"And I'm going through with me promise. I will feast on your guts and eat your brains!"

"You can get another pet."

"There's only one Aclima and twice now you've taken her from me!"

Qeenan stumbled and fell as those words slammed into him

and he understood exactly what he'd done. He tried to attack, but it was useless. Nibo brought his crook down on him over and over, the same way he'd once beaten him with his club. His wrath was absolute.

"Xuri, no!"

He froze as he heard the last voice he'd ever expected to hear again. Felt the most gentle touch on his arm.

Unable to believe it, he turned his head to see Valynda by his side. Fully restored.

"I don't understand."

Thorn gave him a droll stare before he used his thumb to indicate Acheron. "Atlantean god of creation. They tend to come in handy at times."

Acheron jerked his chin at Valynda. "Thanks to Circe, she had a body this time for her soul to return to. Getting the two of them back together wasn't that hard."

Yet it still wasn't over.

Nibo turned back toward Qeenan. "You owe my lady an apology."

Bleeding and shaking, Qeenan pushed himself to his feet. "Our day is still coming, Xuri. If not now, it will. There is only so long you can keep anger contained when you step on people and treat them unfairly."

"You don't correct things by destroying everything. You correct it by working together to make it better for all. For it is better to build than to destroy."

And that had always been the difference between the twins.

Qeenan sighed as he gathered his men and left.

Nibo turned toward the others. "How do we find Adarian?"

"We're tracking him."

"What about Barnet and Rafe?" Valynda held her hand to her forehead to shield her eyes as she scanned the empty ships. "What do you think happened to their crews?"

Bane let out an elongated breath. "That's a question I'm afraid to ask. But we will find out."

Thorn clapped Bane on his back. "For now, let's get this gate resealed."

"Aye to that."

18

New Orleans

"Is the captain sure about this?" Valynda stared at the bustling port city in the newly established country. She'd never understand why Cameron was so fond of this place.

Even though New Orleans wasn't Cameron's home, she and Kalder were already off the ship and exploring. Along with Sancha, who'd suddenly taken up with Jake Devereaux. Those two had become very close lately. . . .

Valynda was a bit more hesitant, especially

since this was where Madoc had told them he'd found Adarian hiding. "Why would he pick this place?"

"Lots of hatred and resentment for him to feed on." Bane pointed to the encampments that dotted the other side of the river. "They have factions from a lot of different nations thrown in together. So much so that they have areas of town they've been forced to designate as neutral zones."

In that moment, she could feel him here. Deep in her stomach.

"Now that we've found him, what are we to do?"

Acheron, Savitar, and Thorn turned to Bane.

"It's a port city," Acheron said. "I have a place on Pirate's Alley so that I can watch him, and I'll establish a larger than normal number of Dark-Hunters, as Adarian's presence will draw a lot more evil here."

Savitar nodded. "I can ensure there's a Were-Hunter sanctuary put here in order to keep an eye out as well."

"And I'll move in my Hellchasers."

Acheron met her gaze. "Between us, he should be covered."

"What happened to Vine?" Bane took his wife's hand. "I want to make sure she doesn't crop back up."

Thorn snorted. "They fed her to Adarian. She didn't last long. Then again, few do. Evil like that, Adarian drains them and eats them whole. It's what a Malachai does."

Mara winced. "I feel for her."

"Why? She killed me and wanted to kill you."

"I know, Duel, but she's still my sister. I didn't want her dead."

Valynda took Nibo's hand, as she knew he could relate to that complicated feeling. "So, this is it, then? We part ways?"

Thorn wrinkled his nose. "Not exactly." He turned her wrist so that she could see her mark wasn't completely gone. Though faint, it still could be seen. "Some of you are still Hellchasers."

"Deadmen," Will corrected.

Thorn laughed. "Yes, Mr. Death—"

"Deeth!"

"Death, you're still Deadmen. But the gates are sealed. So, you're not needed at sea at the moment."

"Futtocking landwalkers." Bart groaned. "Put me neck in the noose."

Sallie scoffed. "Hang that, put me arse in a tavern."

Will pointed to Sallie. "Like *that* option much better. I'm going with me friend here. To Valhalla!"

Shaking her head, Belle rolled her eyes. "Men. You're ever off on some nonsensical point."

"That's the fun of it." Paden adjusted his tricorne. "I guess me and me sister and Kalder will be heading back to Virginia, then."

"Aye." Sadness darkened the captain's eyes. 'Twas the same that Valynda felt in her heart at the thought of losing her friends.

But all things came to an end eventually.

"Hey now," Thorn chided. "This isn't the end. You know that. We're immortal. Most of us. We'll be back."

"Aye. That we will."

Nibo stayed by her side as they dispersed. "And what of us, *mon ange*?"

Her heart fluttered at the way he said that. Most of all, she trembled at the knowledge he'd given her the choice of staying or joining his pantheon. If she said the word, he'd leave his people for her.

But she would never do that to him.

While he might fight with his brother and other family members to the end of time, they were still family. Blood should be thicker than water. She believed that.

So she smiled. "Wherever thou goest, I shall go. Thy people shall be my people. Forever."

He kissed her hand and laughed. "In that case, and given where we are . . . *laissez les bons temps rouler.*"

EPILOGUE

"What are you doing, Cam?" Jaden appeared right behind his sister as she struggled to paint symbols on the walls of her shack that had been built on the outskirts of some backwater hole in the human realm that the humans had dubbed New Orleans.

With a huff, she paused to look down at him from the ladder she stood upon. "Don't just pop in on me without warning, Verlyn! You scared the shite from me!"

"You're not supposed to be here."

"I don't have a choice, do I?"

"We all have choices. Isn't that what you constantly tell me?"

Ignoring his barb, she went back to work. "Return to your masters."

"You can't contain Adarian forever."

"I have to try. He's way too powerful and we can't afford for him to run loose in the human world."

Jaden cursed as he realized what she was painting. "You're going to try it, aren't you?"

"It's prophecy."

"Idiocy, you mean."

"No. Our only hope."

"To create another Malachai whose powers will make a mockery of Adarian's? Are you out of your mind? Haven't you learned yet not to interfere?"

"As it began, it shall end. Monakribos was born of absolutes. An equal division."

"So, what? You plan to sleep with Adarian?"

"Don't be ridiculous."

He wasn't. That was how it'd all begun. A Sephiroth warrior—those who fought for absolute good—had slept with the goddess of absolute destruction and fathered a child. "Then how? In case it's missed your notice, the only Sephiroth left is male. Last time I checked, two men can't physically have a baby. There's only so much bending the laws of nature even you can do, Cam."

"Menyara," she corrected. "And I know. But . . ." She paused to look down at him. "There is a way. A girl born to the Sephiroth."

Jaden's heart sank at the thought. She was talking about the creation of his great-granddaughter. "Do not interfere, Cam. Enough harm has been done to my child."

Children, actually.

And all because of him.

Most of all, he didn't want his great-granddaughter near a Malachai because of one basic reason. All Malachai were born through an act of violence, and the thought of anyone harming his bloodline . . .

"I mean it, Cam. Don't you dare put my children in harm's way."

"Why do you care now? You've never been this protective in the past."

"I like to think I can learn from my mistakes."

"And I want to save this world."

Some days he did, too. Today, not so much. And definitely not at the expense of his sons.

"Don't, Cam. I mean it."

"Fine, then. Go back to Azmodea and fear nothing. Besides, Jared is locked away. Not like I can get to him."

He winced at the mention of his grandson and the curse that had been laid upon him.

Because of me and my stupidity.

He'd been such a fucking fool. Trying to stop prophecy when there was no way.

"Fine, but don't forget what I said."

Menyara watched as Jaden vanished. He was angry now, but . . .

In time, he'd come around to her way of thinking. She would make him understand that this was what they needed to do. With Adarian here, New Orleans had become a magnet for all sorts of preternatural activity. So, she would stay to monitor it.

Most of all, she knew that it would be here that the prophecy would begin. This was where the last Malachai would be born, and either the world would be saved . . .

Or it would end.

Acknowledgments

For my aunt Berta for all the stories in my youth that fueled a love of Caribbean lore and a devout respect for West African tales, traditions, and culture.

To Tish for your unerring guidance and wise counsel, and bag of tricks.

And for my grandfathers, who taught me many lessons about many religions.